She lost her past…

She was utterly alone. There was no one to hide from, no one to impress, and no one to help her. She felt an uncomfortable hollow void in the pit of her stomach. A great fear swept through her, and she began to shake. Her emotions poured out, and she wept without reservation, her sobbing punctuated by deep gasps of air. She knew she could not survive in the jungle. Her food would run out in a few days, and she would starve to death. Most people have something to remember when they die. They can remember old friends and family, satisfactions and regrets, but Jamie had no such luxuries. She realized she would die without even knowing her name.

The Rings of Alathea

The Rings of Alathea

by

Dan Moore

Published by
Dan Moore Productions
Liverpool, NY
www.danmoore.com
www.meridiansshadow.com

Cover art by Jason Moore

ISBN 978-0-9834283-8-1
First Edition: July 2011
9-21-11 Revision
Printed in the United States of America

This book is dedicated to my family:
my wonderful wife Diana, to my sons Chris and Jason,
to my daughters-in-law Gina and Kim, and to my
grandchildren, Garrett, Logan and Liam.

FOREWORD

Thank you for buying and reading this book. Knowing there are people like you who value my work keeps me writing.

I live with my wife Diana near Syracuse, New York. I am a freelance video producer and the proud father of two sons, two daughters-in-law and three grandsons. I have always had the urge to tell stories. I remember reading my early attempts at science fiction to my Uncle Al, who sat with great patience and encouraged me. He was my first literary fan.

This book belongs to my characters. I am their chronicler, giving voice and context to their struggles and dreams. However, I could not have written this book without the support of my wife Diana. Her love is the most amazing thing I know.

Finally, I ask my hard SF readers to forgive some of the liberties I have taken for the sake of this story. This book is intended to be a Science Fiction adventure that is centered on the lives of my characters, not on the laws of physics. I hope I haven't done anything to disrupt the suspension of your disbelief.

Dan Moore
June 2011

CHAPTER ONE

Awakening

The woman didn't know if she was breaking through a chrysalis or sensing her final glimpse of light through a shroud of death. The light was diffuse, milky white. She could hear moaning. Distant guttural murmuring emanated from the edges of her consciousness. The last wisps of a half-forgotten dream slipped away through overwhelming physical sensations. She felt her chest heaving, her hands groping, her head tilting back, her toes fisting as she squeezed her buttocks and tensed her leg muscles. Every joint ached. The sounds were closer now. They were synchronized with her rising shoulders. She could feel something between her lips. Dry lips. Parched throat. A leathery tongue slapping against hard plastic. She was making the sounds.

She pushed her hands down, touching the cold skin of her hips. She could feel the hard bone of her pelvis, the soft muscles of her upper thighs. A chill ran marrow-deep through her body. She began to shake uncontrollably. She felt cold metal touching her skin. She reached up and felt something hard against her numb fingers. She reached down to herself again, searching for her body. She felt her navel and slid her hands down toward her groin. There were tubes between her legs. She felt a rush of fear, then shame. Someone had placed them there. Someone had touched her. She felt violated. She tried to scream and felt something choking her. Her reaching, groping, probing fingers found her mouth and the tubing that passed down her throat. She gagged involuntarily, then grabbed the insulting canula and ripped it out.

Something moved in her stomach, and she tasted acid in her throat. There was a retching cough intermingled with the moans. She felt pressure at the base of her spine as she tried to sit up, but she could not. She managed to roll to one side, her body heaving, jerking, and twisting as bile rose into her mouth. She pulled at the tubes between her legs and then became aware of the pungent odor of urine. The liquid chilled against the cold metal of her coffin, sending another shiver up her spine. She opened her mouth and drew in a ragged breath. Air irritated her throat. Her chest heaved again, her lungs burning like two white-hot bladders bursting with molten lava.

There was the sound of latches surrendering their grip and a rush of air as it coursed over her body. She felt like she was on fire, every nerve firing as harsh gaseous fingers pressed against her hypersensitive skin. She reached forward again; the gauzy light was brighter now. Her cocoon had opened, and she was aware of a larger space. Her body floated upward. She remembered gravity and wondered where it had gone. She yielded to weightlessness and allowed her body to hover, tethered by a few remaining tubes and wires.

* * *

"Something's wrong with this one, Hip." The voice was

masculine, nearby.

"What have we got?" It was another male voice, this time deeper, mellifluous.

"It's a woman."

"I can see that, Carter."

"But this is Jameson Stryker's pod."

"She doesn't look like a Jameson." The voice named Hip groped the woman's groin. "Definitely a woman."

"Sex change?"

"If it is, you can't tell it from the real thing. We'll ask her when she wakes up."

"Damn! Here's another dead one." The voices moved away.

* * *

The woman floated near a cushioned bulkhead in a wide, circular cabin. The walls were white with recessed lighting panels that flooded the space with a soft glow. Someone had dimmed the fixtures, and the compartment took on a dreamlike quality. Her vision was clearing slowly. There were almost three dozen people suspended around the perimeter of the cabin. They were practically naked, dressed in odd utilitarian undergarments, which failed miserably at protecting each person's privacy. Two men were suspended near a large hatchway. They were clothed in azure jumpsuits and soft soled footwear. They were obviously in command: adults surrounded by a bevy of oversized infants in swaddling clothes.

The woman didn't know where to look. She felt awkward, gazing at the bodies of strangers. She glanced down at herself and then realized she was dressed as they were. She adjusted her loose-fitting panties. Too much of her was on display. She looked at her arms. She was skin and bones. What had happened to her? She felt totally disoriented but didn't sense any danger. She had no idea where she was or how long she'd been there. Perhaps she was still dreaming. She yearned for the inevitable sensation of falling that would jolt her from her slumbers, but it never came.

The two jumpsuits floated into the center of the cabin. A man with long, slender fingers and deep-set eyes sucked in a breath. He was going to be the first to speak, obviously the leader. The woman looked at his eyes. She could tell he was on the verge of panic. He fidgeted with his fingers as he struggled with his words. The second jumpsuit was an older man. He was a portrait of serenity. She could tell he was in a far better place than his companion. The nervous man glanced at him, and the calm jumpsuit smiled and nodded, urging him to speak.

"Ah, my name is Carter Lund," he began. "This is Dillard Whitford, our ship's physician."

"Call me Hip," the calm man interjected. He smiled and scanned the cabin, making friendly eye contact with each person. Then he looked at the man called Carter and nodded again. A few of the undead appeared to understand what the man was saying. Most were still drifting in the extended netherworld between sleep and wakefulness.

The woman saw another flash of fear in Carter's eyes. "We have lost a lot of people." He gestured toward the hibernation pods, which occupied almost every square meter of the cabin walls. "There were sixty four of us put into hibernation. The ship's intellect found a suitable planet for us to colonize and woke us up. Unfortunately, thirty-three of us didn't make it."

The woman did a quick head count; there were twenty-nine people circling Carter and the doctor. "Captain Chamberlain died in hibernation with the others." The man looked like a deer caught in the headlights of an oncoming car. "I was his first officer and will be assuming command of our expedition." Carter's voice cracked. He paused, glancing again at Hip. He was obviously scared to death. A cold ribbon of fear slipped down the woman's spine. This man was out of his depth. She needed a leader with confidence, someone to provide a firm handhold in the face of the unknown.

"Our first task is to bury the dead." The woman saw the color draining from Carter's face. "We have two landing vehicles to take us down to the surface. We only need one of them now, so we are going to place the dead in Lander B." The woman shuttered at the thought of handling dead people. The urge to vomit returned, but her stomach was empty.

"Once we've moved the bodies, we'll begin our preparations for landing. We're in orbit over our new home." Carter managed a nervous smile. "We are going to spend the next few weeks recovering from hibernation and regaining our strength. Then we'll take Lander A and descend to the surface. We'll start our new lives." A few people nodded in understanding.

"It's a miracle we're here. Our journey was much longer than we expected, and some of our systems have failed." Several more people shook off their befuddlement.

"I'm pretty handy with a hammer if you want to beat this bucket back into shape." Carter twisted to face the person who was speaking. The man was built like a wrestler, with thick arms and legs drawn together in a compact torso. He had beady eyes, which betrayed a bright, but undisciplined mind. His lips were curled up in a sarcastic smile. "That is, if the engineering crew don't mind me pounding on their precious hardware." The man farted as he let loose a deep, guttural laugh.

"You are…" Carter wasn't sure what to make of the man's offer.

"Stub Andrews, mechanical engineer, sir." He added the 'sir' in an offhanded, sarcastic manner. He had noticed Carter's anxiety, too.

"Do you have any experience with intellects? We're having a few issues with the ship's memory."

"Intellects are like women, Captain." Carter's eyes narrowed. "They put out after you put somethin' into 'em." Stub thrust his hips forward. Everyone got his meaning.

"We're a community here, Stub. I don't want any trouble from you."

"Just makin' jokes, boss. Don't mean nothin' personal by it." The man glanced at a couple of the women. "I'm a pretty funny feller." The women turned away nervously. Carter dismissed the man with a thank you, eager to move on to another question.

"Where are we, Mr. Lund?" A bony woman across the cabin spoke with a hoarse, gravelly voice. She coughed.

Carter twisted toward her. He waited for her to catch her breath. "We're all on a first name basis here, Olivia. Just call me Carter."

The woman nodded. She had penetrating eyes and a scowl that telegraphed her displeasure. She glanced at the other colonists. They were half naked, looking like they'd just come out of cold storage. She adjusted her panties and t-shirt in a vain attempt to achieve a modest level of decorum. Then she squared her shoulders. "We have a right to know where we are." She paused, brimming with presumed authority, and added, "Carter."

The nervous first officer wilted momentarily. "We don't know where we are, but our ship's intellect has guided us to the planet which lies three hundred kilometers below us. It will sustain life. In fact, it's a warm planet. I hope you like a tropical climate, Olivia." She sniffed derisively.

"Why are we here?" The woman heard her voice say the words. Everyone looked at her. Stub Andrews undressed her with his eyes. She felt exposed, wishing she could take back her question.

Carter was grateful for a reason to turn away from Olivia. He paused, a look of incredulity on his face. "You don't remember?"

The woman didn't remember. She felt a flash of shame. She felt small, inadequate, stupid. "I'm a little fuzzy," she murmured. It was the only truth she knew.

"I like fuzzy," Stub muttered.

Carter pivoted in his direction. "I warn you, Stub. Keep your comments to yourself." The heavyset man grinned.

Carter turned back to the woman. "Let me refresh your memory. Astronomers detected an asteroid that was on a collision course with Earth. There was no hope for the planet, so we launched ten pod ships, in the hope of preserving the human race. We were put into hibernation, and the pod ships were instructed to find planets where we could live. Our intellect has a digital record of the world's knowledge. We have everything we need to establish a colony." The woman could feel Carter's confidence swelling. "We are the seeds for a new society, a new world. We are humanity's hope." There was nodding around the cabin. Stub scratched his butt.

Carter's words didn't refresh her memory. The woman couldn't remember the asteroid or the plan to save humanity. Was this man telling her the truth? She strained her mind to remember Earth. She could imagine snapshots of scenery. She understood concepts and language, but she had no recollection of any personal experiences. She couldn't remember her parents or growing up. She didn't know what she'd studied in school, whether she had been married, or if she had children. Her mind began to ache as much as her muscles and joints. "How long?" she asked.

Carter hesitated. His eyes darted around the room. He glanced again at Hip, who gave him a serious look. It was obvious the doctor didn't want to tell them how long the hibernation had been. "We expected to be under for about seventy years." Carter began.

The woman shuttered. Seventy years was almost two generations. She felt the cabin begin to spin. The reality was too much to bear. She had not only lost her memory, she had slept through a lifetime. She felt as if a thief had come in the middle of the night and snatched the very thoughts from her head and then as an afterthought, ripped away years and decades of her life. She glanced at the men and women around her. She felt nothing. Her emotional memories were missing, too. Had she loved someone? Did she hate? Was she a kind person? The emptiness in her chest expanded like a supernova, and then collapsed into an emotional black hole. Her life was trapped deep within her, unable to escape the strong forces that had fractured her consciousness.

"…but it took a lot longer for the ship to find an Earth-like planet." Carter's voice was shaking, his panic lurking just under the surface. He spread his arms and slowly turned in the zero-g, making eye contact with each person. Finally, he came to rest facing her and whispered. "We've been in hibernation for over five hundred years."

The woman didn't remember anything after that. There was no way to accommodate this new information, nothing to give her stability or reassurance. She had no recollection of her past. She didn't know her name. She didn't know where she was, and she didn't recognize any of the zombies floating around her. Now she was being told she had been asleep for half a millennium. She tucked herself into a fetal ball. Her stomach churned. The cabin began to spin out of focus. She felt herself choking as everything went dark.

CHAPTER TWO

Strangers

The woman woke up in a small chamber festooned with medical equipment. The man called Hip was studying her with a skilled doctor's eye. He pressed something to her arm, and she felt a fleeting pinch as something shot into her vein. She jerked her arm away, but it was too late. "That's something for your nausea," he said kindly. She could feel the drug take effect. She studied the man's face. He was a good person. His eyes were warm and he exuded personal concern. "Don't worry about being confused," he murmured. His voice was deep, soothing. Hip attached a sensor to her wrist, taking note of a display attached to the bulkhead. "When Carter woke me up, I had everything turned around, too." The doctor folded his arms and hovered next to her. "What's your name?" he asked softly.

The woman flinched. It was like a loud siren went off in her head. She pulled at the smock that covered her body. She hunched her shoulders and stared down at her knees.

"I thought so," Hip whispered. He put a calming hand on her shoulder. "Don't try to remember. If you knew your name, it would have been on the tip of your tongue."

The woman was silent. She watched the doctor study his instruments. There was an emotional wall around her. A deep inner voice whispered to her. It told her to watch her back, choose her alliances carefully. Something commanded her to take nothing at face value. Did the feelings come from some form of training? Had she been hurt somehow? Was the memory of some past violation kicking in subconsciously and making her paranoid? She hadn't a clue.

"Here's what we know about you…" The doctor disconnected the woman's wrist sensor. "We found you in a hibernation pod that didn't belong to you. Does the name Jameson Stryker mean anything to you?" The name hung in the void of her mind. There were no associations triggered by it, no faces or voices, no connections whatsoever. She kept looking down at her knees. She shook her head. "Well then," the doctor went on. "We've got to call you something. Everyone will be interested in you, and you're going to need a name." The woman began to shake. She wanted to hide, to disappear. "Since your hibernation pod had Jameson Stryker's name on it, why don't we call you Jamie? Would that be okay?"

Jamie. The word meant nothing to her. What the hell, it was as good a name as any. She nodded slowly and said, "Jamie."

"Good. I think it's a nice name," Hip offered. "Not as good as your real name, I'm sure, but it will do until you figure things out." The doctor grew serious. "While we're on the subject of Jameson Stryker, I've got to ask you a personal question." Jamie looked at the doctor, panic rising again from the pit of her stomach. She had enough questions for herself and damned few answers. "Is there any way your real name might be Jameson Stryker?" Jamie didn't understand the question. Her face was shrouded in confusion. "That's a man's name, and you're obviously a woman." Hip gave her a gentle smile and squeezed her shoulder again. "Did you have a sex change?"

Jamie's heart stopped. What was this man asking? She glanced down at herself unconsciously. Hip watched her. Their eyes met and she shrugged. Had she been a man? God, this was awful. She wasn't sure. It's one thing to have no memory, but to forget one's gender? A tear pooled in the corner of her eye. She shifted her hips in the zero-g. Her body oscillated slightly. "Look, Jamie," Hip offered. "I'm your doctor. What you tell me will remain between us. You can be honest."

Jamie swallowed and then tried to lick her lips with a dry tongue. She nodded slowly, "I did." She thought she was lying, but she wasn't sure.

Hip gave her a knowing smile. She wondered if he could see through the lie, but he didn't challenge her. "It was one of those advanced jobs, wasn't it?" he asked. "They modified your skeletal structure and re-plumbed your anatomy."

"Spared no expense." Jamie played along.

"Where did you have it done? Brigham and Women's?"

She shrugged. "I don't remember." She felt the urge to pee.

"I examined you when you were coming out of hibernation." Hip orbited around her. "You don't have any scars." He gazed at her with a professional eye, nodding in appreciation. "It was a perfect piece of work."

Jamie didn't respond. The whole exchange was bazaar. She willed her bladder muscles to relax. Maybe she was schizophrenic. She must have an alter ego that was holding her memory captive. Getting a sex change operation wasn't something a person forgot. Had she been this Jameson

Stryker?

"Have we met?" she managed.

"A long time ago, I think. I sat in on the pre-flight physicals."

"Then you know things about me." Jamie cleared her throat. "Medical things."

Hip's cheeks reddened. "Not exactly. I'm afraid I don't remember a lot from those physicals. I wasn't the one conducting them, and I haven't been able to access your medical records." He exhaled, offering Jamie a whimsical smile. "I'm afraid I'll have to ask you everything all over again."

Good luck. "Now?" she asked. Jamie couldn't remember a single thing about her medical history.

"No." Hip patted her arm. "There's plenty of time for that." Jamie sighed. The doctor could see her nervousness. "You're going to fit right in, Jamie. We're all feeling overwhelmed." Jamie saw a brief, faraway look in his eyes. "Your past isn't as important as your future." Jamie sensed a deep sadness in the man, as though a bandage had been lifted, revealing a profound wound. Who was he trying to convince? It didn't matter. In that moment, she'd give anything to remember who she was.

* * *

The interior of the pod ship was mostly white. Every flat surface was lined with equipment racks tucked between quilted bulkheads. The hibernation chamber was the largest cabin on board. The dead had been moved to Lander B, their empty pods a silent reminder of the risks they were all facing. The large cabin would be their bunkroom and common area until they left the safety of the pod ship for the alien world below.

Jamie hung motionless at the entrance to the hibernation chamber. She wasn't sure she wanted to sleep in her pod. She tried to imagine her inert body lying there for five hundred years. The thought was too big for her. She felt pangs of fear, wondering if a short nap would result in another lost century. She felt the futility of friendship. Even if she could remember loved ones, they were all dead, swept away by the ages. She pulled her arms to her chest, careful to avoid any momentum that would send her body across the chamber. She hugged herself tightly. The emotional wall grew thicker around her. Loneliness enveloped her like an impermeable membrane, making it hard to breathe.

Jamie's companions were hovering by their pods. Each was pouring through items contained in personal effects drawers built into the faces of the units. Victoria Willis was an Amazonian woman with a ghost-like demeanor. She seldom spoke, but was aware of everything around her. She was their security chief. She was a strong woman who had spent years undergoing intense physical training. Jamie translated past her, and Vickie looked up. The woman warrior gave her a dismissive stare and turned her attention back to the items from her drawer.

Jamie continued along her trajectory across the hibernation chamber. A slender man with long delicate fingers nodded to her. "Pay no attention to her," he said, gesturing toward Vickie. "I don't think she's human. She was probably hatched out of an armory on some experimental military base." Jamie grabbed a handhold to stop her forward motion. The man had bright red hair and green eyes. "I'm Russell Wolf." He stuck out his hand. Jamie surprised herself as she reached out reflexively and took it. Their palms met. Fingers touched. The man's hands were very strong, yet gentle. The sensation almost staggered her. She hadn't touched a human hand for centuries.

"Jamie Stryker," she heard herself say. The name would do.

The man's smile broadened. "Everybody calls me Rusty because of my hair. My folks always told me it's red 'cause they left me out in the rain." He didn't give Jamie a chance to laugh. The man must have told the story so many times, he offered it without thinking. "You really don't remember all that stuff about the asteroid, do you?"

"My mind feels like it's full of cotton."

"I know what you mean." Rusty was gripping something tightly in his free hand. The man had pulled back into himself. He exuded a profound sadness for a brief second, and then his big smile returned. "Don't worry. You're going to be just fine." Jamie nodded her thanks and pushed off toward her hibernation pod. What was he hiding? She remembered the doctor's brief melancholy. Rusty had been broken, too. It was a comfort. She wasn't alone in the dark labyrinth.

Parker Davies' pod was next to Jamie's. She was a slender blonde woman with short golden hair and perfectly formed breasts, which floated under the thin fabric of her jumpsuit. Her nickname was Bliss. She exuded sexuality. Her striking femininity was like a magnet, drawing men toward her like cosmic dust in a strong gravitational field. She was erotic as hell. Bliss seemed oblivious to the effect she had on men. She treated them like brothers, moving in close, punching their shoulders, touching their faces. She drove them crazy. Jamie thought it was an act.

Bliss hung by the pod, her legs pointed toward the ceiling of the chamber. Her torso hunched over her open drawer. She was cradling an old photograph in her hand. Jamie paused by her side. She could see the picture over Bliss's shoulder. It was the image of a family: a father with an arrogant smile, a mother with a tired face, and two young girls. The family resemblance was unmistakable. Jamie looked at Bliss's father. His hand was on his daughter's knee. It didn't look like a fatherly touch. "Your family?" she asked softly.

"Yeah," Bliss whispered. Jamie saw a slight tremor in the woman's hand.

Jamie looked at the older child. She could tell it was Bliss. There was a hint of discomfort in her eyes. "You have your father's eyes."

Bliss stiffened. "Everybody says that, but it isn't true. I'm more like my mother, you know?"

"Sorry."

"No!" Bliss pleaded. "Don't worry about it. You couldn't know. My dad and I didn't get along." She clutched Jamie's arm. "I wish he wasn't in the picture. He didn't know how to raise daughters. We sort of brought out the animal in him, you know?"

It was more than Jamie wanted to hear. She changed the subject. "Your sister is pretty."

"Thanks." Bliss paused. "She was great. She's dead of course." Bliss still clung to Jamie's arm. "Do you miss your family?"

"Yes, I do." The words tumbled from Jamie's lips without her thinking. "I'm afraid I don't remember them very well."

"You don't remember your parents?" Bliss was confounded by the thought.

Jamie kicked herself. She didn't want anyone to know about her amnesia. She measured the emotional distance between them. Bliss seemed harmless, even delicate. Jamie liked her. "I've been having trouble remembering things."

"You're lucky, honey." Bliss gave her a hard, sisterly look. "Some memories you don't want to remember, you know?" She released her grip on Jamie and looked back at the photograph. Jamie saw the frightened child inside the voluptuous beauty.

Jamie moved to her left until she was in front of her hibernation pod. She stared at the drawer. She wondered what was in it. Perhaps there would be clues to her past, reminders of who she was. She braced herself on a handhold and unlatched the drawer. It slid toward her. The drawer was like an old safety deposit box with a hinged metal lid. The moment was overwhelming. The items in the box would be links to her past. A photograph like Bliss's might trigger a catalytic memory and bring everything back to her. She might see the faces of her parents and remember her name. She slid the catch and opened the container. It was empty.

* * *

Hip made it clear that no one was ready to go through the rigors of landing on the alien planet below them. Everyone needed several weeks of physical training to bring their bodies back to optimal condition. Jamie struggled on a device that resembled a stationary bicycle, pushing her leg muscles to their limit. She always rode a bike near the wall where no one could sit behind her. Each session, she rode further than the one before. She could feel her strength returning, her muscles recovering their tone.

Jamie focused on her body and the large blank screen in her mind where her memories were supposed to be. She didn't like talking with her fellow travelers. They would ask her questions she could not answer. She lied to avoid the awkward silences induced by her ignorance. She was tired of pretending, so she kept to herself.

Jamie pumped harder against the pedals. Her muscles burned. She thought about the day when Hip asked her about the sex change. She knew she had lied to him. She had no proof, no personal knowledge to back up the feeling, but she was certain of it. She needed the comfort of a few absolutes. She had always been a woman. She was using a borrowed name. Jamie wondered if Jameson Stryker would mind. For the first time in centuries, Jamie laughed. The man had died five hundred years ago.

Rusty with the red hair was on an exercise bike ahead of her. Jamie watched his hips oscillate as he pedaled the machine. He was stripped to the waist. She could see the bumps of his spinal column marching down his back and disappearing beneath the waistband of his shorts. She watched his body move. Shouldn't she feel something? If she was truly a woman, Rusty's beautiful body should have triggered some kind of sexual response. She felt nothing.

Vickie the security chief was on the bike next to Rusty. She pedaled effortlessly. She was never out of breath. She watched the woman's smooth movement and then glanced back at Rusty. She could see the subtle differences in their pelvic structures. Vickie's hips were wider. Her legs pumped up and down at a slightly different angle. Jamie wasn't aroused by either of them. She hoped a physical urging might help her unravel the mystery of her sexual preference. Lingering doubts began to replace the fleeting certainty she had felt.

Jamie slowed her pace, allowing her muscles to cool down. Her exercise period was drawing to a close. Her fingers shook as she unfastened the harness. She pushed away from the handlebars and floated out of the room.

* * *

Jamie was hovering in the wash area a few moments later. An enclosed capsule surrounded her while water sprayed over her body. A suction unit below her feet removed the water as quickly as it entered the chamber from above. The shower felt like being caught in a river of wind-driven water droplets. The chamber had a perforated floor, offering her a footing as the force of the water pushed her body toward the drain in the weightless environment. She luxuriated in the cleansing stream and then punched a button. The water droplets were replaced by a soothing blast of warm air that cascaded over her wet hair and down through her toes.

* * *

Jamie entered the dining cabin. She was dressed in one of the ubiquitous blue jumpsuits. Her hair was still damp, an occasional globule of water drifting away as she moved her head. She propelled herself across the cabin and grabbed a handhold by the beverage dispenser. The synthetic hazelnut coffee was quite good. She filled a bag and rotated in place, scanning for a quiet place to enjoy her daily indulgence.

Thomas Paul was hovering on the other side of the cabin, sipping a bag of warm tea. He caught Jamie's eye and smiled. There was no avoiding him. "Come and join me," he offered. Jamie preferred being alone but didn't want to offend. She drifted over and gripped a handhold to stop her motion. He looked at her hair. "How are you doing on the bike?"

Jamie was surprised. She didn't like people checking up on her. "Have you been stalking me?" she asked with an accusing glare.

Thomas laughed. It was a disarming chuckle. She couldn't help but smile. "I saw your wet hair and thought you'd just come out of the shower. That usually happens after exercise."

Jamie ran her fingers through her hair nervously. It was

simple logic. She nodded.

Thomas took another pull on his bag of tea. "How's your conditioning coming along?"

Jamie rubbed her leg unconsciously. "Okay, I guess. I'm doing better than the first week. I never want to go through that again."

"You're not kidding. I thought I was going to die." Thomas's eyes sparkled. "So, what's your story?"

Jamie stiffened. This was why she avoided small talk. She tried to remember some of the lies she had told her other companions. Sooner or later, she would be exposed by her inconsistencies. She was sure of it. Her body moved in the weightless environment, a tell revealing her emotional facade. She reached up and gripped a handhold. "What do you mean?"

"Everybody has a story. You know… birth, growing up, success, failure, hopes. What brought you here?"

Jamie could feel her pulse rise. "I didn't like the idea of being around when the asteroid hit the Earth."

Thomas almost spit up his tea. "That goes without saying," he said dryly. "I mean, where were you born and what was your family like? Did you have a husband?"

Jamie didn't know how she was going to deflect the man's probing questions. "I'm average," she heard herself say. "There's nothing unusual about me."

"I doubt that," Thomas looked at her deeply. "Everybody's interesting. You just have to listen. Why are you so evasive? Were you running from something?"

Jamie hadn't considered the possibility. Had she forgotten her past because it was horrible? Had she been the victim of some kind of psychological torture? She gave

Thomas a befuddled look. It was easy, given her amnesia. "Maybe," she said. "I could be running from nosey people who try to pry their way into my life." Thomas frowned. "You're the holy man, aren't you?" Jamie wanted desperately to shift the conversation away from herself.

Thomas laughed, shrugging off the insult. Jamie noticed how emotionally agile the man was. "I guess you could call me that."

Jamie had an instinctual disdain for religion. She didn't know where it came from. She wondered if there was a bad experience with a church in her past. She couldn't remember. Jamie had watched Thomas dispense more than his share of pabulum to the other travelers. She hated simplistic answers to difficult questions. She did have a respect for mysteries. After all, she was struggling with one of her own.

Thomas didn't notice the skeptical expression on Jamie's face. He was filled with enthusiasm. "In a couple of weeks, we are going to set up housekeeping on a new world. We may encounter alien life. I'm here to remind us of our spiritual values. My goal is to proclaim the Lordship of Jesus. This is an amazing opportunity to spread the Word of God. We might bring a whole new species to a saving knowledge of Christ. We may lead an entire civilization to heaven."

Jamie thought he was reading from a script. It was as if someone had pumped the words into his head, and he was regurgitating them by rote. "What if the aliens are happy the way they are?" she asked.

"That is impossible, Jamie. No one can be happy without the Lord. God fills the emptiness in every life, alien or otherwise."

"I think you're wrong about that." Jamie regretted the comment, even before she finished saying the words.

"Are you a religious person?" The conversation was shifting toward her again. She swore at herself.

"Sure," she lied. Jamie was fairly certain she wasn't religious, but she knew she'd have an easier time agreeing with him. If she said no, he'd probably try to convert her. After all, she couldn't remember. Maybe five centuries ago she had been a nun.

"Is Christ your Lord and Savior?"

Jamie recoiled at the question. It was none of his damned business. She decided she hadn't been a nun. "What do you mean?" she parried.

"Are you certain of your place in heaven?"

This was getting worse. Jamie didn't know what to do. She couldn't remember what she believed. She wasn't drawn toward prayer. She couldn't recall any transcendent experiences. She had her doubts about the existence of God or heaven. "It's a very personal thing. I'd rather not talk about it."

Thomas gave her an intense, knowing look. "It is personal, Jamie. It's between you and Jesus. You must surrender to Him, if you are to enter the kingdom of heaven." Jamie looked into his eyes. He was saying words from the script again, words from some spiritual director's handbook that were deemed appropriate for frightening unsuspecting people into faith. The man didn't have a clue.

Jamie took a long swig from her coffee bag. "It's time for me to turn in," she said. "Nice talking to you, Thomas." It was another lie.

"Rest well, Jamie." Thomas tipped his flask toward her. It was like a one-sided toast. "And remember, sooner or later you will have to come to terms with Jesus."

She nodded and launched herself toward the hatchway. She couldn't wait to get out of there.

CHAPTER THREE

Descent

C arter Lund liked to end each waking period with a meeting. He called it "checking in." Everyone would gather in a circle like they had done on the first day. Carter wanted them to share what was on their minds. He **went** around the circle, urging each person to say a few words. Jamie always declined. He would ask her if she had something to share and then wait, hoping the uncomfortable silence would compel her to speak. It never worked. Jamie hovered resolutely in place without a word. Eventually, he would move on to the next person, and they would say something to avoid the prolonged attention. Better to say something trivial than endure the scrutiny that came with silence. Jamie wasn't trying to be stubborn; she didn't know what to say. They had come out of hibernation nearly four weeks ago, and she still couldn't remember who she was. What in hell was she supposed to share?

Carter finished his interrogation and folded his hands. Hip floated by his side. The doctor wore a worried scowl. "Hip has some bad news for us." Carter deferred to his companion.

"For the last few weeks, we have been trying to address

an issue with the ship's intellect. It hasn't put us in immediate danger, so we haven't said anything until we understood the scope of the problem. It seems our library is offline. We can't access any of the ship's memory." He paused to let his statement sink in. Jamie smiled to herself. Now there were two of them with amnesia. Several of her fellow travelers had concerned looks on their faces. Olivia Jepson frowned. She wore her disapproval like a war medal, as if she enjoyed it. Bliss was fussing with her hair. She was in another world. Stub was on the other side of the cabin watching her. Nothing was more important to him than a sexy woman.

Hip kept his voice calm. "The ship was jammed full of information before we launched. We were carrying digital copies of every published book. I spoke with the artificial intelligence, and she has no idea where they are. We've checked the intellects on both Landers, and their storage wells have been filled with routine flight data. The intellect can remember back about three hundred years, but that's it. We have lost the collected history of the human race."

Everyone was stunned by the news. A large part of their mission had been to preserve human knowledge. Without the vast store of information in the ship's intellect, they would have to begin again, building a foundation from the precious little knowledge each could remember. The measure of lost history, science, mathematics, and art was staggering. Stub belched and scratched his groin.

Olivia Jepson raised her hand. She looked like a stern schoolteacher who had caught an errant child misbehaving on the playground. "That is totally unacceptable," she chided. Her voice had an edge to it, like chalk on an ancient blackboard.

Hip nodded. "I agree. It's not good."

Olivia's voice became more severe. "We were depending

on that knowledge to establish our new society."

"That's right," Carter replied evenly.

"Weren't there safeguards in place to prevent this from happening?" She gave Carter an accusing glare.

"I'm not a software engineer Olivia, but I'm sure there were. I don't know what went wrong."

"Well you should. The captain is supposed to know." She scanned everyone's faces. "Who is our data specialist?"

This time, Hip answered her. "We had three of them. They all died in hibernation."

"Are you telling me no one has the expertise to fix the intellect?" She said it like a disappointed mother.

"That's right," Carter replied. "Even if the data is still in memory, we can't access it."

"I am very disappointed in you, Carter Lund." Olivia enjoyed pointing out other people's mistakes. "If you ask me, you are a poor leader. You have failed to instill confidence in us, and now you have demonstrated your incompetence."

Hip slid toward her. His face was flush with anger. "Don't you dare question the captain! We owe him our respect!"

The stern woman was caught off guard. She sniffed. "He's going to kill us all."

Hip positioned himself squarely in front of her. "That is enough, Olivia! We're going to survive. Our ancestors solved problems and left a record for future generations. We're going to go down to that planet and do the same thing."

"What do these people know?" Olivia scanned everyone condescendingly.

"More than you give us credit for." Hip met her gaze.

Stub raised his hand. "I got my hammer," he offered blithely. Hip pivoted and gave him a dirty look.

Olivia shook her head. "See what I mean?"

Carter was brimming with determination. "We are going to take Lander A down to the surface, and we're going to establish our colony. We'll solve whatever problems we face." Jamie was struck by how Carter was simply paraphrasing what Hip had already said. "We'll preserve everything we can remember, and we'll rebuild our knowledge base as we go. The loss of the ship's library is a big step backwards, but that doesn't mean we can't move forward."

Jamie watched as Carter continued to address the group. He commanded their attention, but there was something more: they were all drawn to him. They needed him. She studied their body language. Most of them were too scared to notice his uncertainty. Olivia was right. Carter was in over his head. She shifted her gaze to Hip. The doctor was unflappable, a calm presence under pressure. At least Carter listened to him. She shuttered at the alternative. All leaders were flawed, but chaos always surrounded ineffectual men like Carter. She noticed Hip watching everyone's reaction. Their eyes met briefly, and he gave her a confident smile. She offered a slight nod in return, and then Hip's eyes shifted to Rusty, who was floating next to her.

"I have a question, Captain Carter." All eyes turned toward Bliss. "Did we lose all the cosmetology records?" She floated in the zero-g with her legs wide apart. She was teasing a snarl out of her hair. All the men were transfixed. "I need to look good, you know?" Olivia snorted and several others looked away. Bliss was being serious. Apparently, she had not grasped the greater implications of losing humanity's knowledge. "You boys won't be interested in an ugly woman, you know?"

Stub rolled his eyes. "Oh, my god," he swore under his breath. He leaned over to Ben Beck and whispered something. Ben was one of Vickie's security officers. The two men had become friends over the past several weeks and enjoyed making rude comments about the women. Ben laughed. Jamie heard the word "stupid" as the two men smiled mockingly at the young woman. Bliss gave them a dark frown, frustration and hurt written on her face. Stub poked his tongue against his cheek and made an obscene gesture with his hands. Bliss folded her arms across her chest and turned away.

Jamie spoke on impulse. "I have a question." Everyone turned toward her. She cursed herself. The question in her mind would expose her to the group. Once asked, she would never be able to take it back. She drew her knees together and brought them up, as if she was sitting in an invisible chair. "The ship's not the only one with amnesia," she began. "I've been having trouble remembering who I am. I don't even remember my name. Do you know anything about me?" She could hear the desperation in her voice. "I really want to know."

No one spoke. Ben leaned over to Stub and whispered to him again. The two men smiled at Jamie and nodded in agreement. She knew the look. They saw her as an object, something for their amusement. There was an awkward silence, and then Hip intervened. He urged people to speak to Jamie if they had any information. As Carter adjourned the meeting, Jamie heard Stub suggest that stupidity was contagious. No one came forward with any clues to her identity.

* * *

Pod ships weren't designed as sightseeing vessels. The

only viewport was on the flight deck. The massive ship was like a cocoon, holding its precious cargo within its hull. Two Landers hung on the ends of wing-like struts on either side of the vessel. They were hybrid vehicles designed to operate in space as well as an atmosphere. Each resembled a stubby aircraft with a broad fuselage and triangular wings. The Landers were designed to contain an immense amount of food and supplies. They were ugly and powerful, each with a blunt nose and massive engines mounted at the tip of each wing.

Lander B had been converted into a crypt, the dead colonists carefully sealed in body bags and placed within her. She would remain in orbit, docked with the pod ship, a silent reminder of the risks of long duration space flight. Her sister ship, Lander A, was poised for departure.

Jamie had wriggled through the cramped access way and strapped herself into one of the passenger carriers. They were narrow slots along the pressure hull, designed to protect a human body during descent. Comfort had been the last thing on the minds of those who designed them. Everyone was claustrophobic, packed into the Lander like sardines. Hip had given everyone a sedative to take the edge off their anxiety. Jamie felt entombed. She smiled sardonically to herself. Maybe this was her tomb. If the Lander faltered or a fire erupted in the interior of the ship, they would all perish. She closed her eyes and tried to imagine herself wandering through a field of flowers. Where did that image come from? She didn't care. Anything was better than the cramped horror of the Lander.

The rumble of the Lander's engines vibrated the hull. Jamie's hip bone was pressed against the bulkhead, and the vibration shook her skeleton. Her teeth rattled. She brought her arms up to her face and pressed her palms against a cargo container that hung less than four centimeters from her nose.

She thought she could feel the container move toward her. A wave of panic flooded her at the thought of being crushed.

Jamie felt the Lander separate from the pod ship. Lateral thrusters pushed everyone to one side, and then she sensed the ship rotate along its major axis, lining up for the deorbit burn. The ship flew smoothly on its trajectory for a few moments. The interior of the ship hummed from the sounds of pumps and blowers, but everyone was spared from the gut wrenching g-forces. Then the main engines fired, and Jamie was slammed toward her feet. A strap dug into her armpits, and she jammed her knees against the cargo case in front of her. The deafening roar of the engines filled the ship, accompanied by intense vibrations.

The temperature in the Lander began to rise. A rush of warm air coursed through the narrow access way. The smell of burning plastic wafted around her, and Jamie felt something like a burning ember touch her hip. She shifted her body away from the bulkhead and reached down blindly with her hand to feel the wall next to her. It was too hot to touch. The warm wind grew hotter. Now she could smell something melting. She heard a scream, then another. They were going to die.

CHAPTER FOUR
Arrival

No one died. The Lander descended through the thickening atmosphere of the alien planet and set down on a beach of pale green sand. One of the struts sank into the granular surface, canting the ship at an odd angle. One engine, still hot from the descent, dipped into the violet water. A geyser of steam blasted into the air. There was a terrible noise, and the ship's airframe shuttered as the engine disintegrated. The wing, no longer burdened by the weight of the massive engine, rose out of the water. The Lander pitched toward the beach and then came to a rest, squatting unevenly on the shore.

The air was still hot inside the Lander. Jamie sucked in a breath and felt a wave of panic. She didn't want to die, especially by fire or suffocation. She unstrapped herself, yielding to the urge to escape from the ship. She was heavy. It had been a long time since she had felt the force of gravity. Her arms and legs were like lumps of lead. Her panic grew. She slid herself out of the narrow passenger carrier and tumbled down to the decking in the access way. There was no headroom, so she crawled laboriously on all fours toward the Lander's main hatch. She heard a high-pitched hiss, like the sound of escaping steam, and then felt an odd-smelling rush of air course around her. Someone had opened the hatch.

Jamie froze. She didn't know what to do. Would the alien atmosphere kill them? She held her breath until her chest burned. Then she exhaled the last of the ship's air from her lungs and closed her eyes. This was it. Her life was over. She drew in a deep breath. The air was warm, but cooler than the interior of the Lander. It had a sweet taste as it slipped over her tongue. She could feel her lungs expand, and a pleasant warmth in her chest began to spread through her body. She closed her mouth, not wanting to take a second breath until she trusted the first. She relaxed her diaphragm and waited for her body to demand another breath. She didn't breathe again for two minutes, doing so out of habit rather than need. The strange atmosphere was hyper-charged, one breath equivalent to several of Earth's air.

Jamie walked on her palms and knees through the access way. As she neared the main hatch, she saw a shaft of violet light illuminating the last few meters of the passage. She dragged her heavy body into the crowded hold, grasping handholds on containers and bulkheads as she struggled forward. She followed a man in front of her. He was having trouble, too. The odd light grew brighter. Finally, Jamie pulled herself to a standing position at the main hatch. She paused at the top of the ramp, which led toward the surface below.

A dreamlike scene lay before her. A long strip of pale green sand stretched indefinitely into the distance, rimming a violet sea. She walked down the ramp on rubbery legs, wanting to stand clear of the Lander's fuselage. Jamie looked at the lavender ocean and then raised her eyes. Unlike Earth, the sun was setting in the east, kissing the distant edge of the alien sea. A series of golden rings arched across the violet sky, rising to perhaps sixty degrees above the horizon, glistening with reflected light. Two moons hung like sisters beyond the rings. The larger was pale and foreboding, while her smaller sibling was like a mirror, offering a distorted reflection of the planet to those on the surface.

A jungle lay inland of the beach. The odd flora undulated in the gentle breeze. Jamie stood still, like a visitor in an art gallery, transfixed by a beautiful painting. Strange, squatty trees with sinewy branches stood at attention along the edge of the sand. Their triangular leaves seemed hard, clicking together as they oscillated in the air currents that pressed across the water. The plants had no roots. Rather, each had branches spreading along the ground from its trunk, joining seamlessly with its neighbor. A carpet of crimson turf lay beneath the wood. The grass was short and fine, resembling hair. Each strand rippled in the moving air, tiny vortices twisting their way across the blood colored sod. A river broke the shoreline about three hundred meters from where she stood, its water foaming over a small waterfall as it joined the sea. A mist rose where the waters merged, the sun's rays creating a monotone rainbow in shades of violet and purple.

Jamie's legs would hold her no longer. She sat down on the sand to rest. The only sounds came from the water lapping upon the shore and the breeze clicking through the brittle leaves of the trees. There were no birds or insects, no signs of fish or lizards. She dug her hand into the sand, the tiny granules falling through her fingers like an hourglass. Nothing moved. There were no shells or telltale flotsam revealing the presence of animal life.

She looked at the other colonists. Each had descended the ramp and stood awestruck at the water's edge. Most of them had flopped down on the beach, sharing her fatigue in the planet's gravitational field. Jamie wondered if they would survive, thirty-one people posited on the shore of an ancient sea. She and her companions had crawled out of the sky, venturing onto the land of this alien planet. Civilization was beginning again. She questioned how civilized it would be.

* * *

Carter and Vickie took a small contingent into the jungle. They would need a site for the permanent settlement. They returned with great excitement, having found an open area about half a kilometer inland. The colonists would rest under the wings of the Lander and start building their settlement at first light. They wasted no time pulling scores of crates and panels from the Lander. They arranged them under the edges of the wing, forming a perimeter to protect them from any predators that might wander the beach after dark. As light began to fade, everyone lay on the sand, exhausted from their first day. The alien twilight was extended by the sun's rays reflecting on the mirrored moon and the planet's rings.

Jamie sat in a corner of the temporary shelter as Spud Andrews closed the Lander's hatch. The tropical breeze blew inland from the ocean. The temperature was hot, but tolerable. She was grateful they hadn't landed on an ice world. Cold and snow would have made life miserable. Jamie ached. It would be days before she could move around in the planet's gravity without noticing its force. She sat on a thin cushion. Her knees were bent, and she wrapped her arms around her shins. A central light illuminated the heart of the shelter like a campfire, its soft glow tapering off into shadows around the perimeter of the space. There were a few hushed conversations, but most of the colonists sat quietly. Like Jamie, they were exhausted from the landing and the day's work.

Hip and Vickie were huddled around Carter. They spoke in low tones. The captain was obviously unsure of himself as they laid plans for the new settlement. Jamie was sure the triumvirate had formed due to Carter's fear rather than his wisdom, but it was a good mix, nonetheless. Hip brought humanity, while Vickie offered pure cunning. The three came to some sort of conclusion and broke their tight circle. Carter stood near the light and pivoted slowly, surveying everyone's faces. It was time for another meeting. He put his hands together and smiled. The murmuring died almost immediately. "It's been a really good day," he began. "The landing was a little rougher than I had hoped for, but we didn't end up in the water." A couple of people rubbed sore muscles and joints as they remembered the forty-five minutes of terror that preceded touchdown. "As it turns out, we've landed in an ideal spot. Our settlement will be in a clearing a few hundred meters beyond the beach. There's a natural path through the trees. We'll take a couple of the logistics people with us tomorrow and do a complete site survey. Stub and his construction crew will supervise the unloading of the Lander. We'll need to lay some panels on the beach to make a suitable roadbed. With luck, we'll start carrying things to the site by tomorrow afternoon." Carter sat back down. Jamie listened to the hushed voices of her companions. The murmurings lingered for a while and then tapered off.

Jamie lay quietly on her cushion. She could hear her heart beating in her chest. The alien surf sang its endless song, pulsing with the rhythm of the waves as they lapped gently against the shore. She felt the sting of loneliness. She didn't know the people around her. She knew nothing of this strange planet. She did not know who she was. She rolled to one side, letting out a long sigh. There were too many mysteries. She longed for an anchor point, one memory she could use as a handhold. None came. Fatigue defeated her, and she slipped into a dreamless sleep.

* * *

The roots of the alien trees created a tripping hazard through the jungle. Most of them were less than fifteen centimeters in diameter, but they crisscrossed the ground and would make it difficult to carry supplies from the Lander to the clearing. Fortunately, Carter's team had found a natural path roughly halfway between the Lander and the small river. Its labyrinthine avenue wove between the roots, offering a meandering lane void of obstacles. Carter called it the beach trail.

Jamie followed behind Thomas as the colonists navigated back and forth along the trail. The smell of the jungle was sweet. The morning light filtered down through the brittle leaves and cast intricate shadows on the crimson turf underfoot. Odd fluorescent stalks crowned with spherical seed pods flanked the trail. They shimmered as occasional shafts of light struck their luminous sheathing, offering a visual pastiche of blue, green, and orange hues. Jamie was so wrapped in awe at the fantastical scene, she failed to notice Thomas slowing his pace. The man fell into step beside her. "This trail will be great for meditation," he commented.

Jamie was startled by the sound of his voice. "What?" she stammered, feeling a profound disconnect between the man's words and what she was experiencing.

"The trail," Thomas seemed oblivious to the wonder around them. "The way it cuts this way and that is like a spiritual labyrinth. It's a great discipline. It can draw you closer to God."

Jamie shooed the man away. She didn't want to evaluate the efficacy of the serpentine route of the beach trail. She didn't want to think about spiritual practices. She wanted to take in the indescribable world around her, luxuriate in its impossibility.

The winding path through the woods widened out into a substantial clearing, carpeted with the reddish grass and void of trees and roots. It was the perfect place to build their settlement. Carter gathered everyone and asked Thomas to bless the land. The holy man's voice deepened as he intoned the prayer, calling upon all that was transcendent to purify their intentions and establish their new home in peace. He spoke of alathea, which was an ancient word for "truth," challenging everyone to create a society based on honesty and integrity. Jamie winced as he commanded Satan to stay away. She felt like they had slipped back into medieval times, full of fear and mysticism. She wondered if Thomas realized what he was saying. They had a chance to make a fresh start, to lay aside some of the insanities of religion and prejudice and class. Instead, they were invoking the anthropomorphisms of a lesser god, who was in conflict with an imaginary boogeyman.

Jamie didn't close her eyes during the prayer. She felt nothing, no divine nudges or inner spiritual warmth. She was skeptical about the whole affair. Losing her memory had wiped away her assumptions. If she had been a religious person before she lost her memory, she certainly wasn't now. The colonists surrounding her would be no different than any other collection of human beings. Their fate rested with chance. Perhaps prayer-centered lives would have a calming effect on those who were prone to nervousness, but it would not save them from a virulent microorganism or an unanticipated side effect of the alien air they were breathing. Jamie saw religion as an expression of humanity's need for absolutes. She frowned and shook her head. It was always easier to exchange certainty for reality. Jamie shuttered at her own hypocrisy. She wanted to remember, to gain certainty from a reality she had forgotten. She was no different than her companions.

"You say the word alathea means truth?" Carter's voice cut through Jamie's muse. She looked up. Thomas was nodding. "Let's call this planet Alathea, then. It rolls off your tongue, sounds nice." Carter didn't wait for approval. He clapped his hands impatiently. "Prayer time is over, folks. Now let's get to work."

* * *

They had studied Alathea from orbit. Her axis was tilted and there were seasons, but they had landed near the equator, where climatic variations were minimal. They knew she had a rotational period of thirty-two hours. The days were long. There were sixteen hours of light, give or take. The mirrored moon and luminous rings extended the twilight, making the days even longer. The mornings dawned with an early heat, and the temperature rose for almost eight hours until midday. It got hotter and hotter through the long afternoon, until the sun dipped beneath the horizon, having baked her victims for eight more hours.

Their first obstacle was the sandy beach. Everyone labored in the planet's gravity, their feet sinking into the soft granular surface. They took panels from the Lander, and arranged them end to end across the pale green sand. The flat pieces of metal formed a narrow road, over which they would carry the contents of the ship's hold to the tree line. The reddish jungle sod offered them a firmer footing along the beach trail and into the clearing.

By midday, the sun was baking the metal panels. Walking on them was like traversing a bed of hot coals. To make matters worse, the air was uncomfortably warm. Everyone took a break. Jamie sat alone on a case under the Lander's wing. She examined the small food packet in her hand, wondering how many of them were in the ship's cargo hold. They were going to have to grow their own food sooner or later. She ripped open the wrapper and took a bite. It tasted like peanut butter. How did she know that? She could remember the names of flavors and colors. She knew words and basic sentence construction, but she didn't remember any experiences. Somewhere among the thousands of words in her brain was her name. She was pretty sure it wasn't Jamie. She wished it were as easy to remember as peanut butter.

That afternoon, Jamie lost track of the number of trips she had made from the Lander to the clearing. Her jumpsuit was sodden, and she smelled. The subtle sea breeze was barely perceptible and did little to comfort her as she carried a bulky flight case down the ramp from the ship's hold. She dragged it along the makeshift road surface toward the tree line. The box shook as it slammed across the seams between the uneven metal panels. She felt a sharp twinge of pain in her back. Jamie pulled the case with every ounce of her strength, grunting under its burden.

Another colonist whisked by her, making it clear she was in his way. "You forget how to work, too?" he chided. Jamie blushed as two other colonists laughed at the comment. She mustered every last bit of her strength and pulled the case rapidly down a slight decline in the path. The edge of it caught in the gap between the road panels. Jamie lost her grip and the case careened into the soft sand. She fell headlong onto the torrid road surface, skinning her knees and palms.

"How did you ever get placed on this expedition?" The voice was dripping with sarcasm. Jamie rolled painfully to her side and caught a glimpse of Stub Andrews. He was carrying a case on his shoulder. "You gotta pull your weight, Miss Nobody. We all have to do our part." Jamie didn't reply. She grunted and pulled herself up. She staggered over to the case that was now half buried in the sand. "Let's see you sweat, little girl."

Jamie slid the case back toward the roadway as Stub disappeared into the trees. She made little progress, her attempts to gain leverage diminished by the shifting granules under her feet. She cursed the cargo case. She pounded the top of the box as her eyes filled with tears.

Jamie was startled by another set of hands reaching for the case. "Let me help you." It was Bliss. The woman had left her case on the roadway to help her. Bliss smiled. "We can get it." Jamie stepped aside to give Bliss some room, and the two women rolled the case back toward the nearest roadway panel.

"What a pair of weaklings!" Ben Beck emerged from under the trees. Stub must have said something to him when they crossed paths in the jungle.

"Up yours!" Bliss shot back.

"It takes two of you brainless idiots to carry a simple case," was the reply.

Bliss squared her shoulders and stood up straight, facing the man. "Asshole!" she muttered.

"Now that's something you might be good for!" Ben wiggled his hips and trotted back toward the Lander.

They pushed the case against the edge of the roadway and leaned into it. The case tipped up on its edge and slammed down on the hard surface. "Thanks," Jamie gasped.

Bliss smiled proudly. "We didn't give up, you know?"

Jamie nodded as she grabbed a case handle and continued dragging her burden toward the tree line.

* * *

That night, they slept out under the stars. Everyone was exhausted from their eighteen-hour workday. They arranged their cushions close together for security. There had been no sign of predators in the jungle, but Vickie had insisted on everyone staying in the clearing. She and two other security specialists would stand guard through the long night. Jamie folded herself up on her cushion. Her body ached, and she felt a deep exhaustion beyond anything she had ever felt before.

* * *

Jamie's eyes snapped open. Anxiety filled her as every sense went on high alert. It was the middle of the night, yet someone was shouting. She pitched herself up and pulled her legs under her into a kneeling position. She could hear the sound of bare feet running on the thick sod. "Look at that!" someone yelled. Jamie turned in the direction of the voice. A small knot of colonists stood a short distance away. They were looking toward the southwest, over the tree line that defined the edge of the clearing. The ever-present rings hung in the sky, casting a golden wash over the clearing. Somewhere in the jungle, or beyond it, was a greenish glow. It was coming from the planet surface, like the lights of a city illuminating a distant horizon. They were not alone. Something was out there.

CHAPTER FIVE
The Wall

No one slept for the rest of the night. Everyone was unnerved by the thought of aliens roving through the jungle. Vickie was the first to pull a cargo case to the center of the compound. She turned on a lantern, adjusting its intensity and color to offer enough illumination without damaging her night vision. Before long everyone joined her, making a circle around the lamp. They sat, casting worried glances at the mysterious lights and wondering what might jump out of the shadows.

Vickie and her security team kept their weapons close, a small comfort given the potential danger. Jamie was reminded of an old western movie where the pioneers would circle their wagons for protection. Small cliques formed, their members speaking quietly to each other. Conjecture filled the air. Carter sat with Hip and Vickie. It was obvious they were discussing the situation. Jamie sat alone, listening to the urgent murmurings. Anxiety hung like a fog over the group. Everyone was pooling their ignorance.

Carter rose and stepped into the center of the circle. "I want everyone to stay calm," he said quietly. "The worst thing we can do is panic. We don't know what's out there." Jamie was impressed. Carter was acting like he almost believed what he was saying. "It's probably a natural occurrence, unrelated to our presence. It might be bioluminescence or the like. We're going to send a group into the jungle at first light to check it out. Then we'll have some facts." There was another hushed buzz of voices. Carter crossed his arms, waiting for silence. "We'll go mad if we let our imaginations get away from us. Stay focused on what you can see, not on what you fear. We have to find out what those lights mean. Then we'll know what we're dealing with."

Jamie looked around and saw the tension in her companions' faces. There were a few nods. Carter was rising to the occasion. Perhaps he would become an effective leader after all. There he was, standing before the group, exuding confidence. He had a plan. Now, if alien monsters didn't kill them all, everything was going to be all right.

Jamie was struck by a sudden thought. She and her fellow colonists were the real aliens. They had invaded Alathea. Whatever was behind the jungle lights belonged here. Perhaps the natives were worried about the strange creatures who had come from the sky and landed on the shore of their ocean. She began to doubt their moral high ground and their ability to defend themselves.

They stood vigil in the center of the clearing, while the mysterious lights danced like a greenish aurora over the treetops. An adrenaline rush had swept away any thought of sleep. Conversations ceased, and everyone listened for sounds of movement in the jungle. There were none. The glow over the forest continued for several hours and then faded away.

* * *

As morning came, the colonists' anxiety was blended with anticipation. Vickie and her team left the clearing and began their trek through the jungle. Their plan was to journey for half a day in the direction of the lights and return with a report by nightfall. Carter urged everyone to continue unloading the Lander, but no one was in the mood.

A Jungian urge drew Jamie toward the beach. She left the clearing and set out on the beach trail. The landing site by the alien ocean reminded her of an ancient sea where Earth creatures discovered their legs and crawled tentatively to the dry land. Humanity had arrived on this strange shore just two days before. Men and women were finding their legs in the planet's gravity, an echo of common ground in an uncommon place.

Jamie increased her pace as she meandered back and forth along the trail. She vaulted impatiently over several tree roots, anxious to be near the water. Jamie felt at home on the beach and had resolved to spend every spare moment wandering at the edge of the violet ocean. Perhaps it would help her remember who she was.

Finally, Jamie broke through the row of trees, which bordered the strip of sand along the water. She saw a flash of red against the lavender waves. It was Rusty's hair. He stood motionless, gazing into the sky. The rings of Alathea were like a curved ribbon of gold, a sash spread across the firmament like a resplendent highway. The halcyon rings pulsed with color ranging from deep amber to bright yellow.

Jamie drew up beside Rusty and stood quietly, allowing herself to take in the cosmic beauty. She had seen the rings like everyone else. They were always visible, but Jamie had not taken the time to stand silently and drink in their beauty.

"Amazing, aren't they?" Rusty's voice was low, almost reverent. He held a digital canvas in his hand. Jamie leaned toward him and sucked in an unconscious breath when she saw the image on the screen. Rusty had drawn a magnificent picture of the rings. They hung over the violet sea, splashing the wave tops with gold. The painting captured an impressionistic view of twilight, where Alathea's sun had bowed below the horizon, but the rings were still full of unearthly light. The golden wash was soft, creating amorphous shadows and gently overwhelming the purple hues of the sea.

"Rusty! That's beautiful!"

The young man looked down at the drawing and smiled with satisfaction. "Thanks."

"I didn't know you were an artist."

"I was." His words were heavy. "I haven't painted in a long time." Jamie sensed the same sadness she had seen in him on the pod ship. "I couldn't help myself." There was a hint of guilt in his voice.

"Are you worried about the lights in the jungle?" she asked.

Rusty turned. His eyes lingered on the rings until they were lost in his peripheral vision, then he faced her. "A bit, but there's nothing I can do about it. I guess that's why I decided to draw the rings. My art always takes me away from my fear. It helps me stay in balance."

"Balance?"

"There's an old story of a great king who asked his high counselor for a phrase to temper his arrogance and lift him up from despair. The wise man thought long and hard about it. Then he returned to the king."

"What did he say?"

"He said to the king, 'This too shall pass.' For when you are filled with arrogance, you must remember your frailty, and when you are locked in despair, you must remember your power." Rusty smiled. "Balance. Art helps me keep

45

perspective."

He hesitated. There was something else he wanted to say, but Jamie knew he felt awkward about it. Did he want to be intimate with her? She hoped not. She was too confused for that. She didn't want him to ask. She didn't want to hurt his feelings. She didn't want anything to threaten the dawning friendship she sensed between them. "What is it?" Jamie watched as Rusty's face turned as red as his hair.

"I was wondering…" he began. "Do you know Alice?"

Jamie was relieved. "Do you mean the short woman with dark hair?"

"Yeah, I want to get to know her, but we haven't been introduced."

"Sorry, Rusty. I don't know her either, but she seems nice enough. Why don't you walk right up to her and say hello?"

"Maybe…"

"You'll know within a few seconds if she's interested in you."

"Or if she isn't…"

"This too shall pass," Rusty grinned when she said it. "Don't be negative. You're a nice guy. You'll never know if you don't try."

Rusty relaxed. "You're right. I'll do it at dinner." His eyes were full of promise.

Jamie patted him on the shoulder and left him on the beach. Alice would be lucky to have a man like Rusty. She felt the empty spaces in her memory as she retraced the indentations her feet had made in the sand. Had she loved someone? Had she been married? She wandered the beach, glancing up frequently at the rings, while wondering if she had ever worn a ring of her own.

* * *

Vickie and her heavily armed guards returned to the clearing in the late afternoon. Ben swaggered up behind Vickie, brandishing his weapon like the serious kick-ass commando he imagined himself to be. Jamie saw a hint of envy in Ben, as though he thought his role should be reversed with Vickie. She guessed the man didn't like taking orders from women. Vickie glanced at him, and the look disappeared instantly under her commanding stare.

Everyone gathered around to hear Vickie's report. "We went about thirty klicks into the bush before turning back," she said offhandedly. "We didn't see anything. There's a lot of weird plant life and crap out there, but there weren't any tracks or birds, not even a bug." Vickie scanned the group. Her eyes were always moving, taking in her environment, measuring potential threats. Jamie wondered if she ever relaxed. The woman was anal. It made her perfect for her job. You don't want a head of security who takes things at face value. She watched the female warrior scrutinize a man who had his hands jammed into his pockets. Jamie tried to imagine what it would be like to trust no one, always wondering where the next danger was coming from. Jamie sucked in a breath. She was describing herself.

"If there was something out there, we would have seen it." Vickie concluded.

Carter looked relieved. "What's our next step?"

"Not much we can do for now," she replied. "Tomorrow we need to start building a perimeter wall around the settlement. Our safety should be the first priority. We can delay building the sheds and such." The idea of a protective wall sounded good to everyone. Carter and Vickie had a long discussion with Stub's construction crew, and a plan was drawn up for the barricade.

"Vickie will post an overnight watch until the wall is built," Carter announced that evening. "We don't think there's anything to worry about, but we're not taking any chances."

The mysterious lights appeared again that night. They pulsed with varying intensity over the alien treetops. The colonists stood quietly in the clearing, watching the lights and listening for any sign of movement in the jungle. Once again, nothing moved. There were no alien creatures casting eerie shadows in the golden twilight. Jamie noticed a change of mood among the colonists. Fear no longer held them in its grasp. The odd lights were vexing, but exhaustion from the previous night's vigil drove everyone to bed. Jamie was one of the last to surrender to her fatigue. Vickie's team stood watch over the perimeter, their weapons at the ready. In spite of the discomforting lights, all was calm.

* * *

As Alathea rotated on her axis, the rings visible to the clearing became shrouded in the planet's umbra, and darkness fell. Light from the mirrored moon and her lesser companion pierced the night. Soft shadows from the trees stretched across the clearing. The furry red sod was now a shade of gray in the diminishing light. Jamie stirred on her cushion, rolling to one side. She scanned the dark tree line that formed the edge of the jungle. Vickie was walking slowly across her field of view, keeping watch. In the next few days, they would build a protective wall, and the tree line would be obscured. It was going to be a hard job. Jamie was too tired to imagine the long days of physical labor. She closed her eyes and drifted off to sleep.

* * *

Jamie huddled in the back seat of a dark colored car. She was ten years old, and she was scared. It was a cold night, and she had wrapped a blanket around herself, careful to tuck in the edges. A corner was draped over her head, leaving a slit for her eyes. Her mouth was under the cover, her breath slowly warming the air captured under the thick cloth. She reached out of her cocoon and rubbed away the patina of frost that had formed on the inside of the window next to her. She pulled her hand back quickly, grateful for the warmth created by her body under the blanket. She gazed out of the window and across the darkened sidewalk.

The bank building was dark. Its large windows and cold, stone walls stood silently like a mausoleum. There was a faint flicker of light. For an instant, Jamie could make out the counter separating the tellers' booths from the lobby area. She could see a large round clock behind the narrow row of bars that stood at attention along the counter top. It was just after 3 a.m. A car's headlights pierced the cold air somewhere behind her. Jamie slumped down in the seat like her parents had taught her and waited for the vehicle to pass. It didn't slow down. Jamie's shoulders shook under the blanket, half from the cold and half from fear. Her parents had taught her to fear strangers who paid too much attention and avoid police officers at all costs.

Jamie heard a scraping sound from the bank building. Two shadowy figures were at the entrance. She watched them pause, then slip quietly out the door. Within seconds, they were in the car. Her father started the engine without a word. The heater fan spun into life, blowing warmish air into the frigid compartment. There was a clicking sound as he put the car in gear. Jamie felt the car lurch forward. It rolled slowly at first, and then picked up speed. The headlights came on, and she and her parents were on the move again. They would drive all night. They wouldn't rest until they put a hundred kilometers between themselves and the bank.

Young Jamie pulled the blanket more tightly around herself. She wished for a bed she could call her own. For as long as she could remember, she had always slept in the car, or in some ratty motel room. She would pretend to sleep while her parents made noisy love in the bed next to her. She had no toys, no yard, no dresser or tea set. She wasn't good enough for all that. Her father called her excess baggage, and that's what she believed.

* * *

Jamie woke and scrambled to her feet. Vickie turned at the sudden movement. She glanced at her as Jamie stepped away from the sleeping colonists and headed toward the tree line. "Where are you going?" she hissed.

"I've got to pee." Jamie replied in a loud whisper. Vickie nodded and turned on her heel.

Jamie reached the first row of trees and stepped into the darkness beyond. She peeled off her jumpsuit and squatted in the shadows. The soft hair-like grass felt like a deep pile carpet under her toes. She was half awake, still surrounded by the vestiges of her dream. Her parents had been thieves, constantly on the run. They had taken her with them as they robbed and swindled their way through life.

Jamie felt a shiver as she remembered her mother taking her into the bushes by the side of the road. She was no stranger to squatting unceremoniously in the woods to pee. She remembered the impatient look on her father's face when her mother led her back to the car. She had been an accident resulting from drunken sex in the afterglow of a caper pulled in some forgotten town. Jamie ached at the thought. She had hoped for the comforting memories of loving parents and a pleasant home. Instead she was a neglected child, the daughter of common thieves.

* * *

Morning came like a dragon's breath as the air in the clearing became torrid with the rising of the sun. Stub Andrews and his crew laid out the footprint of the perimeter wall, as the rest of the colonists scavenged the Lander for posts and panels. The soil had the consistency of spongy clay, making it difficult to dig holes for the fence posts. Stub manned the digger, and soon the powerful man's skin was glistening with sweat as he wrestled with the machine. The first posts were set by midday, and everyone worked continuously through the long alien afternoon.

Jamie and Bliss had been tasked with carrying tents from the Lander. They dragged them into the settlement and piled them in an open area on the south end of the compound. The tents were erected as night fell, and everyone was grateful for the modicum of privacy offered by their thin nylon panels. The lights glowed once more above the jungle as the weary colonists settled in for the night.

* * *

The wall was nearing completion on the fifth day of construction. The end was in sight, and no one was going to stop until the settlement compound was wrapped safely behind the protective barricade. Fear had motivated them beyond their endurance, and everyone was bone tired from the long days of hard work.

The sun beat down on them relentlessly. The day seemed warmer than any other they had experienced. Jamie paused to wipe the sweat from her brow. Bliss was ten meters away, picking up some leftover construction material. Jamie watched her arch her back. She stretched her arms up toward the sky and then pulled at the sweat-soaked cloth under her armpits. Without warning, Bliss unzipped the top of her jumpsuit and wiggled her arms out of the sleeves. Stub was in front of her. He froze, transfixed by the woman's naked torso. She tied the arms of her jumpsuit around her waist and continued working. Jamie was stunned. She gazed at her friend for a long minute. The scars on Bliss's back took her breath away.

* * *

The wall was finished in the early afternoon. Carter told everyone to rest, and Jamie went to her tent. An empty cargo case served as her bedside stand, and another provided a place to sit. She had laid her cushion on top of a carbon fiber cot and hung a small lantern from a cord that dangled from the peak of the roof. In spite of its Spartan appearance, the tent felt like home. Jamie lay down and closed her eyes, listening to the sounds of the camp. She could hear the faint clicking of the rigid leaves in the trees. Distant conversations whispered to her. Their murmurings were punctuated by the sounds of footsteps and tools clinking together as workers cleaned up.

Jamie could hear Olivia from across the compound. The woman's big voice cut through the background sounds. "I don't care how hot it is," she was saying. "The girl should keep her shirt on." Jamie's curiosity was piqued. Her eyes snapped open, and she slid down to the bottom of her cot, near the flap of the tent. "Just because we're on a new world doesn't mean we throw our morals out the window."

"Let her be, Olivia," another voice was saying. "She's not doing any harm. Look at Hulk. He's got bigger breasts than she has." Hulk was one of the heavier colonists.

"That's different." The pitch of Olivia's voice was higher now. "Women's breasts are sacrosanct. You don't rip off your blouse and let them flop in the breeze."

"Bliss's breasts don't flop, Olivia."

Jamie smiled. Bliss was a beautiful woman. She replayed the scene in her mind. Bliss hadn't stripped down to titillate the men around her. She didn't care if the men looked at her breasts. It was hot, and she wanted to be comfortable. A couple of the other women followed her example. After all, the men had stripped to their waists, why couldn't she do the same? They were living in a tropical environment, and bare breasts made sense. It was the religious folk, like Olivia, who took offense.

"You are right about that," Olivia shot back. "That woman is going to get gang raped. Did you see how Stub looked at her? She's a menace, and some of us might get hurt because of it. Some of these men might get too worked up; we could become collateral damage." Jamie tried to imagine Olivia being straddled by Stub. She chuckled to herself. Olivia's tone grew throaty. "We are not going to become a bunch of uncouth savages." Jamie wondered if a bra and a blouse was all that stood between civilization and the dark ages. Maybe she'd go topless tomorrow.

* * *

The new perimeter wall was almost three meters tall and broken by a large gate, which opened onto the beach trail. The wall created an "inside" and an "outside." Inside was where civilization was supposed to be, where things were normal and relaxed. Outside was, by definition, uncivilized. It was a place of potential danger. They didn't know what dangers might be lurking beyond the wall, but the colonists feared the unknown and had hurried to establish a safe haven for themselves. Jamie noticed how many of the colonists picked up their pace as they neared the new entrance to the compound. They were eager to get inside. She watched the expressions on their faces. She knew the wall was a necessity, but she wondered if it was creating a false sense of danger and security. There was no evidence of any threat in the jungle, only the mysterious lights. However, Jamie saw a real danger inside the settlement; people like Stub and Olivia couldn't be trusted.

The Lander stood outside the safety of the perimeter wall. Carter was worried about the security of the ship's stores. The settlement's survival depended on the food and equipment remaining on the unprotected beach. He telegraphed a sense of urgency to everyone. Storage sheds had to be built quickly to hold the vast supplies held inside the massive ship.

The colonists continued their endless parade, carrying items from the Lander across the plank road to the jungle, and then on the beach trail through the trees to the main gate of the settlement. Jamie neared the beach on one of her return trips to the Lander and paused as she saw Carter standing behind one of the odd trees that flanked the shoreline. He was staring intently at the Lander. Her curiosity was piqued. She stepped off the trail and watched him. She followed his gaze and looked out across the sand. Four women were lugging cases of supplies on the plank road. Their breasts bounced as they lumbered along. Jamie watched as Carter responded, his erection forming an unmistakable bump in the crotch of his jumpsuit.

As they approached the beach trail, Carter orbited the tree trunk, keeping out of sight. The women were several meters apart. Jamie watched him study each one in turn. He was sizing them up like animals in a marketplace. The women meandered into the jungle, and Carter, the objects of his interest now out of sight, stepped out on the beach to fetch another load of supplies. Jamie waited until he was gone before emerging from her hiding place. Carter was on the prowl, looking for a mate.

CHAPTER SIX
The Surf

The Lander had been stocked with two years worth of packaged food, but not all of it had survived the five-hundred-year journey. They estimated there was enough food for about a year and a half. After that, they would have to live off the land. Their four agriculturalists were among the dead, so no one knew how to raise crops. Carter told them that survival depended on planting a successful garden. He made a grand gesture toward the trees. "These things are growing here. Let's try the seed." And so they did. Hip volunteered to take a stab at farming. He recruited Thomas. Jamie and Bliss offered to join them, and the four set out to find a suitable place to plant a crop.

The land surrounding the compound was covered with the ubiquitous crimson grass. The ground cover was laced into a thick, gritty loam, which had the consistency of modeling clay. They remembered how hard it had been to dig the deep holes for the fence posts. They wanted to find soil more conducive to planting, but found nothing but the spongy substance. They selected a patch of land on the seaward side of the compound, between the settlement wall and the jungle. It took them the better part of a day to strip away the reddish grass and expose the underlying soil.

Hip grunted as he yanked a particularly tenacious piece of sod from the garden patch and tossed it aside. "I think we could make bricks out of this stuff," he gasped. "I'm not so sure about vegetables, though." Jamie was nearby, struggling with a shovel to cut the next patch of sod free from the surrounding grass. She was focused on her work, attacking her prey with a vengeance. Hip studied the way she was kicking the shovel. "We haven't talked much since the landing," he said. He stepped closer until he was facing her. "Have any memories come back to you?"

She pushed down on the spade one more time, its blade disappearing beneath the grass. "I had a dream about my parents."

"That's good!" Hip wiped the back of his neck with his sleeve.

"I don't know." Jamie let go of the shovel. It stood at attention, the square of sod tipping slightly. "I was waiting for them in a car. I think they were robbing a bank."

Hip shook his head. "Your parents were thieves? You've got to be kidding."

Jamie scratched her left breast unconsciously. "I could use a little normalcy."

Hip gave her a wry smile. "Said the woman standing on an alien planet."

They laughed. Jamie liked this man. He was bright and kind. She enjoyed his company. "Did you have a family?"

A curtain of sadness descended over him. "I had a wife, but no children."

"What happened?" Jamie knew she was treading on holy ground, but she had shared her secret with him and felt safe asking the question.

"It's a long story."

"I have nothing but time." Jamie pulled off her gloves. "Tell me."

"I lost my wife to cancer. It was awful. I watched her go from a vibrant, athletic woman to an emaciated skeleton." A tear erupted from the corner of his eye. "I loved her more than anything."

"I'm sorry." Jamie regretted being so personal. She put her hand on his shoulder.

"I think it's worse when you're a doctor. You watch your lover waste away, and all your knowledge taunts you. We're trained to help people, to cure people. I wish I could go back and do things differently."

Jamie could feel Hip shaking under her fingers. His vulnerability appealed to her, made her feel less lonely. "But there was nothing you could do."

He shrugged her hand away. "I could have saved her, damn it!" Jamie was startled. Hip turned away. "I was so busy with my practice; I didn't see her symptoms until it was too late." Hip kicked at a clump of sod. "What kind of doctor am I?"

Jamie almost touched his shoulder again, but then thought better of it. "You're human," she said gently. "Life is in real time, and we don't have the advantage of foresight. Sometimes things just happen."

"I know that up here." Hip rapped his head with the palm of his hand. "But I still feel like I let her down when it really mattered." He turned back to Jamie. "I could have saved her all that pain. We could have had a few more months together." Hip looked across the garden, a distant look in his eyes. "After she died, my life didn't mean anything anymore. I thought about staying behind. I was tempted to ride out the asteroid impact and die, but I was afraid the guilt would follow me into the afterlife, or wherever she is, so I came out here to make amends. I thought a suicide mission was just what I needed."

"Sounds like you were running away from the pain."

"That might be true." Hip softened. "But I've learned something: the pain goes with you no matter where you go." A sound made them both look toward the settlement wall. It was Ben Beck making his security sweep. Hip gestured toward him as the guard disappeared around the corner of the barricade. "I know some of the colonists haven't treated you very well."

Jamie sighed. "You'd think they would have cut me a little slack." Hip nodded sympathetically, but said nothing. "Want to know the truth?" Jamie looked directly into his eyes. "It hurts. They latch onto your weakness and never let you forget it. Everything is new here. Why can't we all make a fresh start?"

Hip scowled. "I'd like to think we could be better, but some people don't change."

"Yeah," she agreed.

* * *

The next morning, the foursome returned to the garden. They plowed the rubbery loam and hand-planted rows of corn, tomatoes, and squash. Thomas found an irrigation system in the Lander, and they laid it out between the furrows. Hip and Jamie snaked a long hose through the jungle to the shoreline. A small pump pulled water to the sprinkler heads, which created a fine mist over the garden. They didn't know what else to do. Mother Nature, or whatever name she went by on Alathea, would have to do the rest.

* * *

Jamie was getting used to exhaustion. Every day brought another task, which sapped her strength. The day of planting and setting up the irrigation system left her bone tired. She was sure she had never been a farmer. She might have been a sailor, though. She returned to the shore after dinner, hoping the sea would relax her mind and body. She pulled off her shoes and sat down on the beach, wiggling her toes in the fine grains of sand. Her jumpsuit was damp with sweat. She hadn't bathed in several days and smelled like a dirty locker room. The golden rings that surrounded Alathea arched overhead in the evening sky. The sun was a hair's breadth from the horizon, and the planet's moons had already risen.

Jamie leaned back and lay flat on the sand. A brilliant star, already visible in the gently fading light, stood directly overhead. She thought of the children's nursery rhyme: "Starlight, star bright, first star I see tonight..." What would she wish for? She could wish for a crop in the garden, or ask for Stub and Ben to develop some manners. She could wish for grief to release its grasp on Hip. There were lots of things she could have hoped, but in that moment she wished for a memory that would tell her who she was.

Jamie's revere was broken by the sound of laughter. She propped herself up on her elbows and looked to her right. Two figures were splashing in the surf, a hundred meters down the shoreline. They were knee deep in the violet water, running and laughing. They were naked. Jamie squinted to see them more clearly. It was Rusty and Alice. They looked like two children enthralled in carefree abandon, whipping through the water with wild and innocent joy. Occasionally, one would bend down and skim the surface of the water, sending a drenching spray toward the other.

Jamie stared at them as the couple cavorted in the ocean. She smiled, feeling like she was naughty. She watched Alice's breasts bounce as she ran back and forth. Rusty's genitals swung from side to side. He turned away from her, his smooth bottom caught in the long horizontal rays of the setting sun.

Alice turned suddenly and saw Jamie watching them. A broad smile erupted on her face, and she sprinted toward her. Before Jamie knew it, Alice was less than five meters away from where she was sitting. Alice pulled up short, wearing an impish grin. "Hi Jamie!" Rusty turned at the sound of his partner's voice. He paused without shame, facing Jamie in all his glory. "Come and join us!" Alice shouted.

Jamie was embarrassed. It was one thing to watch two naked people play in the water. It was another to have them stand unashamedly before you and invite you to join them. "No, I couldn't," she replied.

"It's fun, Jamie," the dark-haired woman said. Rusty trotted up behind Alice and took the opportunity to splash her. She giggled and sidestepped away from him. "We had to clean off," Alice offered. "The water is great."

Jamie thought for a moment. She needed to wash. Her smell had been bothering her for more than a day. She glanced down at herself. Why not? She didn't feel any inhibitions. She got to her feet without another thought. "I could use a bath," she said.

"Great!" Alice clapped her hands together. "Let's gang up on Rusty!"

Jamie peeled off her jumpsuit and ran into the surf.

* * *

The end of the day had come and Jamie sat on the cot

inside her tent. She felt clean and refreshed from running in the surf. She was surprised at how natural it had been. Maybe she'd been a nudist in her former life. She had chased Rusty and Alice and was caught up quickly in the fun of the moment. It was innocent play. She had felt mutual respect and acceptance. No one had tried to take advantage of her.

Jamie had hoped the sight of Rusty's body would reinforce her belief that she had always been a woman. He was a healthy man and reasonably endowed, but she hadn't felt any sexual attraction. Perhaps she was too tired from gardening. Maybe she had been a man. Jamie honestly didn't know. She was still a mystery.

* * *

They built a large hanger-like structure in the compound. It had a tubular framework, covered with a tough polymer skin. They drove long stakes into the ground to hold it down. The Commons, as they called it, was like a high tech Quonset hut. They fashioned tables from cargo cases, and flat metal panels scavenged from the Lander. Lamps hung from the ceiling, and a simple food preparation area was set up in one end. They mated a smaller service building at one end of the larger structure, making a perfect place for the storage of food and general supplies. A pair of large doors divided the two spaces.

As twilight fell, Carter called the community together. It was their first meeting in the new Commons. Carter stood in front of the group with Hip and Vickie. His hands were folded behind him, his eyes scanning the faces of his charges. He called upon Thomas to offer a prayer. Jamie watched as most of the colonists bowed their heads. The sharing time came next. A few always had something to say. Most of them, like Jamie, preferred to remain silent.

Olivia raised her hand. She rose from where she was

sitting and strode confidently to Carter's side. Her jumpsuit was zipped as high as it would go, and she had obviously fussed with her hair. Jamie watched her eyes. The woman had been critical of Carter on the pod ship. Now she was enamored by him. She obviously enjoyed standing next to him. Jamie could tell she was the kind of woman who was drawn to power. Olivia probably fantasized about being Carter's first lady.

Jamie could tell Carter didn't share the sentiment. He looked down, and then, as if he could read her mind, he looked up, making eye contact with Jamie. He gave her a fleeting smile. What was that about, she wondered? Men reveal more than they realize when they look at a woman. Sometimes it's where they look. It's easy to tell the difference between lust and friendliness. Stub and Hip sent very different messages when they looked at her. Carter's look was more enigmatic. It sent a shiver up her spine.

Olivia spread her hands. "We have a tremendous responsibility here," she began. "We are setting the foundation for a new civilization. It is time for us to shun the darker side of humanity's past and bring what is good and pure and noble to the forefront of our community." Many of the colonists were expressionless, waiting to see where she was headed with this line of thought. Some rolled their eyes. "We cannot allow immorality here." She paused for effect. A couple of her friends nodded their heads in approval. "If we allow even the slightest infraction, it will lead us down a slippery slope toward debauchery and damnation." Thomas gave her an approving nod. Then she turned toward Bliss, who was sitting near the entrance of the Commons. "We cannot allow women to expose their breasts in public. It's unseemly and makes us little more than animals. If we don't stop this behavior now, we'll descend into a hedonistic tribe of perverts and rapists."

A couple of colonists stifled laughs. Carter gave them an evil eye and quickly restored order. Olivia balled both hands into fists and pressed them into her hips. She had an air of superiority as she continued to give Bliss a cold, hard stare. "We all know who you are." Olivia continued. "Several of our women are guilty, but there is one troublemaker who led them astray." Carter shifted his weight back and forth, unsure of what to say. "We will have decency in this settlement!" Olivia's eyes burned with self-righteousness. Bliss smiled at her. She cupped her breasts in her hands and shook them. Olivia sniffed disapprovingly and looked away.

Jamie felt like a spectator for a moment, and then realized she was one of the women Olivia was accusing. She wondered if she had seen them cavorting in the surf. Alice raised her hand. Carter recognized her, and she stood up. "I disagree with Olivia. This is a tropical climate, and it gets real hot at midday. The men strip to the waist to stay comfortable, and I think we deserve the right to do the same."

"It will ruin our community." Olivia countered. "It's a step toward the abyss."

"I don't think so." Alice didn't flinch. "I think it will have the opposite effect. We have a chance to celebrate what is natural and healthy. We can set the tone for future generations. We can shun the puritanical taboos of old Earth and learn to loosen up a bit."

"We'll all be raped!" Olivia shouted.

"You don't have to worry about that, honey." Stub gave Olivia a lascivious grin.

Alice scanned the men's faces around her. "No we won't, Olivia. The men will ogle us in the beginning, but they'll get used to it. Our bodies are a big part of who we are. Let's treat each other with respect and equality. If the men can strip to the waist, we should be able to."

"You'll never catch me doing that!" Olivia was horrified at the thought.

"Thank God," Ben Beck offered under his breath. A ripple of laughter coursed through his corner of the Commons.

"That is your choice." Alice continued. "But we must have the choice. That's the point." There was a spontaneous round of applause. Olivia blushed. She picked an invisible fleck of dirt off her spotless jumpsuit and stomped out of the Commons.

* * *

Jamie returned to her tent after the meeting and sat quietly on her cot. Lights from the compound cast dancing shadows on the nylon skin of the enclosure. She could hear the murmurings of her fellow colonists. The air was still warm from the long alien day. She pulled the zipper down on the front of her jumpsuit and wiped the sweat from around her neck. She allowed her mind to wander over the day's events. There was so much missing from her past, she enjoyed the act of remembering the smallest of details of her day: the sweet alien air as she woke, the hard leaves clicking in the morning breezes, the rings glowing perpetually in the sky, the smell of the wet sand on the beach. She thought about running naked in the surf with Rusty and Alice. It was her fondest memory of the day, perhaps her best recollection of all.

There was a tapping sound. A shadow fell across the front panel of the tent. It was the silhouette of a man. Jamie instinctively pulled the zipper back up on her jumpsuit. "Who is it?"

"It's Carter. May I come in?"

Jamie heard something different in his voice. He spoke less formally, not as the captain, suggesting a personal inquiry. She glanced at herself in a small mirror and made sure she was presentable. She shifted nervously on the cot. "Come in, sir." Her voice cracked.

Carter opened the fly and entered the small tent. He could barely stand straight in the space, so he hunched over, an awkward smile on his face. Jamie gestured toward a small equipment case, which sat across from the cot. He sat down and let out a long breath. "Thank you," he offered. "I'm still not used to this gravity."

Jamie nodded. Alathea's mass was roughly equal to Earth, resulting in similar g-forces, but their conditioning in orbit had not fully prepared them for the stresses on their muscles. They were all tired at the end of the day, eager to get off their feet. Carter winced slightly as he stretched his legs and pointed his toes. He grasped the sides of the equipment case like a pommel horse and rocked himself back and forth over the flat surface.

"I've got to get a cushion for that," Jamie said to fill the silence.

He shook his head. "It's fine."

Jamie was mystified. Carter had shown little interest in her. "What can I do for you, sir?"

"Don't call me sir, Jamie." He stopped rocking back and forth and lowered his buttocks back down on the case. "We're all on a first name basis."

"Okay." She didn't know him well enough to call him Carter. Using his first name seemed too personal, unnatural. "Did you need something?"

"Everything is good," he said absentmindedly, kneading

his knuckles into the palm of his hand like a mortar and pestle. "I just wanted to stop by."

A knot began to form in Jamie's stomach. She remembered Carter's erection as he watched the women along the beach trail. She was suddenly aware of the cot under her bottom and the enclosed space of the tent. Carter was between her and the tent flap. She wondered if he would stop her if she tried to escape. Did she need to escape? Why were alarm bells going off in her head over this man? She gripped the edge of the cot tightly, driving the blood from her fingers. Carter smiled disarmingly, but she didn't relax.

"I was wondering what you thought about the meeting tonight."

"The meeting?" Jamie hadn't expected this. "I don't know. It was okay, I guess. Which part?"

"I was wondering what you thought about Olivia's concern." Carter seemed embarrassed. "Do you think I handled it okay?"

Jamie was startled by the question. "I don't know what you mean." She gripped the cot a little tighter. Why would the leader of their settlement be interested in her opinion?

"I mean, do you think I should have defended her position?"

Jamie cleared her throat. She didn't like where the conversation was going. Had Carter made assumptions about her? Did he consider her an easy lay? She glanced at the tent flap. The desire to escape stirred again. "I think Olivia is wound a bit too tight for her own good," she said finally. An image of Rusty and Alice running naked with her in the surf flashed in her mind. They had laughed and played together. No one had been hurt. In fact, she had felt respected. The playful intimacy had bonded them as friends. "Alice made a good point. We have to respect each other." She hoped her answer would satisfy him, perhaps teach him a lesson, and he would go away.

"So you agreed with Alice." Carter seemed relieved.

"I do." Jamie was flustered. "I did."

"I thought you might." Carter dropped his hands and massaged his knees. Jamie's eyes followed the movement. She glanced at his crotch and saw the cloth of his jumpsuit move. His penis was swelling. She looked back up at his face. Carter saw what she had done and smiled. "I'm fond of you, Jamie." Carter slid to the edge of the equipment case. "I want to spend some time with you." Waves of anxiety shot through her. She tried to hide her reaction, but Carter saw it. His face fell. "I've offended you."

"It's not you," Jamie stumbled, and then added, "Carter," for good measure. "I'm just not ready." She looked down, noticing she had crossed her arms tightly across her chest. She unfolded them and gripped the edge of the cot again. "I'm still trying to figure out who I am. Until I do that, I can't be with anybody."

Carter grew distant, a barrier rising between them as his erection collapsed. His eyes lost their focus. He began to stand up. Jamie reached out and put her hand on his knee. He flinched as she touched him. "I'm flattered by your offer, Carter." It was a lie. She pulled her hand away and crossed her arms again.

"I saw you at the beach with Rusty and Alice," Carter said softly. Jamie blushed. "It looked like you were ready for that."

"It was innocent," Jamie stammered, wondering why she felt the need to explain herself.

Carter rose and bumped against the nylon roof. The tent rippled from the impact. "I'm sorry to have disturbed you."

Jamie started to rise, and then realized she would be far too close to the man if she did so. "I'm glad you stopped by," she said, but neither of them believed it. Carter was already unzipping the flap of the tent. He stepped through the opening quickly and disappeared into the night.

Jamie rose and closed the flap. She should have known Carter had seen her in the surf. He had been watching all the women. When he saw her in the water, he must have been sexually aroused and hoped she would sleep with him. She pushed the image from her mind. She didn't want a lover, especially Carter. However, he had assumed otherwise, and their association was going to be complicated. Jamie wondered what the consequences of her refusal might be. She was disturbed by the twinge of guilt that lingered in her gut. There was no need to feel bad. She had been honest with the man.

Jamie pulled off her jump suit and lay down on the cot. It was a hot night, so she didn't bother with the thin blanket folded at the foot of her bed. She pulled herself into a fetal position. What kind of person was she? Had she been hard to get along with in her past life? Did she have lovers? She sucked in a breath, reminded of the depth of her disorientation. Had she been a man like Carter? She was momentarily disgusted by the thought, but not convinced of its falsehood. No, a personal relationship was out of the question. Until she could remember who she was, she would have to remain alone.

CHAPTER SEVEN

Settlement Building

J amie walked toward the beach where the Lander stood. She dreaded another day of endless trips carrying supplies and materials to the settlement. She decided to walk along the water before getting to work. She wandered down the thin slice of sand to where she had played in the surf with Rusty and Alice. To her surprise, the couple was there. Alice was sitting in the sand, facing toward her. Her jumpsuit was unzipped. Her skin was wet. Her shoulders were arched back and the morning light glistened on her breasts. Rusty sat across from her, his hands caked with sand. A partially completed sculpture stood between them. Alice smiled when she saw her. Rusty was intent on his work, unaware of her presence.

Jamie approached slowly, not wanting to startle him. She craned her neck over his shoulder to see the sculpture. It was a stunning likeness of Alice. It captured the subtle curves of her body and her carefree spirit. Jamie orbited Rusty until she could see his profile. His eyes were soft as he looked up at Alice. They were adoring eyes. He was a man in love, an artist lost in his muse.

"How does it look, Jamie?" Alice flicked a grain of sand

off one of her nipples.

"It's amazing," she whispered. Her voice spoke in a chorus with the gentle waves kissing the shore. Rusty glanced up at her and smiled without a word, his hands still shaping the pale green sand. "I didn't know you could make sand sculptures with such detail," she said.

"This stuff is different," Rusty spoke softly. "It's a bit sticky when it's wet. It holds together better than anything you find on Earth."

"It's a masterpiece."

Rusty looked up at Alice, his face glowing. "Only as good as my inspiration," he murmured.

Jamie felt like Rusty and Alice were in a luminous bubble. She stepped back instinctively. She did not belong there. The radiance surrounding them was their own, a private bliss. She felt a pang of loneliness mixed with happiness for her new friends. She wished them a good morning and turned back the way she had come.

Jamie went unwillingly to the Lander and gathered up an armful of supplies. She lugged it unenthusiastically to the settlement. She felt like a pack mule caught in an endless loop. She delivered her burden to the Commons and returned to the main gate. She stopped. The beach trail invited her back to the Lander and another load of supplies. She couldn't bring herself to do it. She turned left, deciding to check on the settlement garden. Perhaps there would be green shoots appearing in the grooved furrows. She was surprised to see Bliss kneeling by the edge of the plot, her head close to the ground.

"Any shoots yet?"

Bliss squinted down one of the rows. "There isn't a single

plant, Jamie. I don't know what I'm doing."

"It's been less than a day since we planted them."

"I know. I was just hoping to see something. How long does it take for a seed to sprout?"

Jamie shrugged. She didn't have a clue. "We're pooling our ignorance here. It's probably too soon to tell."

Bliss straightened up to a sitting position. "Maybe the seeds are bad. It's been five hundred years, you know?"

"I doubt it. Didn't they find seeds in the pyramids that still worked?"

Bliss gave her a blank look. "What are pyramids?"

Jamie grinned. She was surprised by Bliss's ignorance, but pleased with her own recollection, not out of superiority, but from gratitude for mental clarity. "The pyramids were in Egypt. They buried the pharaohs in them."

Bliss wasn't interested. "This is bad. We've got to eat, you know?"

"I wish I had been a farmer." Jamie offered. Bliss leaned back on her arms. It was hot under the alien sun. There was no coolness in the breeze. The day was going to be oppressive. Bliss had kept her jumpsuit zipped up ever since Olivia had made her comments at the community meeting. She looked uncomfortable, her sweat darkening the fabric under her arms and between her breasts. "You look hot," Jamie observed.

"Yeah. It's going to be bad this afternoon."

Jamie gestured toward her friend's jumpsuit. "Why don't you unzip?"

A dark shadow crossed Bliss's face. "I can't. It's not proper, you know?"

"Says who?"

"You know. Olivia and her friends. They want proper women here."

"And what does a 'proper woman' look like?"

"Not like me."

"That's bull. You're as proper as the rest of them. Don't let them get to you."

Bliss leaned forward and wrapped her arms around her knees. "That's easy for you to say. They leave you alone. I can't stand the way they look at me. They enjoy passing judgment, you know?"

"Screw 'em, girl. They talk about me, too. I'm the one who can't remember who she is. Do you want the truth? They're scared of us. They're scared of me because I'm a mystery woman. They can't control a cipher. They're scared of you because you are comfortable in your own skin. It has to do with their puritanical upbringing."

Bliss looked up at her. "Puritanical?"

"Straight laced. Squeaky clean." Jamie saw a glint of understanding in the woman's face. "There are basically two kinds of people: the ones who want everything around them to conform to their will and the ones who adapt to things. Olivia and her buddies are the first kind. They want you to change so they can feel safe." Bliss was nodding her head. "You and I are the other kind. We adapt to what happens."

"Like keeping my top on."

"Or maybe taking it off on a hot day." Jamie pulled her zipper down several centimeters, revealing her cleavage. "There's one important difference between those who adapt and those who insist on their own way."

"What's that?" Bliss asked.

"Those of us who adapt, survive."

Bliss grinned.

* * *

For the next several days, Jamie worked with a crew to build a hard-sided storage shed on the south end of the compound near the tents. Stub was particularly brutal. He assigned her to tasks that would make her bend over. He liked to watch her. He would position himself so he could look between her legs. He made suggestive grunts as she moved. He gave her difficult jobs to make her sweat, arousing himself with the odor of her body. Jamie ignored him. She put every ounce of strength and endurance into her work, refusing to let Stub wear her down.

Jamie was grateful when the building was finished. She ached from the physical labor. She walked slowly toward the Commons for the noonday meal. She picked at her simple lunch, more interested in something to drink. The day was hotter than normal, and the afternoon promised to be a furnace. She went to her tent to get out of the sun. Jamie fell on the cot, her legs aching, and her shoulders burning. She rolled over on her stomach, letting her arms dangle over the edge of the bed. Within a moment, she was fast asleep.

* * *

Jamie stood in a gleaming white kitchen. It was spotlessly clean. Bright light poured in through large windows over the sink. She was cutting celery with a small knife at an immense island with a polished stone top. She was garbed in a thin white robe, untied and open. It draped over her breasts, which seemed larger than she remembered. She could feel the cool edge of the island against her belly as she leaned into it.

She looked up and saw the great room, which opened up beyond the kitchen. She remembered the first time she entered the house, how she had marveled at the high ceilings and majestic windows. She could still feel the warmth of the fire from the night before, how it caressed the skin of her shoulders as she sat on the soft rug before the hearth. There had been the odor of pine, mingled with the fragrance of William's aftershave. She remembered the sunset as it surrendered to the moonless night, the sun's red disk casting its final crimson shafts of light across the crystalline mountain lake before dipping behind a ridge.

Jamie looked down at the celery. There was a drop of blood on her finger. She had slipped with the knife. She dropped it and brought her hand to her mouth, her finger tasting like copper with a hint of celery. She looked down at herself. Her breasts were covered in blood. The robe was sodden. She looked back at her hands. They dripped with the crimson fluid. She screamed, her cry echoing through the empty house. Then she saw the bloody footprints winding their way through the great room. They were the impressions of her bare feet.

Jamie left the kitchen and followed the trail of blood down a wide white hallway and into the master bedroom. William's naked body lay punctured and torn on the bed. It was as if a homicidal painter had spilled a five-gallon bucket of red paint on the pure white bedclothes. The pillows looked like marshmallows dipped in the ink of death. His blood cascaded down the dust ruffle, forming sticky pools around the edge of the bed. A kitchen knife stood at attention in the center of his chest, its blade buried hilt-deep between his ribs.

Jamie felt a cool breeze against her wet skin. She shivered as she approached the bed with morbid curiosity. This was her husband. There had been a fight. He had attacked her. Jamie knew their marriage had been filled with violence. She remembered bruises and broken bones. She remembered making excuses for the wounds he had inflicted upon her. She drew closer to the body. His legs were spread; a deep ragged gash was furrowed into his crotch. She remembered castrating him with the knife.

* * *

Jamie jumped up from the cot. She looked down at herself, expecting to see the blood. Her jumpsuit was unzipped to her waist, and she was dripping with sweat. She was alone in the tent. She shook the dream from her senses, remembering how she had laid down to rest. She had spent the morning helping to build the storage shed. It was only a dream, she told herself. Even so, Jamie knew it was more than that. Jamie remembered the house and the lake. She remembered all the times her husband had hit her and threatened her life. She remembered the last night by the fire. She remembered how she had hidden the knife under her pillow, how she had taken it when he had grabbed her by the throat. She remembered being unable to breathe as he tried to squeeze the life from her. She remembered the power with which she had swung the blade as she buried it into his body.

Jamie's hands began to shake. She swung her legs off the side of the cot. Why couldn't she have remembered eating cookies with her mother or playing with a childhood friend? The memory seemed like an evil joke. First she was nothing. Now she was a killer.

She remembered meeting William. She remembered his smile, how he had said all the right things and smothered her with attention. Their wedding day had been beautiful, an elegant gathering on the shore of the mountain lake where the immaculate white mansion stood. They had taken their vows under the same trees that sheltered the killing room where she had taken his life. She remembered the first time he had struck her and then the months of fear, as she lived under the shadow of his brutal domination.

She sat quietly, brooding over the recollection. It was a horrible experience. She didn't like violence, but she remembered how self-preservation had kicked in, enabling her to do the unthinkable to save herself. At least she wasn't Jameson Stryker. She had been a woman all along. There had been no sex change.

Jamie turned the details of the dream over and over in her mind during the afternoon, as she made her circuit from the Lander to the compound and back again. She decided to keep the memory to herself. She might share it with Hip eventually, but right now it was too fresh in her mind. She ate silently at dinner, allowing the new information to sift its way through her consciousness. She paid no attention at the evening meeting. She began to dread new recollections, fearing what they would tell her about her past. What was worse? Hiding in a fantasy or being shattered by the truth?

* * *

That night, the eerie lights appeared again over the darkened jungle. They pulsated and danced across the treetops in shades of green and yellow. At times they receded, as though the source of the light had moved further from the settlement. Other times, the lights seemed to come from just beyond the trees outside the perimeter wall. It was dazzling and unsettling at the same time. Everyone worried about what it meant, but there were no signs of movement, no evidence of any aggressive creature stalking them from beyond their safe haven.

* * *

The next day, Jamie received the unwelcome news that Stub wanted her on his crew to build the settlement's clinic.

She labored through the long morning, digging a trench for the foundation. It was arduous work, digging down through the rubbery soil. It sapped the strength of all who wielded the shovels. Stub had given Jamie a short spade, requiring her to bend over as she dug. Once again, he made sure he was behind her as she worked. She imagined him lying on the bed from her dream, a kitchen knife protruding from his crotch.

Jamie's back was on fire by midmorning. She was grateful when the trenching was complete. She stood back and watched the men pour concrete into the deep channels that outlined the footprint of the new building. By late afternoon, the foundation was cured, and they began erecting the walls.

Jamie sat down to rest on an equipment case near the construction site. The day's heat was not relinquishing its grip. She pulled a water bottle from one of her leg pockets and took a long swig. She saw movement in her peripheral vision. It was Thomas. "Mind if I join you?"

Jamie tried to conceal her displeasure. She didn't like Thomas. She had kept close to Hip while they were working on the garden, engaging the doctor in small talk whenever Thomas drew near. She had been successful in avoiding any meaningful exchanges with the man. Now, it appeared her luck had run out. "Yes," she replied. Jamie did mind his joining her. She wondered if Thomas was paying attention.

The man settled down next to her and pulled a piece of cloth from his hip pocket. He had taken her reply as an invitation. Thomas wiped his brow and then looked intently at her, expecting her to start the conversation. Jamie steeled herself and remained silent, taking another sip of water. She had the advantage. There was nothing she wanted to say to the man.

"It's coming along nicely." Thomas finally offered. He gestured toward the new clinic building. Jamie shrugged and took another pull on her water bottle. "When do you think it'll be done?" Thomas rubbed his hands together. She noticed his soft skin. She could tell the man had never engaged in hard work.

"The framing will be finished tomorrow morning. We'll have the roof on tomorrow afternoon. It'll take a few days to finish off the inside." Jamie was going to tell him it was a much bigger job than it looked, but she restrained herself. She didn't want to trigger a prolonged conversation. She feared she had said too much already.

"You're doing a great job."

Jamie nodded to Thomas, but said nothing further. The man wouldn't know a good job from a disaster. She looked at her hands, wondering if she had been in the construction trade.

"How have you been?" He leaned forward. Jamie didn't know why, but she recognized the posture. He was in his counseling stance.

"I'm fine." Jamie cursed herself for speaking out loud.

"Are there any memories coming back to you?"

Jamie imagined telling Thomas about her dream. I've discovered I'm the daughter of thieves, she would tell him. I'm a cold-blooded killer. She smiled at the thought of his reaction.

"It's good to see you smile."

Jamie frowned.

"You've remembered something." He paused, allowing the silence to goad her into speaking. Jamie panicked. What was she going to say? There was no way in hell she was going to share with this man. She didn't trust him. "Don't be afraid," Thomas encouraged. "Sharing is healthy. You may dislodge some memories."

Jamie took another sip of water and then took her time twisting the cap back on the container. She nodded without looking at him. Then she glanced at the clinic building. "I remembered a house I might have lived in," she offered.

"Fantastic!" Thomas broke into a huge smile. "Tell me more."

God, this is awful. "It was on a lake in the mountains." Jamie could feel the slippery slope that would end with her spilling her guts.

"It must have been beautiful."

"I was very happy there," she lied. She had taken a step back from the verbal abyss.

"Good memories are a blessing," Thomas said. He studied her. "You seemed defensive when we talked on the pod ship." Jamie wondered what Carter would do to her if she killed the holy man. "I chalked it up to your disorientation," he continued. Obviously, Thomas couldn't read Jamie's thoughts. "I was wondering if you had thought more about your faith."

Jamie slipped her water bottle back into her leg pocket. "I don't get you, Thomas," she began. "Why are you so interested in what I believe?"

"Because I am a man of God." He smiled.

"I don't need him." Jamie cursed herself again. The conversation was going to get ugly.

"Everyone needs God, Jamie. It's a universal truth."

"Why?"

"It's simple. If you cut God out of your life, your soul

79

will die."

Jamie knew it was more complicated than that. "I'll take my chances," she said.

Thomas frowned. "Why take your chances when faith in God can offer you immortality?"

"I think the whole "god concept" gets in the way of love." Jamie said it simply and directly. She didn't know where the idea had come from. The words just tumbled out of her. "I don't believe in God. I believe in love."

Thomas looked like the air had been knocked out of him. His face was pale, a look of astonishment on his face. "But God is love," he stammered.

"If that's true, most God followers have a pretty messed-up understanding of love."

"And I suppose you know what love is?" There was a hint of sarcasm in his voice.

Jamie had no idea what she was talking about. She was just trying to rattle the man and make him go away. She conjured up her best smile and took a deep breath. "Love gives life. If a relationship diminishes your life, it isn't loving. That's the only thing that makes sense to me." She drew in a deep breath, trying to remember something about her beliefs, so she could fend off Thomas's unwelcome questions. "I don't want anything to do with the manipulations and meanness of religion." She expected a quick retort, but Thomas was uncharacteristically silent. He looked up at the luminous rings that cut across the violet sky. Jamie could tell he was a million miles away and a hundred fathoms deep.

* * *

They finished a few days later. The building housed a three-bed ward, a small office, an exam room, and a storage area. Hip set up the infirmary with the help of Rachel Bennett, one of Vickie's security officers. Officer Bennett was trained as an army medic, and Hip had quickly recruited her as his assistant. She was a quiet woman with quick eyes and an unreadable face. Jamie thought she would make a great poker player. Hip slapped his hands together enthusiastically when the last items were stowed away. "I feel better now," he said. "Everything is ready for my first patient."

Rachel left the clinic, leaving Jamie alone with Hip. Jamie sat down on one of the beds. "I hope you don't need it for a long time." She paused, gauging Hip's reaction. "No offence, but I've never liked hospitals or doctors' offices."

"None taken," the older man replied. "I'd be glad if no one ever needed it." Jamie always felt better when she was with Hip. She ran the palm of her hand across the blanket covering the bed. She was exhausted. Hip noticed her malaise. "How are you?" he asked.

Jamie glanced around the room, making sure they were alone. "I haven't been sleeping too well. I had a bad dream a few days ago."

"Did you remember something?"

"I think so," Jamie was quivering. "But you know how dreams are. Sometimes they don't mean anything."

"Tell me about it."

Jamie trusted Hip. Over the past few weeks, she had developed a deep affection for him. She could confide in him, knowing he wouldn't pass judgment. "In the dream I killed my husband." Hip's jaw dropped. "I was in a beautiful house. I think it was mine. And there was a trail of blood leading into the bedroom." Jamie wrapped her arms around her chest, as if she was trying to hold herself together. "He was on the bed."

"Sometimes dreams are more symbolic than literal," Hip offered. "The act of killing might mean you are moving on from something undesirable."

Jamie shook her head. "I had been there before. There were odors and the light in the room was very familiar. I think it was real."

"I'm not a psychiatrist, but I know you are desperate to remember things. Maybe you need to believe the dream was real, even though it wasn't."

"Maybe I'm a killer." Jamie felt a weight in her gut as she said it.

"I don't think so. I'm a pretty good judge of character, and you're much too kind for that."

"He was abusing me. He beat me every day. I couldn't take it anymore, and I killed him."

Hip studied her. He sat down next to her and put his arm around her shoulder. "If your dream was real, you were acting in self-defense. It doesn't make you a bad person. You had to protect yourself."

"I hope that's true," Jamie whispered. On impulse, she touched the calf of his leg. She caressed it, feeling his well-toned muscles beneath the cloth of his jumpsuit. Hip's eyes narrowed. He glanced down at her hand and then looked up at her with a soft, melancholy smile. "You are a lovely girl," he murmured. "I must admit a certain fondness for you." He placed his hand on top of hers. "Perhaps if we had met in another lifetime..." His voice trailed off as he gently removed her hand.

* * *

Jamie felt stupid as she left the clinic. It had been foolish to lead with her emotions. Hip had denied her gently, and she understood it. He would always be in grief, spending the rest of his life trying to make amends for his wife's death. His love for her was unbreakable, his guilt a slow poison. Still, Jamie had sensed his wistfulness. They had both felt drawn to each other. His was a friendship she would cherish forever.

Jamie brooded as she headed toward the beach trail. The awkward moment with Hip had confronted her with one of her fundamental mysteries. She still felt an erotic tingling in her body as she thought of him, but her sexuality still perplexed her. Her infatuation suggested she belonged in a woman's body, but still, she was uncertain. She was desperate for human contact, for the warmth of unconditional acceptance. Her yearnings clouded her judgment. She might have been drawn equally toward Bliss, so intense was her need for companionship. Jamie wondered if other people found sexual attraction as complicated as she did. The other colonists remembered their past. They had a sense of cultural and personal context for their gender preferences. Jamie did not.

* * *

That evening, as they gathered under the large curved roof of the Commons, Carter praised them for their work. He told them the compound was beginning to feel like home. They were putting down roots in their new world. "I think it's time for us to take the next step in forming our community," Carter said enthusiastically. "Tomorrow we will hold a lottery at our evening meeting. Each of us will be paired with a spouse." A dozen conversations broke out across the Commons. Carter's idea was not being welcomed. Jamie saw a lot of heads shaking and heard several heated exchanges in the crowd. Vickie stood up and moved toward Carter. She turned and faced the group, her hand resting loosely on her sidearm. An uncomfortable stillness filled the room.

Rusty raised his hand when Carter was finished. "Some of us have already formed couples," he said. "There's no need for us to participate in the lottery."

A series of side comments cascaded through the group. Carter raised his hand for silence. "We agreed to a lottery before we launched. The basic plans were developed prior to our journey, so we would not let emotions interfere with important decisions."

Rusty wasn't buying it. "The people who sent us on this mission crafted those plans five hundred years ago, while Earth was bracing for the end. It's a bad idea that was created under intense emotional stress, and we shouldn't do it." Several colonists began to nod in agreement.

Carter gave Rusty a commanding leer. He stuck out his chin and drew himself up as straight as a ramrod. "I am in command here. The only legitimate couples will be the ones formed in tomorrow night's lottery."

"You can't do that!" Rusty shouted. Vickie stiffened. She ripped open the Velcro restraint on her weapon, her hand ready to pull it from its holster.

"I can and I have already done so." Carter raised his voice. "I am the leader of this settlement. I am here to enforce the rules, and that's final."

"But things change, Carter." Rusty was pleading. "Conditions on the ground are fluid in this kind of situation. People fall in love. It's inhuman to split couples that have already formed."

"We are all going to abide by the same rules, Mr. Wolf. It's not our fault that you and Alice decided to take off your clothes and run around on the beach. You couldn't keep your emotions in check, and the two of you formed an illicit union. The community will not recognize it."

84

"Damn you!" Rusty hissed. Vickie stepped toward him, her fingers closing on the grip of her sidearm. Rusty sat down, a look of hatred on his face.

"We must perpetuate our race." Carter went on. "There must be a structure to our society. We don't have time for love. We must uphold the institution of marriage and make families. We will begin tomorrow." Carter adjourned the meeting quickly before anyone else could challenge him.

Jamie agreed with Rusty. The lottery was a big mistake. She understood the need to procreate. That's what colonization was all about. However, treating everyone like balls in a roulette wheel was ill-advised. The lottery was going to fracture existing relationships and create discord in the community. Beyond her philosophical objections, Jamie didn't want a mate. She would have gladly paired with Hip, but he had refused. She wanted the freedom to choose a companion on her own terms, to fall in love and then decide to partner for life.

CHAPTER EIGHT
Lottery

T he next morning, Carter stood before the colonists like a visionary, his eyes focusing above and beyond his audience as he made his pronouncements. He seemed caught in a state of spiritual ecstasy, perhaps drunk on his own power. Jamie was astonished by what was happening. Carter was treating everyone like children, micro-managing their lives down to the most personal detail. He commanded everyone to clean their tents and bathe prior to the lottery. He asked Thomas to prepare for a group wedding that evening. He asked everyone to comb through the supplies and make decorations for the compound. He insisted on an elaborate celebration.

The colonists' reaction was even more troubling. They took the orders in stride and did as they were told, yielding mindlessly to Carter, as if he was a dictator. They went to the shore and washed their clothes. They bathed in the violet river upstream from the waterfall. By midday, the settlement was adorned with brightly colored bottles and fabrics. Someone fashioned a few strings of lights with painted bulbs. A couple of the women cut tablecloths for the Commons from the textile supplies. The cooks prepared a special dinner with a large tray of cupcakes decorated with bells and hearts for dessert. Why were they following him so blindly?

Jamie was not one of the enthusiasts. She left her tent the way it was and poured herself into her daily chores. She was the only person working, but she refused to surrender to the celebratory mood. There was a lack of authenticity about it. Carter had promoted the idea like a cheerleader for a losing team, selling the impossible idea of success to nonbelievers. Vickie had to stand guard over the group, in case a riot broke out. The excitement was a faux overlay, obscuring the colonists' real feelings. Jamie had seen the carefree attitudes as people greeted her throughout the day, but it was a facade, their smiles quickly turning to worried frowns.

Jamie took a walk on the beach and settled down on a flat rock near the mouth of the river. The stone was warm in the afternoon sun. She leaned back on her hands and gazed at the fine mist rising from the small waterfall where the river dropped into the sea. The waters merged, churning and roiling as the rapid currents of the river met the slowly rolling surf. The energetic river would lose its battle with the calm ocean, the weaker surrendering to the ways of the stronger.

Jamie thought about the wisdom of the river. The lottery would cause turbulence in the settlement. Some would be broken by the overwhelming current of change. Others would embrace it, finding a new reality, much like the river's water merging into the ocean. There would be distress in the colony until equilibrium was reestablished.

Jamie gazed at a rock poking up from the riverbed. It stood its ground in the rapid current, the river diverting around it. The water spiraled into eddies where the rock split the stream, settling back again into the never-ending surge toward the river's mouth. She would be that rock. She would join neither the company of the obeisant, nor the ranks of the broken. She would not accept Carter's dictum. She would stand against the ill-considered lottery. Jamie knew she would pay a price for her obstinacy, but anything was better than being paired against her will.

She looked upriver and took in the whole sweep of the surging tributary. The water always found its way to the sea. The little rock, standing tall in the river, making its protest against the current could not stop it. Eventually, the water would wear it down or knock it over, and the twisting eddies would disappear. A wave of futility washed over her. Jamie could not stop the winds of change. She could only be true to herself.

Jamie's attention was drawn to movement in her peripheral vision. She turned her head and saw Rusty and Alice at the water's edge, perhaps fifty meters down the shoreline. They were naked in the surf, like when she first had seen them, but they were joyless. They stood knee deep in the violet water, holding each other's hands. Their heads were tipped down, lovers saying goodbye.

A flash of memory struck Jamie like a lightning bolt. She saw a woman's face. She was dying. Jamie heard her whisper "I love you," in a soft, breathy voice. She remembered reaching toward her and pulling her frail body to her chest. She kissed the woman on her waxy forehead. Jamie remembered saying her last words to her, "Don't go, Camille! I can't live without you." Jamie could hear Camille's final breath in her mind. She could feel the overpowering emptiness as her lover's life slipped away. She cried out, the sounds of the rushing river drowning her voice as the current coursed its way into the endless ocean.

Jamie was shaking as the echoes of her memory slipped away into the nether world of her mind. She had sat forward on the rock, hugging herself tightly. Once again, she felt herself falling apart. She sobbed deeply, pausing only to gasp for air as another wave of grief coursed over her. What was happening? She remembered their intimacy. She remembered losing Camille. She remembered feeling her body as she died, her soft warmth ebbing away into cold, hard death. "Damn it! Who am I?" she muttered to the alien sea. The sexual clarity of her encounter with Hip now drained away like the outgoing tide. Jamie struggled to her feet, unwrapping her arms from her chest. She looked down the beach to where Rusty and Alice had stood. They were gone.

* * *

Jamie noticed that Carter had rearranged the Commons for the evening meeting. A lone table stood in the middle of the room. Two canisters, labeled "men" and "women," sat side by side on its surface. A small pile of paper, each leaf torn roughly without the aid of scissors, was stacked next to a logjam of pencils. Storage cases were arranged theater style, with a central aisle, on both sides of the table. Carter stood like a priest behind an altar, motioning for everyone to sit in front of him, leaving a field of empty cases beyond the table. There was an expectant hush as he called upon Thomas to offer a prayer. A few glanced around as Thomas invoked the divine.

"We are doing this for the sake of societal stability." Carter stated firmly. "Natural pairing without the formal blessing of the community will lead to anarchy and moral breakdown. Our community is small, and the dangers are too great for us to allow individuals to make up the rules as they go. Men would take multiple wives. Jealousy and conflict would follow. The entire colony could perish. The institution of marriage will be honored on my watch. It is my moral duty to do so."

Carter explained that each person would write their name

on a piece of paper and place it in the canister corresponding to their gender. Once all the names were deposited, he would draw one name from each container, and those persons would be paired. The new couples would sit together in the empty chairs behind the table.

Jamie watched as the first row of colonists moved forward and wrote their names. She was one of the last ones. She walked down the aisle with her head lowered. She paused near the women's canister. Carter's eyes were locked on her as she picked up one of the last slips of paper. She took a pencil and wrote, cupping her free hand over the paper. Then she folded it and dropped it into the container. She turned away without looking at Carter and returned to her seat.

Carter stirred each of the canisters and withdrew a piece of paper from each with a flourish. He read the name on the first slip, and a man stood nervously. Then he read the second, and a timid woman rose from where she was sitting. She looked like a frightened animal, helpless and frozen in fear. Carter motioned for them to approach. They met in the center aisle and walked forward together. Carter directed them to sit on one of the empty storage cases behind him. Jamie watched the man put his arm around the woman's waist. She shifted away uncomfortably. He pulled her toward him. She frowned but didn't resist.

Alice's name was drawn during the third round. She was paired with Stub Andrews. She appeared pale as a sheet as Stub snatched her hand. Her body resembled a toothpick next to his muscular frame. Jamie watched Rusty as Alice took her place with Stub. The artist's shoulders were slumped and his head bowed in defeat.

Carter drew Thomas' name next. He was paired with Olivia. Jamie smiled to herself. Maybe there was a god. They deserved each other: Mr. Holier-than-Thou and the Lord

High Executioner. Olivia was obviously pleased. Thomas wasn't happy.

Rusty was paired with Bliss. He walked forward like a wooden statue when their names were called. Bliss took his hand before they reached the center table. She gripped it tightly as they skirted past Carter to join the group of couples. Rusty's arm was limp. He made no attempt to squeeze her hand in return. Jamie saw their faces for the first time when they turned to sit down. His eyes were filled with despair, hers with joy.

Jamie and Vickie, along with two other women, remained in front of the lottery table. Carter smiled as he picked the final slip of paper from the men's container. It was his own. "Well what do you know, ladies and gentlemen?" He said it like a carnival barker. "We've saved the best for last." Jamie saw Stub grin and whisper something to Alice. She looked terrified. "Carter Lund is to be paired with…" He paused fishing a name from the women's canister. "…with Jamie Stryker." His grin illuminated the room. "Come here, Jamie." He said it like a master calling his dog.

Jamie sucked in a breath. Her hands began to shake. For an instant, she was no longer in the room. Her vision blurred as her blood pressure crested. A throbbing pain shot through both temples. Time turned to molasses. Vickie prodded her to get out of her seat, and she rose tentatively on rubbery knees. "There must be some mistake," she said.

"No mistake here." Carter waved the papers in the air.

Jamie walked forward to the table and stood before Carter. "Give me the names." He wadded the papers in his fist. Jamie reached out her hand. Carter grabbed her fingers, squeezing them together painfully. She pulled away, but he tightened his grip. "Let me go!"

Carter laughed and let her go. He placed the two crumpled papers in her hand. She unfolded them slowly. The first name was "Carter Lund" and the second "Jamie Stryker." She dropped the papers and met Carter's gaze. His face was wreathed in a knowing smile as he gestured for her to join him with the other couples. She shook her head, cursing under her breath before walking around the table. The whole lottery was rigged. She had never written her name on her slip of paper.

* * *

The community wedding service took place a short while later. Jamie was an unwilling bride. She had not bathed, nor had she donned a fresh jumpsuit. She had left her hair unkempt and avoided eye contact with her betrothed. Carter reached for her during the ceremony, but she pulled away, refusing to hold his hand.

Bliss and Olivia were among the few who enjoyed themselves at the wedding. Bliss was pleased with her luck-of-the-draw partner. Rusty was a good and gentle man. Olivia stood proudly next to Thomas like the lady of a fiefdom. She followed his every word and made no attempt to hide her air of superiority. Thomas ignored her and concentrated on the task at hand.

There were no rings to exchange or candles to light. No grand bouquets of flowers were tossed over brides' shoulders. Thomas didn't ask if there was any reason why certain couples shouldn't be joined in matrimony. He simply intoned the basics, cajoling the couples into the public vows of commitment.

When asked to repeat her marriage vows, Jamie refused. Carter frowned, but they both knew her silence was inconsequential in the broader scheme of things. Passive aggressive behavior would not save her from marriage. These were extraordinary times, and personal preferences no longer mattered. Jamie would be wedded because the stability of the settlement demanded it. "I now pronounce that you are husbands and wives," Thomas declared. Jamie was gone in a flash, leaving Carter alone at the makeshift altar, the words of the final blessing receding over her shoulder.

There was no reception after the wedding service. Couples stood awkwardly by each other, speaking in quiet tones. Some snaked their arms around their new spouses. Most of the partners didn't object, but there were few signs of affection. Stub lost no time and began groping Alice. She slapped him, and he laughed, pulling at the zipper of her jumpsuit as she tried to escape from him. As twilight fell, most of the newlyweds lingered in the Commons, trying to avoid the obligatory intimacy of their wedding night. Friends offered each other knowing glances, uniting silently with shared angst.

* * *

Jamie was sitting on the edge of her cot when Carter came to her tent. He stood at the open flap with his fists on his hips. He said nothing at first. Jamie refused to look at him. He was breathing like an angry tiger. She feared a beating, hoping he could suppress his anger.

"You embarrassed me." Carter's voice was coarse and accusing. Jamie was silent. "I know this is an awkward situation, but you didn't have to walk away from the ceremony like that." No response. "We are all in this together, Jamie. We have to create a new society. I know it seems unnatural to you. I know you don't love me. Nevertheless, we have to build families. Make children."

Jamie shuddered. She wasn't sure how she felt about children, but the thought of having sex with Carter nauseated her. She thought about Hip, then Camille. She felt another wave of confusion. She didn't want a man telling her who she was supposed to be, especially this man who liked to take charge and smother everyone under the blanket of his will.

"Come to my tent."

"No!" Jamie snapped.

"It's your home now."

"Never!"

Carter stepped into the tent. He smelled of aftershave and deodorant. The pungent aroma swept over Jamie. She wanted to vomit. Carter stepped toward the cot, and Jamie crouched forward. She wrapped her arms tightly around her chest. He saw her body language and sighed dramatically. Then he settled down on the equipment case across from her.

"I want this to work between us," he said softly.

Jamie looked up at him with angry eyes. "Get out of my tent."

"I'm your husband. It's time for us to be together." Carter reached for her, his fingers open.

"I'll never be with you."

Carter pulled his arms back and gripped the sides of the equipment case. His eyes glazed over as if he was in a trance. "You can't embarrass me like this. I'm the leader of the settlement, and your rebellion is going to undermine my authority. How can I keep the other couples together if you refuse to be with me?"

"That is your problem." Jamie walked her fingers over the skin under her arms, gripping herself more tightly.

Carter's eyes blazed with fury. "It's your problem too, goddamn it!"

Jamie flinched at Carter's outburst. He leaned forward and grabbed her by the shoulders. He pressed them together, forcing her arms more tightly around her chest. It felt like her back would split open from the pressure. She stifled a groan as he brought his face within a couple centimeters of her. She could smell his anger. "I won you fair and square in the lottery."

Jamie pulled her arms free and tried to push him away. "Like hell you did!"

Carter tightened his grip. His fingers were like steel clamps. "It was the luck of the draw."

"There was no luck about it," she spat back at him. "I never wrote down my name."

Carter dropped his hands. If he was sorry for what he had done, he didn't show it. "That doesn't matter now."

Jamie rubbed her shoulders. "It will always matter."

"You are mine, and you will do as I say. You will not embarrass me in front of the others, or else..."

Jamie winced. Carter's voice was cold. He was a powerful man, and she recognized his threat. She was in grave danger. "I will not have sex with you."

Carter put his hand on her head. Jamie wanted to swat it away, but terror filled her. "You'll change your mind." He slid his hand down the side of her face, and then it was on her shoulder, tracing a menacing line down her side and around her hip. Finally, he gripped her knee like a vice. "I am sleeping with you in this tent. In the morning, we'll go our separate ways and be about our business. We will eat meals together, and if you know what's good for you, you will move into my tent tomorrow night."

Jamie pushed Carter away with all her strength. It was like

pushing a tree. She picked up her feet without a word and lay down on the cot, turning her back toward Carter. She was grateful the bed wasn't big enough for the both of them. Carter touched her bottom, and she jerked, pulling her legs up toward her chest. His hand lingered where lovers touch. Jamie dared not move. She tried to close her mind to the violation, fighting sensations of terror and humiliation. Carter laughed as he pulled his hand away and settled down on the ground next to the cot. Jamie held her breath. In the distance, she heard Stub's angry voice and then Alice's scream. Jamie wondered if she would ever sleep again.

* * *

Jamie did sleep. She was visited by another vivid dream. This time she was a child, perhaps twelve years old, and she was running through the woods, followed by her little sister. She ran like the wind, surefooted as she swept past tree and bramble. Her sister called after her. "Slow down! I can't keep up!" But Jamie paid no attention. She sensed an evil in herself, a malevolent spirit that sometimes latches onto older siblings and turns them into familial monsters. She didn't want her sister to catch her. She wanted her to fall exhausted on the brown pine needles that blanketed the forest floor.

Jamie felt no remorse for her actions. In fact, she found pleasure in tormenting the younger girl. She was detached, like a scientist observing the behavior of a rat. Her sister wasn't a person. She was a thing to be poked and prodded. She was an object that existed for Jamie's amusement.

Jamie ran up a steep hill, which crested along the rim of a deep canyon. She sensed that she had been there before. She slowed her pace and stopped a few feet from the cliff's edge. Her sister was far behind her, the young girl's whimpers echoing through the darkening wood. Jamie paused and looked over the escarpment. Hundreds of sharp rocks lined the ground below. A shadow passed over the floor of the canyon, obscuring the hazardous stones. She looked up at the sky. Twilight was falling, and soon it would be dangerous to tread along the canyon's rim.

Her sister's voice whispered through the forest behind her. Jamie knew what she was going to do. She felt a bolt of excitement course through her like an electric shock. She turned and called to her sister. "I'm over here, Lizzie!" Her sister's name was Elizabeth. Jamie paused in her dream to savor the new information. How could she have forgotten her sister's name? The light was failing now. The landscape was losing all of its color in the accelerated timeframe of the dream. The valley below was lost in blackness.

Jamie heard her sister's feet scuffing across the dried pine needles. She could hear her breathing now. "Where are you?" she called. Her voice was cracking. She was on the verge of hysteria.

"I'm over here!" Jamie called out with a strong voice. "Hurry up!" Jamie smiled to herself. She would play a trick on her sister. In a flash, she pivoted and hid herself behind one of the trees that stood at the edge of the cliff. The rapid footsteps grew closer. Jamie saw her sister flash past her.

The young girl ran straight over the edge of the cliff. She tumbled through the air. "Howard!" she screamed.

* * *

Jamie awoke with a start. It was dark. She gasped for breath as she emerged from the dream, gripped by its horror and grateful for its passing. It was another memory. Jamie sucked in a tremulous breath as a singular detail of the nightmare obscured all others. Lizzie had called her Howard. Jamie tried to steady her breathing. She could feel her heart pounding. Once again, she was filled with doubt. Had she been Lizzie's older brother? Had she changed her gender to escape the law? Had she joined the colonists to run away from her past? Jamie shook violently on the bed. She heard Carter's sigh, then remembered the night before. Oh God, he's sleeping next to me! I am in such a mess! She gripped the edges of the cot, willing her body into stillness. She dared not wake him. She was too tangled in her memories for that.

CHAPTER NINE

Alice

J amie rose early the next morning. She managed to step over Carter without waking him and left the settlement quickly. She made her way to the beach and sat, as she often did, on the large flat rock by the mouth of the river. The breeze was already stifling, even though the sun was just peeking over the jungle. She closed her eyes, trying to remember the vestiges of her dream. She had a younger sister named Lizzie. They were running through a forest. She caused her sister's death by allowing her to fall off a cliff. Jamie remembered her fascination as Lizzie's body flailed in midair, then tumbled violently against the jagged canyon wall. She was amused by her sister's death. What kind of person was she? The dream in the white mansion seemed justifiable. She had killed her husband in self-defense. The death of her sister revealed a much darker side of her personality.

Jamie recoiled from the horrible thoughts and turned to Lizzie's last word. She had called her Howard. As the days and weeks progressed, Jamie was becoming more convinced of her womanhood. Still, the girl from her dream had used that name, a distinctively masculine name. No matter how she tried, it didn't fit her. The memory was vivid, the feelings clear, but an inner voice questioned the recollection. She had never been Howard, and she wasn't a monster. Sometimes a dream was just a dream, right?

* * *

Jamie rose from the rock and made her way northward past the Lander. The sun was higher in the western sky. Jamie paused and removed her shoes. The sand was already warm against her feet, but not hot like it would be later in the day. She kept walking, hoping the sea would tell her what to do. Everything seemed so unmanageable: not knowing who she was, the challenges of this new world, and Carter's unwelcome interest in her.

The morning light danced on the waves, as if Nature was laughing at her. She remembered Rusty's story about keeping balance. "This too shall pass," the sage had said. Jamie wanted it all to pass. Right now. She didn't want to return to the settlement. She loathed the idea of spending a single day with Carter. And most of all, she wanted the fog in her mind to lift away and reveal the truth about her past.

Jamie turned around, retracing her footsteps in the sand. The Lander loomed as she approached it, a technological oddity perched on the ancient shore. She approached the ship and stood at the edge of the long ramp, which rose into the belly of the spacecraft. She set down her shoes and poked her feet into them. Then she climbed the ramp and entered the darkened interior of the Lander.

The hold was cavernous. They had taken a substantial portion of the supplies from their stowage spaces, leaving a large open space in the belly of the ship. They had stripped out some of the bulkheads for the compound wall and the storage buildings. Jamie's body ached with the memory of carrying everything to the settlement. The morning light reflected off the sand beneath the ship and filtered softly through the hatchway. Jamie moved slowly in the dimness. She didn't know why she had entered the ship, or what she was looking for, but something drew her. She moved toward the flight deck.

The narrow access corridor had been cleared, and she could walk upright. She entered the small compartment and squinted as the bright sunlight struck her in the face. There were four seats in the cockpit. Two of them were bolted to the deck before a complicated instrument panel, which wrapped around beneath the forward view ports. Behind them, two other seats bracketed the central aisle, each placed before darkened control surfaces. Everything looked complicated, even with the power turned off.

Jamie stepped between the seats and peered through the curved aluminum silicate glass. She could see the place where she had run in the surf with Rusty and Alice. The river was pouring over the small waterfall, a spray of water sparkling in the morning light. She couldn't see beyond the river. The shoreline angled behind the tree line and was lost from view. The distant horizon cut across the violet waters to the south and east. Alathea's golden rings rose majestically into the sky and beyond it.

Jamie stood for several moments, transfixed by the beauty of their new world. Then she glanced down and scanned the instruments. The dark panels scoffed at her, reminding her of the dysfunction of her mind. She sat down in the pilot's seat and gripped the controls. The ship would never fly again. The Lander had done her duty and delivered them safely to Alathea's surface. Jamie closed her eyes and imagined the powerful engines coming to life. She imagined the ship flying high into the morning air, streaking across the sky. Jamie imagined the ship taking her away from Carter and back to Earth, back to her memories and back to the life she once called her own. Hope sprung within her for a moment, then she opened her eyes. The instruments were still lifeless, and the ship was silent.

Jamie left the flight deck. She was a fool. Escapism rarely solved reality's problems; it only postponed the inevitable. She would never remember her past. It was time to stop grieving for what was lost and start a new life. She thought of Carter again. He was her husband. There had to be a way to contest the marriage, but Carter was the only one who could annul it. Jamie's new beginning was looking more and more like a dead end. She hurried back to the hold and down the ramp. The sand was getting warmer under her feet as she turned back toward the beach trail.

Jamie heard a noise as she entered the jungle. It was a human sound, female. She followed it and saw a woman a couple meters off the beach trail. Her back was against a tree. It was Alice. The dark-haired woman was still wearing her wedding clothes. They were torn and soiled. There was blood. Her legs were splayed out in front of her, and her chest heaved with deep, guttural sobs. Alice had been beaten. She had a black eye, and a large patch of her hair had been ripped out of her scalp, leaving a reddened patch of tortured skin. Stub had raped her, the raw brutality of their wedding night leaving scars that would never heal. Jamie knelt down and reached for her, but Alice jerked away.

Jamie's first instinct was to tell Rusty about Alice, but then she realized he would confront Stub. The artist was no match for the construction engineer. The bastard would kill him. She marched back to her tent and found Carter still sleeping next to her cot. She kicked him unceremoniously in the leg, and he sat up with a start.

"What? What's going on?" It took him a moment to realize where he was. "Oh, Jamie. I remember now. Did you sleep well?"

Jamie ignored the question. "We've got a big problem, Carter."

"What?" He was still shaking the cobwebs out of his head.

"It's Alice. Stub beat the shit out of her last night. If we don't do something, he's going to kill her."

"He's a bit rough around the edges, but she'll adapt."

"Rough around the edges? Are you crazy? That man is an animal. Alice is hiding in the jungle off the beach trail. She can't take another night with that bastard."

"What do you want me to do? We're a small group of people. We need everyone. I can't split them up. They'll still see each other anyway."

"You should have thought about this before you had your lottery, Carter. You don't just mash people together into couples. People like Stub are dangerous."

"I'll keep an eye on him. If I see him cross the line, I'll talk to him about it."

"That won't do any good. He's an abuser."

"It's the only way, Jamie."

"You are such a coward." Jamie looked down at him. She stood like a titan at his feet. He flinched at the invective and then lowered his eyes. Jamie knew she had drawn blood. She spun on her heals and left him sitting on the ground.

* * *

Jamie found Hip and Bliss at the garden. She told them about Alice, and Hip rushed to the clinic for his med case. "Be careful, Hip. She's real shook up. She may not like a man touching her."

103

"I'll be gentle," he called over his shoulder.

Bliss stood by the barren garden and wept. Jamie took her hand, but said nothing. The shadow of a dark memory was etched on the woman's face. Suddenly, the marks Jamie had seen on Bliss's back made sense. She had been abused, too.

"What are they going to do about Stub?" She whimpered.

"I went to Carter, and he said he'd talk to him about it."

"That won't work. He'll beat her again." Bliss spoke from firsthand experience.

"I know." Jamie didn't know what else to say.

"We've got to stop him."

There was a rustle in the grass, and both women looked up. Ben Beck had rounded the corner of the wall and was eyeing them as he walked by. He looked at Bliss and pretended to fondle his breasts. He laughed and moved on.

"How do we do that?" Jamie asked.

"We kill him."

Jamie was fascinated by the thought of killing Stub and only mildly repelled by its brutality. The image of Alice bloodied and bruised came to her. Maybe she could do it. She remembered the rush she had felt when her sister fell to her death. She might even enjoy killing him. Both women were taken by the transcendent gravity of the thought. They turned their attention to the garden, working in silence as thoughts of murder ruminated in their minds.

The garden had not changed since they planted it. There was no sign of growth. The seeds lay dormant in the alien loam. Jamie scooped out one of the corn seeds. There was no sign of germination, no radicle or coleoptile emerging from the shell. Jamie broke the silence. "This isn't working."

Bliss touched her gently on the elbow. "Have you ever been beaten?" she asked softly.

Jamie thought of the white house by the mountain lake. "Yeah."

Bliss looked off into the jungle. "You never get over it, you know?"

* * *

Jamie came upon Hip later that morning. He had scoured the beach trail, but didn't find Alice. There was some blood by the tree where Jamie had seen her, but the woman was gone. Jamie busied herself by fetching more supplies from the Lander. She paused several times on the beach trail near the place where her friend had been, but there was no sign of her.

At the midday meal, Hip and Carter stood in the Commons near the entrance to the service building. They were engaged in a heated discussion. Hip was shaking his head while Carter glared at him. Jamie watched from across the room. She didn't want to eat with Carter, and the argument was a perfect diversion. The two men grew more agitated and pushed their way through the door leading into the service building. Even though they were out of sight, their voices could still be heard above the lunchtime chatter.

A few minutes later, Hip slammed his way through the door and made a beeline out of the Commons. Carter emerged and called to Stub Andrews. Jamie's stomach convulsed as she saw the man, full of swagger and machismo. At first, she thought he was speaking to him about mistreating Alice, but soon it became evident that Carter had a construction project for him. He had etched a diagram on a digital tablet and was gesturing enthusiastically. She watched Stub's skeptical reaction. He scratched his scalp and shook his head. Carter raised his voice in a frustrated growl. "I don't care. I want it done by dinner." His commanding tone left no room for discussion. Stub grimaced and left the Commons.

Jamie watched as Carter scanned the room. Their eyes met, and he walked in her direction. She braced herself, but he paused at Vickie's table instead. He said something about building a fire and told her to gather items that would burn. Jamie heard him say something about chopping trees. It was clear he wanted Vickie's men to get some firewood. There was nodding around the table, and Carter smiled. Then he turned toward Jamie. She was tempted to get up and walk away but thought better of it. There was no telling what the man would do if she embarrassed him again.

"It's going to be a marvelous evening," he cooed as he sat down across from her. "We're going to have a grand ritual with a bonfire and dancing."

"A ritual?"

"You'll see, baby." Jamie hated being called that. "It'll sweep you off your feet."

"I can hardly wait." Her voice dripped with sarcasm.

Carter squeezed her shoulder and left the Commons. She flinched as his fingers pressed a tender spot left by his angry grip the night before. The man had forgotten about it. She rubbed the sore muscle. She was grateful for his preoccupation with the evening's festivities. Carter had a short attention span, and if she could distract him at the right moments, perhaps she could hold him at bay.

* * *

That afternoon, Jamie scoured the jungle between the settlement and the beach looking for Alice. She worried about her friend, but realized that she was probably safer in the jungle than she would be with Stub. She thought about her conversation with Bliss. Could they kill Stub? Jamie was surprised at how quickly the answer occurred to her. They could kill him if it meant saving Alice.

Jamie emerged from the jungle near the Lander. Stub was there, working with his team as they took several pieces of conduit from the fuselage. They were laughing among themselves. Stub grabbed his crotch and danced like a monkey in the sand. The others roared, shaking their heads. She heard one of them say, "He's crazy," and another reply, "But he's in command." Jamie turned back toward the jungle. One of the builders dropped a piece of pipe, and it made a loud clattering sound. Jamie was startled.

"Hey!" Jamie stopped at the sound of Stub's voice. She turned slowly. "Come over here and give us a hand." Stub gestured between his legs, and the other men laughed. He pointed toward one of the long metal tubes. "Take one of these back to the compound." Stub gave her a menacing look. He was a dangerous man.

"Sure," Jamie replied cautiously. She approached the pile of pipe and grabbed one of the conduits. She picked it up. Stub laughed as she shifted it in her palm to fine tune the balance. She turned away from him quickly and headed back toward the settlement.

"You can handle my pipe anytime, babe!" he called after her.

Jamie wasted no time crossing the beach. She didn't want to be anywhere near the man. A shadow crossed her face as she hurried toward the tree line. She turned toward the ocean and looked up. A swiftly moving cloud obscured the sun.

* * *

Everyone gathered in the compound that evening. A

large fire had been lit, which cast flickering shadows across the crimson grass. It was a warm evening, and everyone wondered why Carter had insisted on such a hot fire. A large post-like structure had been constructed in the middle of the compound. It was made from the conduit Jamie had helped carry from the Lander. The slender pipe had been fashioned into a hollow, cylindrical framework, perhaps half a meter in diameter. Sheet metal had been attached to the outside of the frame, forming a smooth metallic skin. The sculpture, if it could be called that, stood about three meters tall. Long strips of cloth were attached to the top of it and hung limply down to the ground. No one said a word as they took in Carter's creation. Their eyes were locked on the pillar. It was shaped like a swollen phallus. The long shaft had a bulbous head near the top where the cloth streamers were fastened.

"What is it?" Olivia wondered.

"Haven't you ever seen a penis before?" Bliss laughed.

"It's a maypole." Rusty shook his head.

Carter stood next to a table filled with cups and a large pot. "Come and drink, friends! It's time to celebrate and dance!" He ladled out a cupful of the brew and took a long sip. "Ah, it's good!" He gestured for everyone to come toward him. Jamie stayed at the back, watching suspiciously. Several of the men drank Carter's libation. They nodded enthusiastically at the flavor. Others came forward, and soon everyone was enjoying the intoxicant. Before long, inhibitions began to melt away. Within an hour, the settlers were giddy, waving their arms in exaggerated gestures and laughing raucously.

Jamie kept to the periphery. She didn't want to drink. Reality was already a moving target for her. She watched as Stub finished his cup and wheeled around toward the beverage table. Bliss was drinking voraciously, the alcohol numbing her reason. She pranced around, overcorrecting her movements as she descended into a drunken trance. Rusty tried to take her drink from her, but she cursed him and zigzagged across the compound.

Jamie scanned the group for Alice but didn't see her. She wandered over by the tents. There was blood on Alice's cot, but she wasn't there. She presumed her friend was still somewhere in the jungle. The daylight was fading, and she was worried.

Jamie saw Hip standing next to his new mate when she returned to the party. He looked up as she took up her station at the edge of the crowd. He wore a melancholy look. Their eyes met for an instant, and he tipped his head. It was a private moment, surrounded by drunken revelry. Jamie felt an ache in her stomach. They had been so close to something beautiful. She wished he had accepted her romantic gesture that day when they were alone in the clinic. Now, they were both thrust into loveless unions. She gave him a broad smile and placed her hand over her heart. Hip bowed slightly as he returned the gesture. Then his new mate pulled him away, and he disappeared into the throng.

Carter urged the crowd to gather at the pillar in the center of the compound. He made the women stand around the cylindrical structure and gave each of them one of the cloth streamers. Then, he formed the men into a second circle around the women and distributed the remaining strips of cloth. Carter was jubilant. He raised his cup in a toast and spoke with a strong voice. "We shall dance," he declared, slurring his words together. "We shall dance for sex with our partners!" There was a whoop of laughter from the men. Carter gave Jamie a suggestive look, and she turned away. "We shall dance for many children and abundant crops in our garden!" He took a long pull from his cup and then threw it to the ground.

Jamie thought it was going to take a lot more than dancing around a maypole to make things grow in the garden. Getting everyone drunk and working them into a sexual frenzy was another matter. No wonder Hip had been angry at Carter. Their leader was playing with fire. Not only had he pressed everyone into ill-advised unions, now he was igniting everyone's primal instincts. A lot of people were going to get hurt. Most of them would be women. Jamie shuttered as she realized Carter would probably rape her before the night was over.

Carter stood at the base of the sculpture, and everyone started to dance in a circle around him. The women moved in a clockwise direction, while the men took the reverse track. They lowered and lifted their cloth ribbons as they passed each other, weaving the strips around the pole. The men howled, and the women squealed.

Bliss was bouncing around the circle with drunken abandon. She dropped her streamer and pranced toward Carter. She threw her arms around the sculpture and wiggled suggestively. The men howled with delight. She unzipped her jumpsuit and let the upper portion of it dangle around her waist. The crowd yelled enthusiastically as Bliss fondled her breasts and kissed the maypole. She had just started to wiggle out of her pants when there was a blinding flash of light and a great clap of thunder. The compound shook. The drunken colonists didn't react at first, thinking the lightening was part of Carter's extravaganza. Then there was a second flash and a rumble more powerful than the first, and everyone began to scream.

A great wind began to whip the alien trees and snap the nylon panels of the tents. The table where Carter had placed the pot blew over in the wind. Cups scuttled along the ground. The pot spilled, and the strong drink flooded across bare ground in wind-driven rivulets. Everyone stampeded across the compound toward the Commons and the storage sheds, pushing and shoving their way like a herd of frightened animals. The raw power of the elements pierced the most primitive parts of their brains and sent them rushing mindlessly toward any shelter they could find.

Carter left Bliss clinging to the pornographic maypole as he followed the others to safety. Jamie hurried toward her friend. Bliss was clinging to the thin sheet metal of the sculpture. What moments before had been an erotic gesture, was now a death grip. The violent wind had caught her loosened jumpsuit and turned it into a sail. The gust picked up her body, her feet leaving the ground. Bliss screamed, the sound lost in the maelstrom. Then the wind pulled the jumpsuit from her ankles, and it disappeared across the compound.

Jamie dug in her heels and pushed toward the frightened woman. Another strong gust caught her as she reached Bliss's side. She threw her arms around the sculpture. The storm exhaled like a gargantuan beast, and then paused. Jamie released her grip, pulling Bliss to her side.

"We've got to get under cover!" she shouted. Bliss nodded feebly and turned her hips away from the maypole. She clung fiercely to Jamie. The storm's fury rose again. The two women stumbled toward the Commons. The winds accelerated to hurricane force, knocking them to their knees. A piece of the settlement wall ripped away and hurtled toward them. Jamie pushed Bliss to the ground as the sharp metal whipped over their heads. Bliss was hysterical. Jamie looked up. The Commons was at least thirty meters away. They would never make it.

Jamie looked behind them at the storage shed near the tents. It was much closer than the Commons. She scrambled to her feet and grabbed Bliss under the arms. The woman was

111

dead weight in her hands. She pulled her friend up and tucked the naked woman under one arm. Bliss was almost unconscious. If they didn't get to shelter, they would both die in the storm. Jamie pulled Bliss around, her limp body pivoting against her hip. "Walk, goddamn it!" she shouted over the wind. Bliss stirred, and the two women staggered toward the shed.

Jamie and Bliss were less than three meters from their refuge, and their strength was tapped out. Bliss collapsed again. Jamie could hardly stand. She dropped to her knees, using her body to shelter her companion. Occasionally, the random cruelty of nature offers a reprieve to her victims. For a brief moment, the storm held its breath, and the winds subsided. Jamie looked up into the twilight sky and saw the thick, dark clouds roiling overhead. She grabbed Bliss by her arm and mustered all of her remaining strength. She jerked the other woman to her feet and pushed forward.

The door on the supply shed caught in the jamb and refused to open. The wind began to rise again, and Jamie knew she wouldn't have a second chance. Either the door would open, and they would be safe, or the door would resist, and they would die. She lowered Bliss to the ground and grasped the latch in both hands. She took a deep breath as she felt the hurricane regaining its fury. Jamie pulled on the door again. It flew open. Loose items in the shed were sucked out of the opening and spiraled up into the wind. Something heavy struck Jamie in the head. She staggered backward, consciousness slipping away from her. She caught herself and reached to her side, pulling Bliss through the doorway. The wind caught the door and smashed it against the side of the building, whipping Jamie into the shed. She tumbled over Bliss's inert form.

The wind howled through the open door-frame, the hurricane's song accompanied by the percussive banging of the door as it swung wildly on its tortured hinges. Somewhere in the back of her weather-beaten brain, Jamie knew the door would be torn from its casing if she didn't close it. She grabbed at one of the storage shelves that lined the walls and pulled herself up again. She threw her body into the open doorway and clawed at the frame as the storm reached full fury once more. Jamie was reaching for the door when the wind caught it and slammed it into the casing. She pulled her fingers out of the way, just as the door crashed against the jamb. She grabbed the inner latch as the door bounced open, pulling with every ounce of her strength. The door closed, and the latch clicked into place, making the loveliest sound she could imagine. Then Jamie passed out.

CHAPTER TEN
Storm

J amie was surrounded by a churning violet mist. She felt herself floating, as if on a winged boat suspended in midair. She could not see beyond the swirling vapor, only indistinct shadows where its density blocked a mysterious light. She sensed the presence of others, people standing beyond her luminous bubble. She did not recognize them. She heard the muttering of their voices. She couldn't make out the words, but she knew they were speaking to her.

Jamie felt no fear. In fact, her misty cocoon was a comfort. It was as if she was in her mother's womb, surrounded by the mellifluous sounds of an unseen world. They were purring to her, offering her the suggestion of a post-partum life beyond the veil of her knowing. The voices were calling to her, defining her, embracing her.

Then silence descended. It was the total absence of sound and sensation, a void in life's medium, a pause between the heartbeats of existence. The silence jolted her. Every sense came alive, attending to the existential absence. Jamie waited. She floated bird-like on currents of violet air, wrapped in alternating folds of darkness and light. A whisper wrapped itself around her silence. "You already know who you are," it said. Jamie's eyes snapped open, the specter dissolving like April's snow.

* * *

It was dark inside the shed. The wind howled just beyond the thin sheet metal skin of the enclosure. The rigid leaves of the alien trees made a deafening sound, clicking and clacking like rhythm sticks on steroids. Jamie could hear sand, probably from the distant beach, pelting on the shed and grinding its surface. Some of the fine grains seeped in through cracks in the doorframe and loose seams in the walls.

There were ominous sounds outside the shed. The storm was tearing away at the settlement. Jamie could hear ripping nylon and metal pipes banging and twisting against each other. There was a horrible crashing sound from the direction of the Commons, and she thought she heard a scream, carried by the hurricane. Something struck the outside of the shed, sending vibrations through the structure. Jamie prayed the foundation would hold. The thin walls of the storage building presented their only defense against the alien fury.

Jamie reached out and touched Bliss's leg. The woman was where she had fallen. She crawled past her body and found a rack of shelves near the back wall of the building. Jamie remembered putting some blankets there when they stocked the shed. She grabbed an armful of them and felt her way back to Bliss's side.

Jamie rolled up one of the blankets and placed it under her friend's head. Then she covered her with another. She turned toward the entrance and used a couple more of the blankets to block some of the leaks where sand was accumulating inside the shed. She wrapped the last blanket around herself and lay back down. It wasn't cold, but the blanket gave her a sense of security, another layer of protection. She settled in but didn't sleep.

115

A suggestion of grayish morning light filtered in around the door. Bliss woke. The continuous roar of the storm had awakened her. She pulled the blanket around herself and gazed at Jamie with large, fearful eyes. "What happened to my clothes?"

"You were drunk."

Bliss dismissed the explanation, distracted by the wind that was shouting outside the door. "There was a storm?"

Jamie grinned at the understatement. "A hurricane on steroids," she shouted back.

"Where are we?"

"In the shed near the tents," Jamie replied over the pandemonium. "We just made it."

"You were dragging me." Bliss's head was clearing. "Thanks."

"You would have done the same for me," Jamie yelled.

"Any food?" Bliss pivoted around and scanned the shelves that lined the shed.

"We're in luck. We put a lot of excess food supplies in here." Jamie rose to her feet and wandered further into the storage space. Within a moment, she returned with a couple of packaged meals. "Don't eat anything that smells funny or has fur growing on it." Five hundred years was a long time, even for meals ready to eat.

"Where are the others?" Bliss looked worried.

"They ran for cover when the storm hit. I saw some of them head for the other supply sheds and the clinic, but most of them went to the Commons."

"Do you think they're all right?"

Jamie shook her head. "I don't know. I heard a terrible crash and maybe some screams. I think something big collapsed out there, but I don't know what."

Bliss pulled her blanket even closer. "How long do you think this will last?"

"I have no idea."

* * *

The storm lasted for days. The winds never ceased, although the banging sounds diminished. Jamie assumed everything that could move had been swept away. Nothing was left to make noise in the gale. There was a small leak in the roof, and Jamie caught the rainwater in a can. They had food and drink and the darkness of the shed. Jamie used a spare blanket as a curtain and cleared one of the back corners of the shed for a latrine. She hoped the storm would end soon. The smell was going to be horrible before long.

The maelstrom cast the settlement into a perpetual twilight, and they lost track of time. The winds howled. The women huddled close together to hear each other's voices over the storm. "I hope Alice is okay," Bliss pulled her blanket tightly around her shoulders.

Jamie was pessimistic. "I didn't see her in the compound."

"Maybe she was in her tent."

"I looked. There was no sign of her." Jamie couldn't hide her worry. "I hope she wasn't out in the jungle when the storm hit."

"She'll be alright," Bliss said confidently. The thought of death did not come easily to her.

"I hope so." Jamie preferred Bliss's fantasy to what she knew to be true. She tried to shut the thought of Alice's death

117

out of her mind. She had been a lovely woman, and they had become friends. If Alice had not been paired with Stub, he wouldn't have raped her. She would have been at Carter's party and would be riding out the storm with Rusty. Stub was as responsible for her death as the hurricane. "Bliss?"

"Yeah."

"Why do you have scars on your back?"

"I said yes to the wrong man." Bliss's voice was thin, childlike.

"What do you mean?"

"You may not know this, but I'm a bit flirty." Bliss said it with complete seriousness.

"I never would have guessed." The dark shed hid Jamie's smile.

"There was this guy. He was rich, and he liked me. I thought he cared." Jamie could sense her friend's pain. "He asked me to marry him, and I said yes. It was a beautiful wedding. One of the guests was a movie star; can you imagine that? I felt like I had stepped into a storybook, and I was a magic fairy queen.

"He beat me on our wedding night, just like Stub and Alice. I never saw it coming. He was nice, and then suddenly he got rough with me. He was on top of me and…" Bliss shuttered at the memory. "…and he started hitting me." She paused for a long while, the storm's winds a fitting accompaniment to her story. "I wanted him to like me, you know? Isn't that stupid? I let him do it. He was careful to leave bruises where people wouldn't see them."

Jamie thought of her own desperation that led her to kill her husband in the white mansion. "But he was hurting you."

"We all get hurt."

118

"But that isn't what a marriage is supposed to look like."

"It took me a long time to realize that, you know? He beat me every night for two years. He shared me with his friends. That's when I realized I had to get away."

"You left him."

Bliss nodded her head. "Yeah."

Jamie put her arm around her shoulder. "We'll try to find Alice when the storm is over." She could feel Bliss relax into her arms. "Find her or not, we'll take care of Stub, too."

* * *

The wind abated slightly on the eighth day, and Jamie cracked open the shed door. She peeked through the narrow opening and then snapped the door shut again. She sank down on her haunches next to Bliss.

"What did you see?" her friend shouted above the rising babel of the hurricane.

Jamie didn't answer her right away. She was terrified.

"What did you see?" Bliss repeated, shaking her.

"The Commons is destroyed." Jamie managed. "The roof is gone. Only the side building is left."

"It's gone?" Bliss's eyes were as big as saucers.

"Ripped apart. I think I saw one or two of the other storage sheds, but there's nothing else." Jamie looked at her companion with cold, dead eyes.

They had traveled into the unknown on a journey spanning five hundred years. They had lost half of their companions but had managed to land successfully on this alien world. They were adapting. They were beginning new lives. And now this gargantuan storm had swept everything away. It had wiped almost every sign of their presence from the landscape and continued to pound them with relentless, destructive power.

"What are we gonna do?" Bliss asked helplessly.

"We're going to stay in here."

"It's my fault, you know?"

"That's ridiculous. People don't cause storms."

"Olivia and Thomas told me I was a sinner. They said that if I kept showing my breasts, God would reveal his wrath. I didn't listen. I made God angry, and He destroyed everything." Jamie stifled a laugh. "It's not funny!" Bliss pouted.

Jamie hated the way people used God as a club, playing on people's fears. "Bliss, it's not your fault. You're not the only one who's exposed her breasts around here. Anyway, Olivia and Thomas are full of shit. God isn't mad at you."

"You mean it?"

Jamie felt like she was making headway. "I do."

"Other people exposed themselves?"

"I was one of them."

Bliss was impressed. She looked hard at Jamie, obviously undressing her in her mind and imagining the transgression. "So maybe you caused the storm."

Jamie let out a long sigh. She should never underestimate humanity's need for cause and effect. "That's right, Bliss. Maybe I'm the one God hates." It was absurd, but for an instant, she wondered if it was true.

* * *

The storm subsided on the twenty-first day. It had been

three weeks of hell. Jamie awoke from a restless sleep and was startled by the silence. The light was noticeably brighter. She shook Bliss awake and went to the entrance of the shed. A small berm of beach sand had accumulated in the threshold. The two women pushed the door open with some difficulty and then stepped out into the bright sunlight.

Jamie and Bliss stood crestfallen. The perimeter fence was gone. The tall panels had been ripped away, leaving an occasional crooked post sticking out of the ground. Likewise, there was no sign of the tents or the bonfire Carter had set on the night when the storm began. Three storage sheds still stood in the clearing; each badly scratched and dented by days of windblown sand and flying debris. The clinic building was the least affected by the storm. It had been built with deep footings and extra structure in its walls and roof.

The Commons was in shambles. It looked like the bare ribcage of a prehistoric behemoth. The Kevlar roof had been peeled away, and the contents of the hall had been swept from the interior of the structure. The small service building, which had been attached to the Commons, had a pronounced lean. Its walls were no longer vertical, and there was a depression in its roof where the underlying structure had failed. Carter's pornographic maypole still stood in the center of the compound as a perverse reminder of the night of the storm. All the cloth streamers were torn away. Sand from the beach had polished the metal sheathing of the sculpture, leaving the phallus shining in the morning sun.

The door of the clinic opened, and Vickie stepped out, followed by Stub and Ben. Jamie was relieved when she saw Rusty sitting on the ground near one of the sheds. Bliss rushed to his side and hugged him. He stared straight ahead, hardly acknowledging her. Olivia appeared and sniffed disapprovingly at Bliss as she waltzed by her.

Carter was the first to emerge from the misshapen service building. Jamie watched as he slumped his shoulders at the sight of the devastation. His hair was wild, and his jumpsuit was stained and wrinkled. His eyes were dull as he wandered the shattered compound. Jamie saw streaks of red on his forearms. The man had scratched at himself until he drew blood. "Hip!" he shouted. "Where are you?" There was no answer.

"Carter!" It was Vickie. Carter swung around like he was drunk, trying to locate where her voice had come from. "Over here in the Commons!" Jamie followed Carter as he trotted toward the twisted wreckage. Vickie was squatting next to a body pinned tightly under the collapsed structure. It was Hip.

Time dilated as Jamie came to a stop near the body. Tears erupted from her eyes, and her legs refused to support her. She fell to her knees, unable to fathom the tremendous loss. Hip had been more than a friend. She had loved him. Jamie felt like she was looking at his body through a long tube. Her field of view had collapsed, excluding everything and everyone except the body of her friend. Someone touched her shoulder, but she was numb. She had to be dreaming again. This could not be true. Hip could not be dead.

Jamie's initial shock began to fade. She could hear Carter's voice. It sounded distant, though he was right next to her. "No, God!" He whimpered. He was shaking uncontrollably, holding his head in both hands. "What am I going to do, Hip? I need you!"

Jamie watched Vickie grab him by the arm. Everything was still in slow motion. "Get a hold of yourself, sir!" She commanded him.

Jamie's head cleared. She wiped her tears away with her sleeve. When she took her arm away from her face, Carter was pleading with Vickie. "Can you wake him up?"

"Wake up who, sir?"

"Hip. I need him."

Vickie crouched down next to the man. "Hip is dead."

"No!" Carter pushed her away and stood up. He ran out into the compound, almost tripping over Jamie as he rushed passed her.

"Hip!" he shouted. "Where are you?"

Vickie straightened her shoulders and planted her fists on her hips. "I want everyone to form a circle around me!" Her voice was commanding. It cut through the chaos, and everyone responded reflexively. Jamie struggled to her feet, only now realizing that Bliss was by her side. Olivia stood next to Vickie. Thomas was next, his face drawn and empty. Olivia stroked his hand like he was a pet dog but paid no further attention to him. She looked at Jamie accusingly. "Aren't you going over to comfort Carter?" she asked. Jamie shrugged, but said nothing. Carter was at the tree line, calling for Hip. Jamie was going to stay right where she was.

Vickie took a moment to study each person's face. "By my count, there are only fifteen of us left. We lost sixteen souls in the storm. I don't need to tell you we're in a bad way. We've got to assess the damages. Ben? Take a few people and inventory the supplies here in the settlement." Ben nodded at Stub and a couple of others. They excused themselves and headed toward the clinic. Vickie gave Jamie a determined look. "You take Rusty and Bliss to check the Lander. We're going to need tools and material to fix the buildings. Find out how many tents are left in the hold." Jamie nodded automatically. Vickie was a born leader, evoking confidence when it was needed most.

Jamie and Bliss crossed the compound and headed toward the place where the entrance had been. Rusty followed listlessly behind them. The gate was gone. Nothing was left but one of the posts, which was bent at an odd angle. Jamie shuttered as she imagined the force necessary to do such damage. They found the beach trail and followed it toward the shore. The storm had combed the red grass. They left matted footprints where their feet compressed the curried blades.

"Where were you?" Rusty asked.

"Bliss and I were in the shed near the tents." Jamie paused, and then corrected herself. "Where the tents used to be. And you?"

"I was in the Commons. It was terrible. We got in there, and within five minutes, the wind tore off the roof. Several of us ducked into the service shed as the building collapsed. We lost seven or eight people in there."

"Hip?" Jamie spoke softly. A great void in her chest ached with every thought of him. She wanted to stop and grieve, but there was no time. Recovering from the storm preempted her emotional needs.

"He stayed in the Commons to help some of the stragglers." Rusty spoke like he had witnessed a holy thing, an example of transcendent courage.

"Shit." Jamie didn't swear often.

Rusty stopped. "Have you seen Alice?"

Jamie dreaded his question. "I haven't." She studied her friend, wondering how honest she should be. "The last time I saw her was the afternoon of the storm. She was in the jungle near here."

Rusty began to scan the trees that bracketed the path.

"She must have gotten back to the compound before it hit."

Jamie put a firm hand on his shoulder. This was going to be the bad part. "I don't know, Rusty. I didn't see her after that."

Bliss encouraged Rusty with a lie, rather than saddening him with the truth. "She's okay. I know it."

Rusty perked up, but his eyes betrayed him. "Yeah," he murmured. "Me, too."

They reached the edge of the beach. All the metal panels that had been laid down in the sand were gone. They turned toward the place where the Lander had been and stopped dead in their tracks. The beach was empty. The Lander had been swept away in the storm.

CHAPTER ELEVEN
Aftermath

T he storm had erased almost all of their brief history on Alathea. Jamie thought the shattered settlement had a familiarity to it. It was like her mind. The basic landscape was still intact, but all the embellishments, like her memories, were wiped away. If a person died, leaving no trace of their time spent among the living, had they lived at all? Hip's body was the only evidence of the dead. All the others simply vanished in the whirlwind. Jamie wondered if they had been illusions.

They buried Hip beneath the crimson sod at the north end of the clearing. Almost everyone stood silently around the grave, remembering the kind physician. Carter was the exception. He was oblivious to it all, wandering in the jungle, refusing to believe his friend was dead. Jamie had never felt such sadness. She had come to depend on Hip's counsel. She remembered working with him in the garden and the day when they had finished the clinic. She had wanted their friendship to become an affair, but Hip's heart was elsewhere. He carried the guilt over his wife's death to his grave. He had no room for anyone else. He was that kind of man. Jamie bit her lip as they filled in his grave. All that was left of Hip were the echoes of his compassion reverberating in her mind.

The sun shone brightly overhead, and the alien air smelled sweet and clean, but there was a dark emotional cloud that enveloped everyone like a chilling fog. Vickie stood at parade rest near the head of the grave, serving as the temporary leader until Carter sorted things out. Olivia gripped a makeshift cross with whitened knuckles, her lips drawn into a hard, thin line. Stub and Ben were silent, leaning on the shovels they had used to fill the hole. No snide remark could deliver them from the cold, hard reality of death. This singular grave symbolized the final resting place for fifteen other friends and colleagues who had disappeared in the storm. When half of society dies, no one is left untouched.

Vickie gave Thomas a nod. The holy man looked down at the mound of dirt but said nothing. "Thomas." Vickie's voice was soft, but commanding. He looked up at her with empty eyes. "We could use a prayer about now."

Thomas twisted his fingers together and cleared his throat. "I, I can't do this," he mumbled.

"Yes, you can. We need a prayer," Vickie urged him. "We've lost friends here. We need to know God took them for a good reason." There was an almost indiscernible catch in her voice.

"I can't believe God took Hip or anybody else." Thomas spread his hands.

"The devil caused it!" Olivia was standing next to Thomas, leaning on the homemade cross. "We are caught in the clutches of Satan himself."

"No!" Olivia jumped at Thomas's rebuke. "This has nothing to do with God or Satan or religion. It was a storm! The winds ripped away everyone who was out in the open. Hip died trying to save one of our friends. It makes no sense."

"Put it in a prayer, Thomas." Vickie wasn't going to back down.

"I won't pray to a god who's done this." He whispered the words under his breath.

Olivia was astonished. "What did you say?"

Thomas raised his voice. "We're all afraid. The storm reminded us of how powerless we are. You want God to be in control. You want me to tell you that God has a reason for all of this. I rode out the storm, praying for an answer, and you know what God said? Nothing! There isn't a good reason, spiritual or otherwise, for what has happened. Hip is dead. Our friends are dead. That's the way it is. As for God, I'm done with him. You can believe what you want to, but I can't pretend anymore." Thomas left them and strode with a purpose back toward the clinic. Olivia composed herself and then raised the makeshift cross like a scepter. Her voice became stately and dignified as she offered a lengthy prayer, asking God to forgive Thomas and protect them all from Satan's power.

* * *

Thomas wasn't the only one to lose his innocence in the storm. The illusion of living in an idyllic tropical paradise was shattered for everyone. They were scratching out an existence on the back of some mythic beast that could contort its body at any moment and destroy them all. They were powerless over the elemental forces in this alien world. The Lander was gone, and with it, their extra supplies and construction materials. The perimeter fence could not be replaced. They would have no protective enclosure, no sense of security. There were no tents, no clothes, and no seeds to grow food. The food they had brought with them would last but a few months, and then they would die.

Vickie put everyone to work cleaning out the storage sheds and clinic building. It was a filthy job, removing human excrement and getting rid of the smell. That night, they pulled cargo cases from the buildings and arranged them in a circle near the center of the clearing. Ben Beck dug a fire pit and built a small campfire. Everyone sat around it in silence, emotionally and physically drained. Carter drifted back into the clearing as the daylight failed. He joined the circle around the fire, but kept to himself, eying the trees at the edge of the clearing as though Hip would suddenly emerge from the jungle. Jamie was bone tired and retired early, making her bed in the supply shed where she and Bliss had weathered the storm.

* * *

Jamie was wearing a white lab coat. She was a doctor. She had risen early and made her rounds at the hospital. She had just performed gall bladder surgery on a twenty-eight-year-old man. Now, she was sitting in a doctor's office. Her colleague, Dr. Samuel Finch, sat behind a large wooden desk. A piece of glass covered the desktop. She felt guilty and anxious. A pretty woman sat next to her in an upholstered chair. The doctor was fingering a sheaf of papers. "I'm very sorry," he was saying. "The cancer has metastasized to your liver."

Jamie heard the woman next to her gasp. She reached out and clasped her hand. She was her wife. "How long?" the woman asked.

The doctor leaned forward and placed the papers on his desk. "Six months. Maybe seven."

Jamie and the woman stood. They were both shaking. The doctor came around his desk, and the three of them paused by the door. "I'm so sorry, Mrs. Whitford." The doctor squeezed the woman's arm and then turned to Jamie. "Hip, I wish I could have given you better news."

* * *

Jamie woke with a start. The dream had nothing to do with her. It was about Hip and his wife. Hip had told her how he had missed the telltale signs of her cancer. He carried the guilt with him for the rest of his life. He had vowed never to let another patient down. Jamie had been thinking about him all day. Dreaming of him made sense, yet she was astonished by the clarity of the vision. Hip's death was finally hitting her. He had honored his vow to the death, attending to the needs of others. She hoped Hip had forgiven himself before he died.

Jamie reached out and felt the metal wall of the shed. She touched her face with her hand. She needed some fresh air. She stumbled quietly out of the supply shed. Alathea's golden rings cut a luminous swath across the starlit sky. They cast a warm glow over the darkened landscape. The mysterious lights were shimmering over the jungle. She stood and watched them.

Suddenly, something tickled at the edge of Jamie's consciousness. Something was there, a presence. She shivered with fear. Something was in the jungle, and it wasn't human. The sensation lingered for a moment and then diminished quickly, like an echo receding into the sounds of the forest. All of Jamie's senses were on alert. She could hear the subtle clicking of the alien leaves in the nocturnal breezes. Then she heard a crackling sound behind her. She turned slowly. Carter and Olivia were sitting alone by the dying embers of the campfire.

* * *

Carter was moody in the morning. He and Vickie were at

the fire circle eating breakfast together when Jamie emerged from the supply shed. They were engrossed in a serious conversation, probably having to do with their current predicament. Vickie was hunched over, speaking directly to him. Carter, however, was preoccupied with the jungle. He kept looking over Vickie's shoulder at the tree line.

Jamie made her way to the clinic building where they had set up a temporary kitchen. As she reached the door, Olivia stepped out with two cups of steaming coffee. She gave Jamie a disapproving look and made a beeline toward Carter. Jamie paused at the doorway and watched the woman hand him one of the cups. Olivia glanced over her shoulder and gave Jamie a smirk before sitting down next to him. Jamie breathed a sigh of relief. Olivia had stolen Carter from her. She was welcome to him.

Jamie glanced at Vickie. Olivia had interrupted their conversation, and she wasn't pleased. Vickie asked Carter a question, ignoring their uninvited guest. Jamie watched as he glanced at Olivia before replying. Carter was looking to her for counsel. She had replaced Hip as his new advisor. This wouldn't bode well for the settlement.

Jamie entered the clinic. Bliss was there, getting her breakfast. They took their food outside and sat together on a cargo case that someone had dragged out of the building the previous day. Jamie struggled to tear open a small package of crackers. "How's Rusty?" she asked her friend.

"He's far away, you know? I talk to him, but it's like he's not even there."

"Is he asking about Alice?"

"I think he realizes she's dead. Nobody could have survived in that storm."

Jamie nodded sadly. "Maybe he's coming to grips with

it."

"I dunno, Jamie. He's in a really dark place, you know?" Bliss said it wistfully. "I wish somebody would love me that much."

"Give him time, Bliss. He'll come around." Jamie said it, but didn't believe it.

* * *

After breakfast, the remaining colonists gathered listlessly around the fire pit. Carter made no effort to buoy morale. He sat quietly, gripping his coffee cup in the palms of his hands and staring at ground. Vickie glanced at him uneasily, waiting for his direction. Carter rolled the empty cup back and forth, unaware of the people around him. His torch of leadership was extinguished, as cold and dark as the charred ground where the fire had burned on the night of the storm. Olivia was sitting next to him and nudged him gently. When he failed to respond, she nodded at Vickie, who took offense at Olivia's presumption of power. The security officer shrugged off her reactivity and got everyone's attention.

"Today, we are going to rebuild the perimeter wall," she said in a strong, commanding voice. Carter didn't react, seemingly indifferent towards the idea. Jamie heard several sighs of relief. The storm had left everyone feeling more vulnerable, and they were eager to regain a sense of security. Vickie told them they would cut down some of the trees near the clearing and fashion a post and rail fence. Stub had come up with a design that reduced the height of the wall and the size of the compound to make construction more manageable.

Everyone worked with a purpose, except for Carter, who remained at the fire circle as if standing vigil for Hip. They took saws to the tree line to harvest the timber. The wood was soft, like pine, and the first tree came down quickly. They cut the branches from the trunk and rolled the wooden cylinder to the spot where the new wall would begin. They set aside the stouter branches for rails. Building the fence made them feel less like victims and more like pioneers, tested by the winds of fate but not broken by them. Even so, building the second wall was much harder than the first. There were fewer people to share the task, and digging holes for the posts was backbreaking work.

Stub focused on the construction of the fence, and Jamie gave him a wide berth. The sight of the man reminded her of Alice, whimpering in the jungle by the beach trail. She wanted to kill him and rid their little society of his mindless brutality, but she knew everyone was needed for the colony's survival. She shuttered at the thought of him fathering offspring and teaching little boys how to become men.

* * *

Jamie was crossing the compound on the fourth day when she noticed a change in the jungle. Trees were losing their leaves. The odd triangular foliage was piling up on the ground beneath them, leaving bare branches zigzagging into the air. The empty trees looked foreboding and dangerous, like the barren and craggy residents of a foggy moor on Halloween.

The colonists stopped their work to survey the dying trees. "What would make them do that?" Thomas wondered out loud.

"Maybe it's a change of season," Olivia suggested.

"Then why aren't all the trees dropping their leaves?" Vickie asked.

Everyone fanned out into the jungle. They studied each tree, looking for the cause of the die-off. There were no signs of insect damage or fungal growth. They waded through the fallen leaves, looking up at the empty branches. Jamie reached the nearest living tree about thirty meters into the jungle. The barren trees were grouped together near the place where they had harvested wood for the new fence.

"You are one beautiful bitch." Jamie spun around at the sound of the voice. It was Stub Andrews. He was leaning against one of the dead trees, undressing her with his eyes. "Want to have some fun?"

"No!"

Stub stepped toward her. "A few minutes ain't gonna bring these trees back to life. Why don't you and me go a little deeper into the woods?"

Jamie backed away. Stub climbed up on one of the tree roots that ran across the jungle floor. He teetered for a moment, and then stretched out his arms and caught his balance. He grinned at her and began to traverse the wooden shaft like a tightrope walker. Jamie looked down at his feet.

"It's the roots," Jamie said. Stub paused, bewildered. "Hey, everybody!" she shouted. "Come over here!" Stub stepped off the root as the rest of the colonists gathered. "I know what's killing the trees."

Carter pushed his way to the front of the group. "What did you find?" He gave Jamie a cold look as Olivia drew next to him.

"The trees are tied together through their roots." Jamie pointed down at the ground. She traced the root that Stub had been standing on. "This root runs between two of the dead trees. They aren't independent plants. When we cut down the trees for the fence, we cut off the supply of nutrients to all the trees down the chain." Jamie led the group to one of the trees they had cut down. Its roots fanned out on the surface of the ground, merging with the nearby trees. Ben Beck took a shovel and dug around the stump. There was no taproot.

"Damn!" Vickie swore. "She's right. All the trees are one big plant."

"Maybe they communicate with each other." Thomas glanced at the dead trees. "I've heard plants can do that."

"I hope they don't get mad at us for cutting them down," said Vickie. "The last thing I need is a stand of angry trees."

* * *

The perimeter fence was finished after two more days of hard work. Everyone felt better as Vickie secured the main gate. As twilight fell, they gathered around a campfire that was kindled by leftover limbs and twigs. The flames danced over the glowing embers. Once again, the ghostly lights appeared beyond the clearing, washing the compound in shades of green and yellow. Jamie looked at her comrades, huddled together in the flickering light. She questioned the value of the fence, having seen no sign of danger. Nevertheless, Jamie respected the fear of uncertainty. It had become her constant companion since waking from hibernation.

Carter stood by the blaze as if in a trance. He looked like a living cadaver as the shadows danced across his pale cheekbones. His eyes were focused above and beyond them, looking into the shadows beyond the glow of the fire. His voice was lifeless and void of confidence. "I think I did us a disservice with the lottery," he mumbled. Carter glanced at Olivia. She nodded, urging him to continue. "I've been talking to Olivia, and she's convinced me that we should turn back the clock and release everyone from the pairings." Bliss gave Rusty a panicked look, but he paid no attention. "People should choose their own mates." Carter said it offhandedly, as if he had no further interest in the matter. He glanced at Jamie with empty eyes. "I want us all to be happy." He twisted his fingers together nervously and sat back down.

Olivia was sitting close to Carter. Her shoulder was pressed firmly against him. Jamie nodded to herself. The conniving woman had convinced Carter to dissolve the pairings, so she could be his mate. She wanted to be the first lady of Alathea. Jamie was relieved. Olivia had saved her.

Jamie saw the dejected look on Rusty's face. If the lottery had never taken place, Alice would be alive, and they would be together, the artist and his muse. She watched Bliss, looking small and scared as she clung to Rusty's arm. She adored the man, but he could never love her. The pairings had been the only thing holding them together.

Olivia rose from her seat. Unlike Carter, her voice was piercing and strong. "I have something to say." She waited, as if wanting her subjects to stop and attend to their queen. "Tomorrow we will begin again. After breakfast, we will remove the abomination standing in the center of our compound." Olivia gestured distastefully toward Carter's maypole. "We will take it down and destroy it." She turned toward Bliss. "And from this day forward, there will be no nakedness in public." Bliss's face turned red. "As long as I am here, we will be wholesome and civilized!" Olivia had taken control. She glared condescendingly at everyone, daring them to challenge her. Stub shook his head, the motion catching Jamie's attention. He looked up and gave her a toothy grin. Jamie glanced away.

Carter rose to his feet unexpectedly, motioning for Olivia to sit back down. He was a man possessed by an uncontrollable desire, which rose up within him and seized control of his mind and body. An odd twitch contorted his face whenever he took a breath, and he constantly shifted his weight from foot to foot, as if he was about to burst forth into a maniacal dance. Olivia gave him a begrudging frown, obviously vexed by his crazed demeanor. "We have to mount a search and rescue mission." Carter began. His voice was stronger now. "One of us is lost in the jungle." Jamie thought about Alice. Perhaps Carter was finally acknowledging her friend's disappearance. She glanced at Rusty, who was now looking intently at the man. Hope was dawning on the artist's face. Carter spread his fingers, his hands resembling great spiders hanging from his wrists. "Our friend Hip is somewhere out there," he squeaked. Jamie saw Rusty's face darken. He brought his hands up to his head and leaned forward, his elbows on his knees. "We'll leave at first light." Carter's face twitched again.

Olivia jumped up. "What about that maypole? We have to tear it down."

Carter grasped her arm with a firm hand. "We'll do that later. Our first priority is to find Hip."

Vickie rose slowly from her seat and approached the odd couple. "Hip is dead, Carter. We found his body in the Commons, and we buried him."

"That is a lie!" Carter's legs were in constant motion, dancing to an unheard melody. "You buried somebody else," he shouted. "It wasn't Hip. He's out in the jungle."

Vickie looked at the man sadly. "It was Hip. We all saw his body."

"Sit down, Vickie!" Carter thundered, his voice becoming resonant and powerful. "We aren't going to abandon our friend! You of all people should appreciate that. I will lead a team into the woods at dawn."

There was no dissuading him. Jamie glanced around the

circle. Concern was written on every face. Carter had lost his mind.

"Okay," Vickie said softly. Jamie could see she was trying to calm him. She slumped her shoulders, forcing her body out of its military stance. She folded her hands like a penitent thief begging for mercy. "We'll do what you ask. I'll recruit a team and we'll go out after breakfast."

"I said dawn!" he snapped. "We will leave at first light!"

"What about the maypole?" Olivia's manipulations were disintegrating right in front of her. She grew petulant. Jamie expected her to stomp her foot and throw a tantrum.

"It can wait!" Carter pushed her away violently. Olivia stumbled backward, almost falling into the fire. "I need Hip. Don't you understand?"

For the first time, Jamie saw fear in Olivia's face. The stern woman gave Carter a wide berth as she went back to her seat. No one breathed. Carter strode out of the circle and walked to the perimeter fence. He put his arms through the rails, leaning silently for a moment, his focus riveted on the tree line, which was barely visible in the diminishing twilight. The spectral glow over the jungle transformed him into a ghoulish silhouette. "Hang on, Hip!" he shouted. "We're coming for you!"

Stub broke the silence around the campfire. "What a loon!" he muttered under his breath. He's as crazy as a left-handed screw in a right-handed whore!"

"Shut up, Stub!" Vickie commanded him.

"But he's nuts," Stub shot back.

Jamie could see Vickie's internal conflict just beneath the surface of her military bearing. The security officer knew Stub was right, but Carter was still the leader. She squared her shoulders and pivoted slowly as she spoke. "It won't do us any harm to take a walk in the jungle. Once Carter realizes Hip is dead, he'll be better."

* * *

Jamie lay down to sleep in the shed. The weight of her body had formed an impression in the spongy floor. She found it fairly comfortable as her hips settled into the depressions, and she pulled the blanket up to her neck. There was a scraping sound, and the shed door opened. Jamie sat up, squinting in the semidarkness. "Who is it?" She feared it might be Stub. The look he had given her at the campfire had been full of sexual menace.

"It's Bliss." Jamie relaxed. "Rusty doesn't want me." She said it like a lost child. "He told me we were done." Jamie heard her friend sobbing. "He's such a good man. I wanted him to like me, you know?"

"It's not about you, Bliss. He was in love with Alice long before you were paired. His heart was already taken."

"But she's dead." Bliss was pleading with the fates.

"That doesn't change how he felt about her." Jamie remembered the look on Rusty's face as he formed Alice's sand sculpture on the beach. "They were madly in love."

Bliss didn't answer for a moment. Jamie could hear ragged breaths as her friend fought back her tears. "Can I sleep in here tonight?" She whimpered finally.

"Of course you can." Jamie found another blanket, and the two women settled down for the night. The maelstrom that had held them in the shed had passed, but now, new storms were rising.

* * *

Jamie dreamed she was floating through the pod ship.

139

The gleaming white walls surrounded her. She was on the command deck and could see a million stars puncturing the ink-black void of space. She pivoted effortlessly and propelled herself down the main corridor toward the pod chamber. No one else was there. She entered the large cabin and studied the sixty-four hibernation pods. One of them was open. She knew instinctively it was her own. She floated past each cocoon. Her fellow passengers were submerged in their artificial slumbers.

Jamie stopped in front of one of the pods and gazed at the placid face of Captain Michael Chamberlain. She entered a code into the pod's control panel and shut off the life support system. His body twitched slightly, but he did not wake up. She watched his life drain away, leaving an empty cadaver on a cold, hard bed. An alarm chimed, and Jamie muted it. She smiled as a feeling of immense power coursed through her.

* * *

Jamie jerked awake. For a moment, she was disoriented. Then she remembered lying on the ground in the supply shed. She listened intently. Bliss's breathing was slow and steady. She wasn't on the pod ship. She had not killed Captain Chamberlain. The dream had nothing to do with her missing past. It was only a nightmare.

CHAPTER TWELVE

Expedition

J amie was pleased when Vickie asked her to join the expedition. She didn't feel threatened by what they might find in the jungle. In fact, she welcomed the opportunity to venture beyond the tree line and see their new home. Her amnesia had forced her to wrestle with uncertainty and mystery. The more they learned about Alathea, the better their chances for survival.

Spending a couple of days on the trail with Stub was another matter. He had raped and beaten Alice. Jamie could still hear her friend's screams. Now Stub was focusing his attention on her. He was a dangerous man, and Jamie vowed to keep her distance from him. Carter and Vickie took the lead, and Jamie waited for Stub and Ben to go ahead of her. It was better to keep him where she could see him. She and Thomas took up the rear. They left the others at the compound gate and skirted the new perimeter fence before hiking into the jungle.

They journeyed all morning. At first, the terrain was surprisingly uniform. Then they found clearings in the dense forest, oases of brilliant color. They were carpeted with the ubiquitous crimson grass and festooned with the fluorescent flowers they had discovered on the beach trail. The flowers, caught in the sunlight, became luminescent with intense hues, painting the open areas with their iridescent colors. Whenever they came upon a clearing, Jamie wanted to pause to take in the breathtaking sight, but Carter was oblivious to the wonder around him and kept urging them forward.

Jamie sensed a change in elevation. The land was inclined, rising slowly from sea level as they marched inland. She stepped over an unusually thick root and looked up into the canopy that spread above her, obscuring the sky. An occasional sunbeam filtered down, illuminating the forest floor like a spotlight. Jamie looked into the depths of the jungle. All the trees looked alike with their shared root system and odd triangular leaves. It was hard to tell one spot from another. If they weren't careful, they would lose their way.

Every hundred meters or so, Carter would stop and call for Hip. Each time, he shouted his name three times at the top of his lungs. Then, while his voice still rang through the forest, he would add, "We're coming for you!" No one challenged him. Vickie stood patiently by his side while Stub and Ben hung back, exchanging whispered sarcasms. Thomas was lost in thought, ignoring the whole affair. Jamie felt like someone playing along with a delusional mental patient. She might have found it amusing if the crazy man wasn't in command.

Jamie's legs burned from the hours of walking. She bent down at every opportunity to rub her calf muscles. Stub watched her with enthusiasm, but said nothing. Jamie stayed close to Thomas. He was no match for the burly womanizer, but she didn't want to be alone. She could tell Stub was waiting to catch her by herself, and she wasn't going to give him that opportunity.

By midday, they had trekked about 30 kilometers into the

jungle. Vickie and Ben looked like they could go on for hours. Everyone else was glad to take a break.

"I don't see any rocks," Jamie observed as she ate her simple lunch.

"There is some hill country to the south of here," Vickie reported. "We even saw a small mountain. However, there are no animals of any kind. No insects. No rodents. Nothing."

"What makes the lights?" Thomas asked.

"I think the trees fart," Ben offered with a grin. "This damn place gives 'em indigestion. They pop a lot of methane or somethin'. It burns after dark, and that's the glow we see."

"Very scientific," Vickie deadpanned. "You're a regular genius, you know that?"

"That's what my mother always said."

Jamie couldn't tell if Ben was being serious or not. Everyone laughed, but Carter was reticent. He ate his lunch unconsciously, his eyes scanning the surrounding terrain. "We'll get you, buddy," he muttered to himself.

Jamie kept Stub in her peripheral vision. She sensed movement and glanced in his direction. The degenerate was staring at her. He was chewing with his mouth open, and Jamie could see pieces of food rolling around between his teeth like socks in a clothes dryer. Jamie looked away in disgust.

Thomas was sitting on a root nearby, meticulously folding a food wrapper. Jamie looked at his hands, wondering if he was making an origami figure. "How are you holding up?" she asked.

Thomas wadded up the piece of plastic and shoved it into his backpack. "Okay, I guess. It's good to get away from the settlement."

Jamie noticed his hands shaking. She had wanted to talk to him after Hip's burial, but he had been particularly morose, and everyone had been busy with the fence. Now was as good a time as any, she decided. "So you're not religious anymore?"

Thomas hesitated, collecting his thoughts. "I guess not." He looked deep into the jungle, but his mind's eye was turned inward. "I'd been feeling wrong for a long time, like I was lying. I was afraid to be honest with myself." He paused. "Remember when the clinic building was going up? We sat and talked." Jamie nodded. "Something you said got to me. You said 'the whole "god concept" gets in the way of love.' I knew it was true, but I had built my life around a set of orthodox beliefs. Then I got paired with Olivia. She's the personification of everything I hate about religious people. I didn't want to be like that. Do you know what I mean?"

"I do." Jamie wondered if she had misjudged the man.

"Then the storm hit. I sat in the clinic day after day, reexamining my beliefs. I watched Rusty fall apart over Alice's death. When you see raw human emotion like that, it affects you. I listened to the simple answers Olivia offered to him, the same ones I used to give to people. I realized I had been a coward. I hid behind the trivial answers to protect myself from the pain and uncertainty. I was too afraid to face the truth."

"God's truth?"

"No. My truth. Being real. Having integrity." Thomas kneaded his hands. "I've spent most of my life defending things that don't ring true. I'm not going to do that anymore."

Jamie still seethed over what Bliss had told her. "Bliss told me you threatened her with God's retribution if she didn't keep her shirt on. She thinks she caused the storm."

Thomas sighed. "I was wrong. I shouldn't have told her

that."

"You should talk to her and set things right. She's still pretty confused and feels a lot of guilt."

"Yeah."

"Okay everybody." Vickie had finished her meal and was stuffing wrappers into her backpack. "If we turn back now, we'll be home by nightfall."

Carter shook his head. "We go on. I'm sure he came this way."

Vickie was about to object, but she bit her tongue. There was no arguing with him. She rose to her feet. "You heard the man. Let's keep going." Everyone slung their packs over their shoulders and pressed on through the jungle.

* * *

It was mid-afternoon when Jamie felt the presence. It was the same feeling she had experienced in the compound. Someone or something was out there. It was like a diffuse muttering in her brain, a dull sense of danger. She felt a shiver go up her spine, and she turned quickly, expecting to see some ugly monster peering at her from behind a tree. She knew they were being watched, although there were no signs of life beyond the vegetation in the jungle.

"Jumpy?" Thomas looked at her quizzically.

"Yeah. I feel like we're being watched, but there's nothing." Her eyes roamed the dense forest.

Thomas patted her on the shoulder. "We're alone out here, Jamie. I think you're imagining things."

"Probably." She wasn't convinced.

They walked on in silence. Carter continued stopping periodically as he had done before lunch. He would call Hip's name three times and then shout, "We're coming for you!" Even though they knew Hip was buried in the north end of the compound, everyone would stand still, listening for a response. Carter had no doubt that his friend was out there. Jamie wondered if he was sensing the presence she felt. Perhaps they were interpreting the same sensation in different ways.

Jamie picked up her pace in order to catch up with Vickie. She forgot about Stub and the man swatted her buttocks as she passed him. Jamie gave him a dirty look and doubled her pace. Stub and Ben laughed.

Jamie drew abreast of the security officer. "Do you get the feeling we're being watched?"

Vickie went on alert, glancing intently around them. She kept walking, but scanned the jungle in every direction. Then she relaxed. "We're alone out here. Did you see something?"

"It was just a feeling. Maybe I'm going crazy."

"I doubt it." Vickie smiled. "Fear can stir up your senses something fierce. It can make you sense things that aren't there. You've got to turn your fear into awareness. Let it in. Stop feeling it and start picking it apart with your mind. Thinking will destroy most of the fear. What's left will be worth worrying about."

Jamie thanked her and slowed her pace. She gave Stub and Ben a wide berth as she returned to the back of the column. Was Vickie right? Was she letting her fear take over? She didn't think so. Something was nearby, and it knew they were there.

* * *

They found a clearing in the late afternoon as daylight began to fade. The glade was awash with the vibrant hues of the alien flowers. They decided to stay there for the night, against Carter's better judgment. He would have continued on in the dark if Vickie hadn't put her foot down. Jamie was thrilled by the chance to linger there, surrounded by such beautiful plants.

They made a small campfire and ate their dinner in silence. Carter grew morose, cutting everyone out of his little world where Hip still lived and the expedition had a real purpose. He stared into the flames and spoke silently to himself. Jamie watched him move his lips, but couldn't make out the words. She had no doubt that he was talking to Hip. Stub and Ben shared a few raunchy jokes, amusing only themselves. Vickie sat stoically, her senses projected beyond the edge of the clearing into the surrounding jungle. Their security was her first and only concern. Her inner soldier never rested.

Jamie settled down next to Thomas. He gazed at the fire, rubbing his hands unconsciously. She thought about their conversation at lunchtime. He had changed. He was no longer wearing a mask. She was seeing the real man for the first time. Jamie was surprised her comments had affected him so deeply. She didn't want the responsibility that came with changing a man's life. She might have ruined him. She had no special wisdom. Her moral compass was shrouded in fog. She had a vague sense of what was right, but she couldn't remember why she felt that way. She was like one of the people in Plato's cave, watching the dancing shadows of reality. The blind one was guiding the sightless.

* * *

The campfire dwindled down to glowing embers, and everyone settled in for a restless night in the jungle. Jamie rolled out her blanket some distance from the others. She had no desire to be near Stub and Ben. She divided her blanket in half and lay down in the fold like an unzipped sleeping bag. She put her head on her backpack and took a long, deep breath of the sweet jungle air. The thick sod felt good under her tired body. She stretched her legs, working out a knot in her calf.

The jungle lights ignited with a fearsome beauty. Back in the settlement, the lights appeared inland. The short stretch of jungle that stood between the compound and the sea remained dark. However, out in the middle of the wood, the greenish yellow lights danced above the trees in every direction, flooding the clearing with an eerie glow. "Damn, that's strange!" Ben's voice was an octave higher than normal. Jamie rolled over. He was propped up on his elbows, trying to look in all directions at once. "I'm glad this ain't the first time I've seen these things. It would have freaked me out."

"It's doin' a damn good job of freakin' me out anyway," Stub growled.

Jamie pitched over onto her back and stared up at the sky. The stars were faint pinpricks in a sea of slate green, painted by the luminous glow. Alathea's golden rings swept across the heavens like a regal monarch's sash. She felt her fatigue taking over, pushing her away from consciousness and out onto a tranquil sea. Jamie felt herself floating, and asked her slumber to grant her a calm nocturnal journey. Her eyes were heavy, and her body was worn from the day's journey. She closed her eyes and slipped into the netherworld that spared her from troubling dreams and offered her the gift of deep, restful sleep.

* * *

Jamie's eyes flashed open. A strong hand with meaty, rough skin was pressing down on her jaw. It covered her mouth and she couldn't scream. Fierce eyes filled her field of vision, and she smelled old sweat and fresh urine. It was Stub.

His was lying prone on top of her; his legs spread to the outside of her knees. She could feel him pressing down on her stomach. She jerked her body in a vain attempt to escape, but he was too heavy and strong.

Stub arched his back and rose to a sitting position. His knees were jammed into her midriff; one hand still clamped over her mouth. Jamie grabbed his arm in both hands and pulled with every ounce of her strength. It didn't move. He grinned fiendishly at her, and she tried to punch his face. Her fists fell short. She was completely helpless.

Jamie had to keep her wits about her. She looked at Stub's chest. It was bare. A thick coat of black hair covered his breasts. The man was an ape. She looked down at his waist. Stub was naked, his swollen member lying flat on her stomach.

"I'm going to get a taste of you, bitch!" he hissed. Stub took his free hand and ripped the zipper out of Jamie's jumpsuit. The cloth parted from her chin down to her groin. He reached up and licked his fingers and then rubbed the disgusting saliva against her breasts. "Nice rack you got." It was a horrifying whisper. He reached down and tore the jumpsuit from between her legs. "You're nice all over."

Jamie relaxed. She knew she was powerless to stop him. He would hurt her if she fought too hard. Her mind was racing. What do I do? What can I do? She needed a weapon. Suddenly, she remembered the small knife she had slipped into the outside pocket of her backpack. She reached both hands over her head, her breasts rising. Stub grunted with satisfaction, totally distracted. He rocked to the side on one knee and brought the other down between her legs, forcing them apart. "This is gonna be sweet," he murmured. He lowered himself down, ready to rape her.

Jamie found the knife with her right hand and gripped it

tightly. Stub's head was now within reach. She brought her hands down swiftly and pressed the sharp blade against his neck. His smile was replaced by a look of surprise. Jamie pressed the tip into his Adam's apple. For an instant, she held his life in her hand. She could cut him and watch his blood and breath mingle as his life drained away. She couldn't do it.

Stub saw her hesitation and his smile returned. "You're a little coward." His voice was low and menacing. He hit her hand so hard she could feel her knuckles slam together. The knife flew off into the crimson grass. "I'm gonna do ya, and then I'm gonna cut ya," he hissed. Jamie could feel the heat rising in his body. She felt him pressing himself between her legs. She closed her eyes, surrendering to the inevitable.

CHAPTER THIRTEEN
Mantles

There was a horrific sound, like a side of beef being hit by a baseball bat. In the same instant, Stub's hand released its grip on her jaw, and he rolled to one side. Vickie stood over them with murder in her eyes. "Goddamn you, Stub!" she shouted. "When are you going to learn about women?"

Jamie covered herself with her blanket, but made no attempt to move. Stub was lying on the ground next to her. Vickie had knocked the wind out of him. He gasped for breath and came up on his knees. Vickie took a step forward. "You are one sorry excuse for a human being." She spat out the words.

Stub leapt to his feet. Jamie's knife was in his hand, and he lunged at Vickie, throwing all of his weight into the thrust. Vickie saw it coming. She stepped to one side at the last possible second and gave the big man a shove as he flew past her. She pivoted around and grabbed his knife hand from behind. She pressed down on his wrist with every ounce of her strength, and there was a sickening crack as the bones shattered. Stub screamed in pain as she pulled the knife from his useless fingers.

The others were awakened by the commotion. They arrived just in time to see Vickie kick Stub over onto his back. "Get up!" she commanded. The man gave her a murderous look, but did as he was told. She ignored his nakedness and stared straight into his eyes. "You owe this woman an apology."

Stub held his broken wrist against his chest. He was still reeling from the speed with which Vickie had subdued him. "I don't apologize to bitches," he managed.

"Do you want me to break the other wrist?" Vickie stepped toward him fearlessly. "It would be no trouble."

Jamie saw fear in Stub's eyes as he looked down at her. "I'm sorry," he offered.

"Tell her you'll never touch her again." Vickie prodded.

Stub looked defeated. "I won't touch you again."

Jamie didn't respond. Vickie moved closer to Stub until her face was a few centimeters from him. She reached down and grabbed his penis, squeezing until the man grimaced. "Now listen to me carefully. I know what you did to Alice and what you tried to do here. If you ever force yourself on a woman again, I'll cut this off." She gave his genitals a shake. "Do you believe me Stub?"

The big man's shoulders slumped. "Yes, ma'am."

"Good." Vickie let go of him and wiped her hand on his chest. "Now let's get back to bed. I think Jamie has had enough for tonight." She turned away from Stub and gave Jamie a wink. She glanced back at him to make sure he was moving. The man waddled across the campsite like a big bear. Vickie gave Jamie her knife back. "Are you okay?"

Jamie was shaking like a leaf. "I'll be fine."

"Let me know if he bothers you again. If he does, I'll

make sure he squats down to pee for the rest of his life." The two women smiled at the thought. Jamie thanked her, and Vickie walked away.

Jamie pulled herself up on her knees. She put the knife back into the side pocket of her pack. She could still smell Stub's odor on her ruined jumpsuit. She pulled out a clean one and put it on. She hung her blanket on a low branch to air out and then lay back down on a fresh patch of grass.

Jamie had never seen Vickie in action before. The woman was amazing. She had skills and was a fearless warrior. In contrast, Jamie thought about the moment she pressed her knife into Stub's neck. She couldn't bring herself to kill him. She wasn't a murderer, even if her fleeting memories suggested otherwise. Jamie rubbed her jaw. She was going to have a bruise in the morning.

* * *

The following day, they pressed on through the jungle. Vickie kept a close eye on Stub, making sure he would not retaliate for the previous night's embarrassment. He didn't say a word all day, favoring his broken wrist. Ben distanced himself from the man, not wanting their friendship to affect Vickie's confidence in him.

They entered a grove of trees in the late morning and found a plant they had never seen before. It was shaped like a teardrop, perhaps two meters in diameter. The pointed part of the bulbous plant was on top and had a fibrous cap. The rounded end sat on a bowl of twisted branches, similar to a robin's nest. The body of the teardrop was made of incredibly delicate wooden fibers, woven in an open pattern. The interior of the bulb seemed empty.

"It's kind of like an old-fashioned propane lantern," Ben observed, "the ones with the glowing bag tied over the gas

153

spout."

"A mantle," Thomas offered.

"A what?"

"The bag was called a mantle. It held the gas as it burned."

"Yeah, one of those." Ben nodded his head.

"Looks more like a birdcage," Vickie muttered.

"We haven't seen any birds," Jamie replied. She touched the side of the plant. Her finger easily pierced the hollow bulb. "It's very fragile." She pulled her hand away carefully.

They called the odd plant a mantle. Ben glowed with pride for having suggested it, even though Thomas had been the one who knew the term. They moved on. Throughout the day, they found several more of the plants. They were never clustered together, always sitting alone in a clearing, surrounded by the alien trees.

By late afternoon, Carter's voice was getting hoarse from calling Hip's name. Even he was beginning to doubt the success of their expedition. The time came for dinner, and Vickie insisted they would not travel after nightfall, so they stopped in a small clearing. They didn't build a fire. They made camp near one of the strange mantle plants and prepared their evening meal. Everyone sat down on the ubiquitous tree roots and ate.

As twilight fell, Vickie took Carter aside. They walked a dozen meters from the group and engaged in a long, animated conversation. Ben kept to himself. Stub's rape attempt had cooled their relationship. Jamie and Thomas examined the mantle. It was similar to the others they had seen, but there was a different pattern in the weave.

When Vickie and Carter came back, Carter told them they

would be returning to the settlement in the morning. He wasn't happy about it, but everyone else was relieved. He sat down dejectedly near the mantle. He took out his knife and began fashioning a walking stick from a piece of wood he had harvested from a low tree branch. He stripped away the bark and trimmed off the smaller branches that protruded from the shaft. He took some thin nylon filament out of his pack and wrapped a handle about a third of the way from one end. It was a handsome job. Ben complimented him, but Carter didn't notice.

Twilight faded slowly, and the brightest stars began to peek through the darkening sky. Thomas was settling in for the night, his back nestled against one of the trees. Jamie approached him, her blanket draped over one shoulder. "Mind if I join you?" she asked. Thomas was taken aback. He blushed, and then Jamie realized how it sounded. "I didn't mean that!" She smiled awkwardly. "I mean, is it okay if I sleep next to you?" It sounded even more like a proposition. "That didn't come out right, either! What I mean is," she glanced over her shoulder at Stub, who was already fast asleep. "I'd feel a lot safer."

Thomas understood. "I don't mind at all. Pull up a root, and make yourself uncomfortable."

Jamie settled down next to him and pulled her blanket over her. They sat without a word, both sensing a vaguely erotic tingle. Vickie was slowly encircling the perimeter of the camp, keeping watch for anything that might be moving in the jungle. Ben was lying on the ground a short distance away, snoring with deep guttural breaths. Carter sat against a tree on the far side of the clearing. He gripped his new walking stick in both hands. His eyes were open, but he was locked in a trance, oblivious to everything around him.

* * *

Jamie dreamt of a blinding light. The vision woke her. The jungle lights had appeared again. The sky pulsated with the familiar greenish-yellow glow, but this time the light filled the clearing. It was all around them. Jamie rolled over to find the source of the illumination. It was the mantle plant. The teardrop-shaped cavity was filled with a cold, green fire that did not burn. The light was growing brighter as the luminous plasma churned and boiled within the delicate structure. The plant seemed alive as it hurled its beams into the jungle and up toward the sky.

The murmuring voices returned. Jamie squeezed her temples and closed her eyes. The muttering was still indistinct, but louder now. She felt like someone else was in her mind. The sensation was overwhelming. Moreover, the voices were associated with the light.

Carter leapt to his feet and let out a primal scream. He acted like man possessed by a demon. He jumped and swore, then grabbed his new walking stick and waved it like a club. He ran toward the glowing mantle and swung the staff horizontally. It hit the side of the luminous globe and ripped through the delicate fibers like a hot knife through butter. The light disappeared, as matted pieces of broken weave rained down on the jungle floor. The plasma, now released from its containment, dissipated like an electric cloud. The camp was cast into darkness. Jamie felt a sudden void in her consciousness. The walls of her mind seemed to retreat into the darkness, creating an emotional vacuum. The voices were cut off abruptly, and there was nothing but silence.

* * *

Carter was standing next to the shattered mantle as the others gathered around him. He turned and looked at Vickie, an astonished look on his face. "The damn thing startled me," he explained. "I was asleep when it turned on."

156

Jamie stooped down and picked up a fragment of the mantle. The delicate fibers disintegrated in her fingers. "You killed them!" she said.

Carter dropped the walking stick. "I thought it was a monster."

Jamie couldn't take her eyes off the plant, which had collapsed in upon itself. Carter had been the monster, acting out of pure rage. He was a dangerous man.

"It's too easily broken, anyway," he muttered. "Something that fragile is just asking to get shattered."

Jamie stepped toward Carter. "So you're blaming the plant for what you did."

"Damn right!" He picked up the walking stick again. "We have to take every threat seriously, or we won't survive."

"That plant wasn't a threat."

"How do you know?" He glared at Jamie. Vickie positioned herself near Carter, ready to snatch the staff from his hand if he made a menacing gesture.

"Okay, everyone," Vickie announced firmly. "The excitement is over. Let's get some sleep. We have a long walk tomorrow."

Jamie backed away from Carter. She didn't want to enrage him further. She went back to where she had been sleeping and settled in under her blanket.

Thomas lay down next to her. "Why did you say 'them?'" he whispered.

"What do you mean?"

"You referred to the mantle as 'them.'"

"I dunno," she rolled over, putting her back to the man.

She pulled the blanket tightly around her arms. The voices were silent. The stillness in her mind was like standing alone in an immense room, the great space holding ancient whispers that still echoed from the rafters. That's what she had meant by "them." She had been frightened by the sensation at first. Now she longed for it. The voices represented something larger than herself. She yearned for a bridge to something real, a link with her past. Jamie rolled on her back and looked up at the sky. All the jungle lights were gone.

* * *

The leaves began to fall before dawn. The hard triangular foliage stung Jamie's face, making sleep impossible. The others were scrambling to their feet, covering their heads with their blankets to avoid the onslaught. "What in hell is going on?" Ben whimpered.

"It's the leaves," Vickie shouted. "Just cover your head and ride it out."

The noise was deafening. The leaves clicked and clattered from branch to branch, creating a sound like rain on a tin roof. The cacophony increased as the leaves spun wildly from the branches and slapped against those that had fallen before them. There was no light, except for the golden wash from Alathea's rings. The dying leaves were shiny and caught the light, creating the illusion of a thousand diamonds cascading from the sky.

When morning came, Jamie found herself half-buried in the dead foliage. She remembered seeing pictures of children rushing and jumping into piles of autumn leaves. She felt a brief kinship with them as she pushed the rigid triangles aside and got to her feet. Just as snow transforms the Earth with its crystalline blanket, the jungle looked like a different place. The leaves covered the reddish grass, changing the color pallet of the landscape. However, the greatest change was overhead. The alien trees stood barren, their naked branches offering empty hands to the sky. They seemed to be mourning the loss of their children, the living dead cursed to stand a hopeless vigil in a fractured wood.

"What the hell?" Even Stub was subdued by the radical change around them.

Thomas was looking up into the empty branches, slowly turning around. "Carter did it," he said quietly. "He killed the trees."

Carter heard him. "I did no such thing." The crazed man balled his fists and sneered defiantly at the former holy man.

"You killed them when you smashed the mantle." Thomas said it evenly, as a matter of fact. "I think the mantle plant was the taproot for all the trees. It was the heart of the organism. Remember how the trees died as a group back at the settlement?" Everyone nodded. "That's what happened here, except you didn't just kill part of the network. You killed the entire plant."

"I was angry!" Carter's legs began to pump up and down, possessed by some psychological tremor.

"I'm not arguing the morality of what you've done, Carter. I'm just telling you what I think happened."

Vickie interrupted them. "Better gather your things. It's going to be a long trek out of here."

Jamie pulled her pack from under the ocean of leaves. She joined the others, and they set off on their trip back to the settlement. Vickie led the way as they crunched through the wasteland. It took them fifteen minutes to reach the last of the barren trees. The familiar surroundings of the jungle engulfed them once more as they padded quietly over the crimson sod and under the lush canopy of branches.

* * *

Carter was unusually silent during the return trip. Not once did he stop and call Hip's name. He fell into the rhythm of the trail, palming his walking stick and getting lost in thought as he strode behind Vickie. Jamie took up the rear of the column, grateful to have no one behind her. She paced Thomas, who hiked several meters ahead of her. She reached out with her senses, hoping to hear the voices once more, but she was greeted by silence.

* * *

They reached the settlement late the following day. They marched through the main gate, and Jamie felt everyone relax. They had returned from the dangerous outer world and were now snuggled safe inside their post and rail enclosure. The illusion of safety was a powerful thing. The others greeted them happily, asking for news. No one spoke of Stub's attempted rape or of Carter's destruction of the mantle. They reported what everyone wanted to hear: the jungle wasn't dangerous, they discovered the source of the strange lights, and Hip, of course, was nowhere to be found.

Carter's maypole was gone. Olivia had insisted on its removal. She had badgered the remaining colonists into action, and they had toppled the obscene sculpture. They had tied ropes around it and dragged the phallus out the main gate to the place where the garden had been. Prudence and modesty reigned once more in the settlement.

Jamie took a head count. Only eight people had greeted them in the compound. Someone was missing. Then she realized who it was. "Where is Rusty?" she asked.

"He's been moping around," Bliss offered. "He keeps mostly to himself, you know. He doesn't want to see me anymore, so I've left him alone."

Jamie made it her mission to find Rusty. She stood in the center of the compound and looked everywhere. He wasn't in sight. She checked each of the sheds, but he wasn't there. Where could he be? That was the wrong question. It was better to ask where he would go. The right question led to the obvious answer. Jamie set off toward the beach trail.

Jamie looked up at the trees as she strode purposefully toward the beach. She no longer took them for granted. Who could have imagined how interconnected everything was? She was sure Carter never expected his act of violence against the mantle to kill two hundred trees.

Her thoughts returned to Rusty and Alice. Their love had been palpable that day on the beach. Rusty had to be there. It was his place of connection. She broke through the tree line and felt the warm sand against her feet. The sun was still a diameter above the far horizon, cutting a golden path across the restless sea. She turned to her right, where she had seen Rusty and Alice playing in the surf. Rusty was there, sitting naked at the water's edge.

Jamie trotted through the sand toward her friend. She passed his jumpsuit lying in a jumble where he had tossed it. As she drew near, she could see a discoloration in the water. Her stomach clenched. Something was very wrong. Jamie stopped behind Rusty. He was sitting with both legs out in front of him, his hands folded on his lap. She could see the calf of one leg. There was a red stain on his skin. The water lapping up against his groin had a pinkish cast. Jamie rushed around him and dropped to her knees. A knife lay on the sand, where it had fallen from his fingers. Both of Rusty's wrists were slashed, and rivers of blood coursed down his legs and into the alien sea.

CHAPTER FOURTEEN
Accusation

R usty was still alive. Jamie bound up the cuts on his wrists and threw the knife into the sea. As she pulled him out of the surf, his legs plowed deep furrows in the sand, which filled quickly with red-stained water. She grabbed his jumpsuit and used the sleeves as makeshift bandages, attempting to stem the flow of blood from his wrists. She ran back to the settlement for help, and some of the others came to carry him to the clinic.

Rachel Bennett had succeeded Hip as the settlement physician. Rusty was her first case, and she was visibly nervous as she tended to his wounds. Jamie stood in the doorway, watching the medic's hands. They were shaking. Rusty was laying on one of the beds in the clinic. His blood coursed from his wounds, leaving red trails on the sheet before dripping on the floor. Jamie wished Hip were still alive.

By nightfall, Rusty was resting quietly. His wrists were cleaned, the cuts sutured and covered with fresh bandages. Rachel had sedated him, and he lay motionless on the bed, his arms tied down to prevent him from tearing open his wounds. Rusty was placed on suicide watch and would not be left alone. Jamie had volunteered for the first shift and had no intention of leaving his side. She understood his hopelessness. He was an artist, a man who led with his feelings. He had fallen in love with Alice, and her loss had been too much for him. The lottery had ripped his muse from his arms. Her death in the storm had pushed him over the edge. Jamie listened to his slow, steady breaths, grateful he was still alive.

Jamie was awakened the next morning by Rusty stirring in his bed. She smiled at him as he opened his eyes. "Good morning," she said cheerfully.

"Where am I?" His voice was weak. He raised his left hand to touch his face, but the restraints prevented him from doing so. The strap pulled against his forearm, and he winced. He looked down at the bandages around his wrists. His face was tormented with confusion.

"You're in the clinic. Do you remember what happened?"

"I, I was on the beach." Rusty frowned as the incident flooded back into his mind. He looked down at his bandages again. "I wanted to die."

"You were almost dead when I found you, you idiot."

Rusty stared at his hands. "You wouldn't understand."

"I do understand. I've lost a lover. It was terrible."

Rusty looked at her. "You're remembering things?"

"I've been getting bits and pieces of memories: flashbacks, really. They don't make sense, but I'm in them. They're glimpses of my past."

"You loved someone?"

"It was another woman." Jamie wasn't sure how Rusty would react, but he nodded. "She was terribly sick."

Rusty retreated into himself, as though the thought

triggered something that pained him deeply. "It happened to me, too," he whispered.

Jamie took his hand gently. "She was a beautiful woman," she continued. The memory was clear. She could see the image of her beloved in her mind. "She had hair the color of honey, and her body was slender and perfect. I loved the way she moved, the way her voice sounded, the way she looked at me."

Rusty was transfixed. "How did you lose her?"

"She died from a degenerative disease. She wasted away. I quit my job to be with her. Every day, a little more of her was gone." Jamie was shaking. "When she died, I thought about suicide. I almost did it, too."

Rusty's eyes were filled with tears. "What was her name?" he asked.

"Camille."

Rusty pulled his hand away from her. "That isn't possible!" Jamie could see the cords in his neck. He pulled against the restraints and writhed in the bed. His face turned red as he gave her a look of pure hatred. "Get away from me!"

"Rusty…" Jamie reached for his hand again, but he pushed it away, grimacing from the pain.

"What are you doing?" Rusty looked like he had seen a ghost.

Jamie was astonished. "What do you mean?"

"You stole my memory! Camille was my wife. I watched her die, not you!"

"But I was there. I remember it clearly. I feel it like it was yesterday." Jamie felt a deep angst blow through her like a chilly wind.

"But it happened to me, damn it! You have no right! Go away!" An ice wall descended between them. Jamie was immobilized by the implications of what Rusty was saying. "Somebody!" he shrieked. "Get her out of here!"

Jamie could hardly breathe. In one second she was sharing a moment of pain to comfort a friend, and in the next he was accusing her of stealing his memories. Her grip on reality began to slip, and she felt herself spinning. The room filled with people. Vickie muscled her way to Rusty's bedside. "What's going on?"

Rusty was agitated, his body twitching under the covers. He pointed an accusing finger at Jamie. "She read my thoughts! She told me all about my wife's death. She couldn't have known about it. Nobody knows about it!"

Vickie turned to Jamie. "Is this true?" The camaraderie Jamie had felt when the security officer had rescued her from Stub was gone. Vickie was all business.

Jamie's legs felt like they were made of rubber. She gripped the edge of the bed and willed herself to stay on her feet. She wasn't sure anymore. "No," she lied. "I was trying to comfort him. I told him about the time when my lover died. Her name was Camille."

Stub was standing by the door. "Now I understand," he snorted. "She's one of them."

"Shut up!" Vickie commanded. He grinned, but said nothing further.

"It's a lie," Rusty hissed. "My wife's name was Camille. I painted a picture of her on her deathbed."

Jamie sucked in a breath. She remembered painting the picture. "Maybe he's right," she mumbled. She sat down in the chair next to the bed.

Vickie stepped closer to her, studying her face. "When did this memory come to you?" She asked the question like a prosecuting attorney.

Jamie put her hands to her face. She squeezed her head, as if trying to force the memory from her mind. "It was the day of the lottery. I had gone to the beach. I saw Rusty and Alice saying goodbye to each other. That's when it hit me."

"You thought it was something from your past."

"I did."

"And now you think it might have been Rusty's memory." It was a statement, not a question.

Jamie put her hands in her lap and looked up at Vickie. "Maybe it was, but the memory was so vivid. I remember painting the picture as she lay there. Her head was wrapped in a white scarf, and her eyes were closed. She looked like she had just told me she loved me. The light fell on her left shoulder, catching the folds of her bedclothes. I was taken by how the color of her skin changed as her life slipped away."

"Damn you!" Rusty tried to get up, pulling weakly at his restrains. Rachel had both hands on his shoulders, urging him to lie down. Rusty ignored her, focused completely on Jamie. "That's exactly how it happened. She's reading my mind!"

A ripple of fear coursed through the group. Several people moved away from Jamie, as if she was radioactive. Vickie kept her composure. "You were near Rusty when you remembered this."

"I already told you that." Jamie saw Vickie's cold logic in the question. She feared where the questions might lead. Everyone was watching her, concern etched on their faces. Jamie was defensive. "If it was Rusty's memory, I don't know how I could have known it."

"You've been remembering other things?"

"Yes." Jamie looked pleadingly at Rusty. He turned away from her. "I was telling Rusty that I was remembering things."

"Tell us about them," Vickie asked coldly.

There was no way to avoid the interrogation. She sighed. "I remember sitting in a car, waiting for my parents to finish robbing a bank." The color drained from Vickie's face. "We lived out of that car and slept in run-down motels. I remember my mother taking me into the woods by the side of the road to pee."

"That is impossible!" Vickie pulled her out of the chair. Her strong hands gripped Jamie's upper arms like a pair of metal clamps. The security officer slammed Jamie against the wall. "You are reading our minds!" she shouted, her military bearing evaporating in the heat of anger.

"No." Jamie squealed. "I just remember things from the past."

Vickie's gaze was murderous. Jamie watched as the woman took a breath and remembered her military training. Her grip relaxed slightly. "Ben, get over here." The security guard was hesitant as he approached. "Bind her hands and take her outside. Lock her in the shed at the edge of the compound. I don't want her near any of us." Vickie pulled Jamie away from the wall and twisted her body so Ben could tie her wrists. She nodded to one of her other security people, and the two men grabbed Jamie under the arms and escorted her out of the building.

Ben pulled her across the compound. "Can you read my mind, Jamie?" He squeezed her arm until she cried with pain.

"No, I can't!"

"We don't want anybody messing around inside our heads. Do you understand?" Jamie gasped as he jabbed his thumb into her biceps. "Something spooky is going on with you, and we're going to stop it." He and his companion pushed her through the shed door. "You aren't going to like it." Ben slammed the door. Jamie tumbled to the floor as he secured the latch. Her act of compassion had become a capital offense.

* * *

During the weeks since waking up from hibernation, Jamie had struggled to recover her missing identity. She had questioned everything. When the memories began to emerge through her gauzy befuddlement, she grabbed onto them. They were like rungs of a ladder, permitting her to climb out of her amnesic pit. The conflicting nature of her recollections had troubled her, especially when it came to her gender. Nevertheless, knowing something, even though it was vexing, was better than knowing nothing at all. She thought she was making progress. The memories were like points of light that promised to illuminate her past. It had never occurred to her that the memories might not be her own, and that incomprehensible thought shattered her sense of self.

She lay on the floor of the shed. She felt soulless. Her heart was beating, and blood was coursing through her veins, but she was an empty husk, a short-lived plant born of seed sewn in shallow ground. Jamie felt like a detached bystander, eavesdropping on other people's lives but never experiencing anything authentically her own. She was like one of the dead alien trees whose root system had been chopped off. She was nothing.

Jamie drifted into a restless sleep. Once again, she was surrounded by a violet mist. The murmurings, which had retreated into silence when Carter destroyed the mantle plant, surrounded her once more. They were more distinct now, dancing on the edge of intelligibility. She sensed syllables, but not words. She was going mad. She was descending into schizophrenia. It was only a matter of time before the voices would become multiple variations on her own fragile self. She would phase in and out of each one, lost in a labyrinth of personalities from which she would never escape.

Jamie opened her eyes, pushing away the mutterings of her subconscious. She would not surrender to the maze. She would not enter the rabbit hole and lose herself. She would fight to be a whole person, no matter what the cost. Jamie sat up, almost convincing herself that things would get better. Then she realized she was deep in her soul's abyss. She was already trapped in the maze, the voices emerging from the dark recesses of her mind.

* * *

It was several hours before anyone came to the shed. Jamie heard noises outside her prison door. "Get back!" It was Ben's voice. The latch clicked, echoing off the metal walls, then the door swung open. Jamie relaxed when she saw Thomas and Bliss enter the shed. "Are you sure you know what you're doing?" Ben asked them.

"Don't worry about us," Thomas replied. The security officer swung the door shut and rammed the latch home. Jamie's visitors slid a couple of cargo cases over to her and sat down. Bliss took her hand and stroked the back of her fingers. "How are you doing?" she asked.

"I'd say I've been better, but I can't remember when that might have been." Jamie laughed sarcastically.

"They're talking about banishing you from the settlement."

"Great. Does that mean I have to forfeit the safety of our fine perimeter fence and face the terrible danger of the jungle?"

Thomas smiled. "It can get lonely out there."

"Haven't you heard? I can read people's minds. I can be halfway across the planet and still attend all of Carter's meetings."

"There's a punishing thought," Thomas mused.

"You aren't acting like you can read our minds." Bliss stared at her friend intently.

"I can't. I just have memories, which piss people off. First there was Rusty, and then Vickie acted like I had revealed her deepest, darkest secret."

"I saw how she reacted," Thomas agreed. "Do you think her parents were thieves?"

"I don't know. Maybe it was her memory. Up to this point, I thought I was remembering who I was. I've been so desperate to know about my past, and now it seems I've stolen everybody else's memories. I'm back to ground zero. I haven't a clue about who I am."

"You sensed my doubt that day when we talked about faith," Thomas observed. "What you said resonated with how I was feeling. I was hiding, and you saw right through me."

"Could be, but I was also expressing my opinion. Maybe that was all there was to it."

Thomas nodded as another thought occurred to him. "You remembered a house on a mountain lake. Where did that memory come from?"

"I lied to you. It was a horrible memory." Jamie was apologetic. "You said it must have been wonderful, and I agreed with you. I didn't want you to pry any further. I thought it was the best thing to say."

"It worked." Thomas rocked back on the cargo case.

Jamie sighed. "The truth is, I lived in a mansion. It was next to a mountain lake. It was pure white inside."

"Did you remember the great room with the high ceilings?" Bliss asked.

Jamie's mouth dropped open. "Yes."

"Was William in your memory?"

Jamie's chin began to tremble. "I remember making love to him by the fire."

"Do you remember when he beat you?"

"I remember every time he hit me." Jamie's body began to shake.

"And did you go into the master bedroom?"

"I did."

"What did you see?"

"I saw his body. The knife. The blood."

"Did you see how I castrated that son of a bitch?" Jamie's eyes grew wide. Bliss nodded sadly. "That's right, girlfriend. It happened to me." Bliss leaned into her and gave her a hug. "William gave me those marks on my back. He's the one I told you about in the storm, you know?"

Jamie pushed Bliss away. "Aren't you afraid of me?"

"Oh, no! You stood in my shoes. You felt my pain. You are my friend. How can I be afraid of that?"

Jamie wept.

171

* * *

Ben came to the shed the next morning. "Carter wants to see you," he intoned. Jamie squinted into the bright sunlight as she followed him out of the door. It could have been a beautiful day, but she knew better. Everyone was afraid of her. Thomas and Bliss had probably tried to calm their fears, but Jamie knew it wouldn't make any difference. The others had retreated into their reptilian brains, where everything was about survival. They would not be in a forgiving mood.

The colonists were waiting for her in the middle of the compound. They sat on the cargo cases that encircled the fire pit. Vickie motioned for Ben to bring Jamie into the center. She stood by the fire pit, surrounded by her accusers. Carter sat with Vickie on one side and Olivia on the other. Everyone looked nervous except Thomas and Bliss. Jamie could tell by their body language that they were wondering if she could read their minds. She smiled at the irony. She couldn't read their minds, but she knew exactly what they were thinking.

Carter gave her an intense, disapproving look. "I have called this meeting to figure out what to do with you. The moment we woke you up on the pod ship, I knew you were going to be a problem. Hip told me I was wrong, but he's not here to defend you. Vickie and Rusty told me what happened yesterday, and we'd all like to hear your side of the story."

Jamie cleared her throat. "I meant no offense." She looked at Rusty, who had been brought out of the clinic. He sat quietly; his bandaged wrists lay on a pillow Rachel had placed in his lap. He was staring down at his feet. "I am," she looked at Rusty. "I was Rusty's friend. I found him on the beach when we returned from the expedition. I sat with him in the clinic. I knew how sad he was and related something I thought would comfort him. It was something I remembered about myself. I was wrong. Somehow, it was from Rusty's past, and he got very upset. I can appreciate why it scared him." Rusty looked up at her. "I'm really sorry, Rusty. I didn't mean to hurt you." He looked back down at the ground.

"When Vickie came in, she asked me if I had other memories. I did. I told her about waiting for my parents in a car. I guess that memory didn't belong to me either."

"It was Vickie's memory?"

"You'd have to ask her."

"It was mine!" Vickie shouted at her. "No one knew that except me. How did you know?"

"It came to me in a dream. It was our first night in this clearing. The strange lights had appeared, and you were on guard duty. I saw you walking the tree line as I fell asleep. That's all I know."

Vickie frowned. "Let me get this straight. You remembered Rusty's past while watching him on the beach, and you stole my memories after watching me patrol the clearing."

"I didn't steal them."

Olivia spoke up. "You ended up with something that belonged to someone else. That's stealing." For her, life contained no gray areas.

"I didn't ask for the memories," Jamie explained. "They just came to me."

Olivia sniffed. "You stole these memories while you were in close proximity to their owners. Is that correct?"

Jamie wondered if Olivia had been a prosecutor. She spoke like a lawyer. "Yes, that's when they came to me." She immediately regretted saying yes.

"She can read our fuckin' minds!" Stub snarled the

comment. Carter looked like he was going to cut him off, but said nothing. The colonists were nodding in agreement.

"You know I can't do that, Stub." Jamie stared the man down. "If I could read your mind, I would have known you wanted to rape me." Everyone looked at Stub, who shifted uncomfortably in his seat. "Do you really think I can read your mind?" Jamie took a step toward him.

"Guess not."

Jamie turned away from Stub and scanned the group. She raised her hands in a pleading gesture. "That is your answer. I can't read your minds. I just remember things from the past."

Bliss stood up. "She's telling you the truth. I went and talked with her last night, and she remembered a secret from my past. It was something I've never told anyone, you know? Even so, I'm not afraid of her."

"The bimbo ain't got no thoughts to steal," cracked Stub. He looked around, hoping the others would appreciate his wit and forget his attempt to rape Jamie. No one laughed.

Olivia looked at Bliss like she was a grease spot on a freshly polished floor. "Not all of us share your wide-eyed, innocent point of view," Olivia stated flatly. "In the real world, when you go around half-naked, you get raped. When you let mental peeping toms look into your mind, they take advantage of you."

Bliss pulled at her collar. "She's a good person."

"I'm not sure you would know a good person if you saw one," Olivia shot back. "Jamie doesn't know who she is or what she's done. I think she's a danger to us."

Jamie could tell most of the colonists shared Olivia's sentiments. She spread her hands. "I'm no threat to any of you. I'm just trying to sort out who I am. I've been a good worker, and I have never intended harm to anyone." She looked at Rusty, who was still staring at his feet. "Rusty, you know that. I apologize for offending you." She turned to Vickie, who was standing outside the circle with her arms crossed. "Vickie, you've stood up for me. You know I'm a good person. I'm sorry if I gave away your secret. I thought I was talking about myself." Jamie turned slowly, making eye contact with every person. "Please. You all know me, as well as I know myself. I'm not a threat."

"That's the problem!" Stub hissed. "You don't know who you are. We don't know you at all. You're a mystery. You could be a killer!"

Everyone began to talk at once. Most of them were agreeing with Stub. Carter raised his hand for silence. "That is enough! I think Vickie put her finger on the problem. You steal memories when you are near to us. You are invading our privacy and upsetting our community. We can't tolerate that."

Jamie felt a cold wave of fear wash over her. Survival was on everyone's minds since the storm, and now she was being singled out as a threat. "I won't share anything else."

Carter got to his feet. The pitch of his voice began to rise. "That is not good enough. If you remain here, we'll all wonder what you have taken from us. We can't trust you."

"Banish her!" Olivia chanted. Others joined in the rhythmic judgment. Bliss and Thomas protested, but to no avail. Almost everyone was calling for Carter to throw Jamie out of the settlement.

Carter called for silence and turned to Rusty. "What do you have to say about this?"

Rusty looked up at him. He looked distant and broken. His eyes were empty, his face a portrait of despair. "Throw her out," he mumbled.

"No, Rusty! You can't say that!" Jamie rushed toward him, but Ben leapt to his feet and grabbed her by the arm. Jamie tried to pull away from him, her eyes still locked on the artist. "You're my friend!"

Rusty had been looking at Carter. He turned his head, his vacant eyes locking onto Jamie. She froze, no longer struggling against Ben's vice-like grip. Rusty looked like a soulless apparition. "Get rid of her," he said. He turned away from her and looked back down at the ground.

Jamie sank to her knees. "I didn't mean any harm," she cried. "Please..." She lowered her head. The voices of her companions began to swell, encircling her with their judgment. "Banish her!" Jamie sensed them getting to their feet and moving closer to her. Their fear wafted over her like foul incense.

Carter raised his hand for silence again. "The people have spoken. We want you out of the settlement within the hour. Put your things in a backpack. We will give you a week's worth of food. Don't ever come back." Jamie knew it was a death sentence.

* * *

An hour later, when Jamie arrived at the main gate, Thomas and Bliss were the only ones there. Carter and the others watched her from the far side of the compound, not wanting to get any closer.

"I'll leave food for you beyond the tree line," Thomas promised.

"Don't get in trouble," she urged him. "I'll figure something out."

Bliss gave her a tight hug. "I'll miss you, Jamie."

"You, too," Jamie managed. Then she turned and strode

through the gate, leaving the danger of the settlement and entering the uncertain world of the jungle.

CHAPTER FIFTEEN

Encounter

J amie was drawn to the alien sea. She took the beach trail for the last time and made her way to the shore. She headed south along the thin stretch of sand that divided the jungle from the water. She took off her shoes and walked barefoot on the fringes of the reddish sod. The shore would be her highway into the unknown. She felt alone, disconnected. Rusty's dismissal had struck her like a sword of ice. It had cut through her. The cold shaft had punctured her heart and had frozen the blood in her veins. She was freezing to death, a living corpse wandering numbly through the winter of her soul. She didn't see the brilliant sun. She didn't feel the warm sea air on her face. She was oblivious to the grass and sand between her toes. Those sensations were for the living. She was already dead.

Jamie rested at midday. She lounged breast-deep in the water, longing for the day she had joined Alice and Rusty in the surf. It had been a moment of innocent pleasure. She had felt a kinship with Alathea and her friends. Now the water taunted her, intensifying her pain and reminding her of things lost forever. She cursed herself for sharing the memories. If she had known she was trespassing into their minds, she would have been like a priest in a confessional, carrying their secrets to her grave. Waves of guilt and grief washed over her like the violet surf. Jamie screamed, frustration and remorse hammering her gut. She returned to the beach and rinsed the sand from between her toes. She took up her journey again because there was nothing else to do.

The sun beat down on Jamie through the long afternoon. Her jumpsuit had dried from her venture into the water and was now sodden with her sweat. She remembered Bliss stripping to her waist and how Olivia and the others had looked down their noses at her friend. She paused under a tree whose branches cast a shadow over the beach. She was kilometers from the others. Who would care? Suddenly, in an act of private defiance, she unzipped her jumpsuit and let the upper portion of the garment fall to her waist. The moisture on her skin evaporated in the sea air, cooling her. She walked a few steps, and the jumpsuit began to slide off her hips. She tied the arms snugly around her midriff and pushed onward.

The day grew hotter still. Jamie stooped at the edge of the ocean and filled her palm with water. She drank eagerly, savoring its subtle sweetness. She stood up again and fisted her toes in the sand. Jamie glanced down at her breasts. She was proud of her body. She thought of Carter's advances, how he had rigged the lottery to be her mate. She didn't like the man, but she was pleased that someone had been interested in her. She wasn't as pretty as Bliss. Her breasts were smaller than her friend's. Women like her didn't get too many second glances. Even so, she could have pleasured a man. She could have borne babies and fed them on her bosom. She felt emptiness in her chest, an ache from things that might have been. She was going to die alone. There would be no more glances, no lover, no children.

She reached upward toward the sky and arched her back, working out a kink in one of her shoulder blades. She looked at Alathea's rings, which swept across the sky like golden ribbons. They disappeared behind the horizon, where the sea became one with the heavens. On impulse, she untied the arms of the jumpsuit and let it fall to the sand. She stepped out of it and stuffed the garment into her pack. The warm air caressed her as she pushed forward on her journey. She didn't intellectualize about her nudity. It felt natural in this unnatural place, suggesting a oneness with the breeze and the sea. Jamie needed to feel close to something. That was all that mattered.

* * *

Jamie lay down that night on the pale green sand, making her bed on her blanket with her pack as a pillow. The rhythmic whisper of the ocean was like an ancient lullaby. She wept quietly, feeling like a child lost in the forest of time and space. She looked up at the sky filled with nameless stars. They were her sisters, siblings with no names in an indifferent universe. She wondered if anyone would ever discern their patterns and group them into constellations. Would someone name them someday? Would she ever remember the name her mother must have uttered on the day of her birth?

Jamie felt small and insignificant. She reached out to the sky. "Who am I?" she asked the heavens. "Tell me what to do." She dropped her hands and held her breath, hoping for a reply. Only the ocean answered, its waves lapping gently upon the shore. There were no voices murmuring in the corridors of her mind.

* * *

The next morning, Jamie came upon a wide river whose waters divided the beach, making it impossible for her to continue her seaside journey. It was much larger than the river near the settlement. She decided to follow it inland and bid farewell to the sandy beach and the ocean's violet waters. Long branches hung over the banks of the river, casting continuous shadows on her path as she trekked into the virgin forest. Patches of fluorescent flowers poked up through the crimson grass, offering splashes of color. Before long, her way was obstructed by tall plants resembling bulrushes, which clogged the river's edge. Jamie moved deeper into the jungle to avoid them. She walked more slowly than she had on the seashore, picking her way over the thick roots, which resembled immense snakes slithering from tree to tree across the forest floor.

Jamie saw her first mantle plant in the midafternoon. It was almost identical to the ones she had seen during Carter's expedition. She stopped and examined the intricate weave that formed the odd plant's hollow bulb. The design was different from the one Carter had destroyed. She continued on her way, pausing to study each of the mantles as she happened upon them.

Jamie's legs grew weary in the late afternoon. She put down her pack near one of the mantles and sat on a stout root, which radiated from the base of the plant. She swung one leg over the radix, straddling it like a horse. Images of Lady Godiva passed through her mind, and she smiled. She rocked back and forth on the root. The smooth bark was cool, gently caressing her inner thighs. She cleared her mind and willed her heart to slow its beating. She wanted to hear the voices again, to connect with something greater than herself. There was nothing.

She was about to dismount the root when she felt an odd sensation. It was a vibration of some kind in the wood beneath her. She listened intently. The river was babbling nearby, and the leaves rustled faintly. The breeze was singing, its breath evidenced by a subtle movement of air. Jamie pitched forward on her wooden steed and stretched out on top of the root. She wrapped her hands around it and put her ear against the bark. There was a faint rushing sound, deep within the plant. It was like water moving slowly through a pipe. That was exactly what it was, she concluded. Jamie was hearing the sound of nutrients passing through the root, giving life to all the trees around her.

* * *

As daylight began to fade, Jamie made camp near a large mantle. It was easily twice as tall as any of the others she had seen. The roots, which spread outward toward the surrounding trees, were at least half a meter thick. There were no overhanging branches above the mantle plant. The surrounding trees had refrained from growing above their bulbous mother, deferring to their source of life.

Jamie rolled out her blanket near the "bird's nest" under the mantle's cage and ate a modest supper. Then she lay down, once again stuffing her pack under her head. In another life, Jamie might have read a book or watched a video, but after hours of walking in the jungle, she was content to lie down under the stars and rest. She could see the violet sky through the leafless channel above the mantle, its color fading on its optical journey toward night.

Jamie felt the isolation of her exile. She was utterly alone. There was no one to hide from, no one to impress, and no one to help her. She felt an uncomfortable hollow void in the pit of her stomach. A great fear swept through her, and she began to shake. Her emotions poured out, and she wept without reservation, her sobbing punctuated by deep gasps of air. She knew she could not survive in the jungle. Her food would run out in a few days, and she would starve to death. Most people have something to remember when they die. They can remember old friends and family, satisfactions and regrets, but Jamie had no such luxuries. She realized she would die without even knowing her name.

She sat up on her blanket and pulled her knees up to her

chin. She grasped her shins and wept like a lost child. She called out to a mother she didn't know. She pleaded with the universe. Finally, she surrendered to the darkness that was gathering in the jungle around her. The shadows enveloped her body and soul, casting her into a pit of despair.

* * *

A breeze stirred the trees, their leaves gently clicking together, and then the lights came. Jamie pulled herself up and stood by the mantle plant as its hollow cavity ignited. At first, there was a pinprick of light at the base of the woven teardrop. It seemed to emanate from some underlying root that sprung out of the tangled nest below the basket-like plant. The tiny dot of light expanded. Jamie gazed through the fibrous mesh. For a moment, the growing light illuminated the inside of the cavity, revealing the texture of the far wall of the bulb. The interlaced stems drank in the light and then, in a seamless symbiotic gesture, began to emit traces of yellowish mist. The light jumped like a lightning bolt in the plant's secretions, and the mantle's lamp came alive with greenish fire. Tongues of cold, luminous plasma danced and roiled in the mantle's belly.

Jamie stepped back, startled by the intensity of the glow. She looked down at her arms. Her skin was a monochromatic rainbow in shades of green. Jamie closed her eyes, but the light was bright, penetrating her eyelids. She returned to her blanket, seeking a shadow on the jungle floor. The base of the mantle plant shielded her, and she looked up into the sky above the alien beacon. Alathea's rings were faintly visible through the dazzling light.

An alien presence surged into her, like air into an oxygen-starved lung. The murmurings returned, louder than ever before. And then there was a voice. "You are not alone," it said. Jamie didn't hear the voice. The words appeared in her mind like an idea. "You are not alone," said the idea again.

"Who is it?" Jamie cried out, certain she had gone mad.

"You are not going mad, young one."

Jamie gasped at the exchange. She was conversing with something unlike anything else she had ever known. It had invaded her mind. The idea was reading her thoughts. Jamie felt two opposing emotions. On the one hand, she felt violated, as if a thief had broken into her inner sanctum and was touching her private things. On the other, Jamie felt a great sense of relief. If this was real, a stranger had come to her, and she was no longer by herself. "What is happening to me?"

"You are empty." The truth of the words struck her like a mighty wind. Jamie exhaled as tears coursed down her face. She was empty. Hollow. Broken. Afraid.

"You don't have to be afraid," said the idea. "We will not hurt you."

"I know," she responded. And she did know. The presence was not a threat. Even so, she was confused. "But I don't understand."

"Understanding is relative," replied the idea. "Once you completely understand, there is nothing else to know, and you begin to die."

"Do you understand?" Jamie was still mystified.

"We try to understand."

Jamie sat up and looked at the mantle plant. For some reason, beyond her knowing, the light emanating from the bulb had changed, and she could look at it. She was mesmerized by the glowing plasma. "What are you?"

"We are not a what. We are a who."

Jamie started to laugh. "This is a dream, and I'm stuck in a Dr. Seuss story."

The idea laughed with her. "We are not a figment of your imagination. We are real. We are alive."

"Why are you talking to me?"

"You are listening. Therefore, you hear us." The mantle's light pulsed, dimming down briefly and then glowing brighter again. "There is something you must do."

A brief, but jarring vision slammed into Jamie's psyche, dumbfounding her, then the mantle plant's light began to fade. She felt a flash of panic. The mental image she had received demanded urgent action, but she didn't want to be cut off from the idea that had invaded her mind. "Don't go!" she cried.

"There is no time to waste, young one," the idea whispered. "If you will put yourself in our hands, we will guide you."

The vision left her with no alternative. "Of course," she said to the mantle. Jamie rolled up her blanket and pulled her backpack over her shoulder. Then, as the mantle's light evaporated, she set off on a new journey through the darkened jungle.

* * *

Jamie walked all night. Alathea's rings cast an ethereal glow through the leaves and branches overhead. She picked her way through the semidarkness, over countless roots and across a dozen small clearings. The jungle, which had seemed indistinct and labyrinthine before, felt familiar. An unfathomable inner voice was guiding her toward her destination. Like an animal following an invisible scent, she could tell at a glance where she needed to go.

Jamie pressed on through midday, eating her lunch as she trod through the deep wood. The crimson sod was thinning, and the trees were less dense. Sometimes she would mount a long tree root like a balance beam. She felt like a young girl as she stretched her arms and walked the length of it, hopping off with an exuberance she had not felt before.

The elevation of the jungle floor began to rise. Jamie's calf muscles ached as she ascended the incline. Before long, she came upon a rocky place. Vickie had reported seeing hills beyond the jungle. Jamie wondered if this was the small mountain she had mentioned. The ubiquitous carpet of red sod became sparse clumps of grass, interspersed with harsh rocky soil that punished her bare feet. Jamie paused and put on her shoes. She moved on, carefully navigating across the rough and uneven terrain.

The rocky ground became steeper as Jamie climbed the sloping face of the modest mountain. The path switched back and forth as she picked her way higher and higher. Jamie's field of vision rose above the treetops. For the first time, she saw the broad expanse of the jungle. The odd trees covered the landscape as far as her eyes could see. She turned and saw the violet ocean to the east. Then she looked up, her breath taken away by the immense beauty of Alathea's rings. Without the trees masking the horizon, she saw the full sweep of the golden ribbons as they arched majestically across the sky.

Jamie looked down at the rocky slope beneath her feet, not wanting to lose her balance. She had climbed to a significant height, and a fall would probably kill her. The inner voice whispered in her mind, urging her forward. She picked her way around a large boulder and traversed a narrow ledge that was barely wide enough for her to walk. Jamie took careful steps, eager to pass beyond the escarpment to a wider path she could see beyond the boulder. She kept her eyes trained on the shelf of rock, trying to ignore the valley a hundred meters below her.

Jamie stopped. Her fear crested within her, her hands shaking against the protuberances in the rock face. She closed her eyes, concentrating on her balance.

"Look down," whispered the idea.

Jamie shuddered. It was the last thing she wanted to do. "I can't!" she cried.

"You must look down," it said again. "You cannot help unless you overcome your fear."

Jamie took a deep breath and opened her eyes. She turned her head and gazed at the expanse of trees stretching eastward toward the alien sea. Then, ever so slowly, she tilted her head until she was looking down the jagged face of the mountain. A woman's body was lying prostrate on another ledge, perhaps five meters below her. It was Alice.

CHAPTER SIXTEEN

Insanity

J amie forgot her fear. She scanned the face of the cliff, looking for a way down to Alice. Seeing none, she pushed forward along the narrow escarpment. She stepped on a loose stone, and it clattered down the rock wall. She froze, her fear returning. Finally, Jamie reached the wider path. There was a jaggy notch before her that descended perhaps two meters into the face of the mountain. She had a short piece of rope in her backpack. She took it out and tied a large knot in one end. Then she forced the knotted end of the rope into a narrow crack in the rock. It held.

Jamie slung her pack over her shoulder and carefully descended into the notch. She kept eyeing the valley below her. She gripped the rope tightly, until her feet found the rough rock at the bottom of the crevice. Jamie crept toward the edge of the cliff. The ledge where Alice lay was another three meters below her. Beyond it was open space, a straight fall to the base of the mountain. Jamie's stomach somersaulted. She looked at the far end of the notch and noticed another crack in the rock. She wondered if she could slide her body into it and use it as a step down to the shelf below. She didn't see any alternatives.

Jamie lay on her belly and backed over the narrow crack. She bent at the waist and let her feet dangle into the crevice. She pushed with her hands and eased herself down into the opening. She gripped the upper edge of the notch and then slipped as the full weight of her body dislodged her fingertips. Her body dropped suddenly and wedged into the crack. Her feet were still fifty centimeters from the bottom of the crevice.

Jamie swore to herself. She could feel the pressure of the rock, squeezing her chest like a vice. She was stuck. The straps of the pack cut into her underarms. The pack! Jamie hadn't considered the thickness of it when she gauged the width of the crevice. She ripped the Velcro straps free and dropped to the bottom of the cleft. Alice's ledge was only a half-meter below her. The rock shelf was wider than it had appeared from above. Jamie approached her friend with a measure of confidence, staying near the face of the cliff. She knelt next to Alice and checked her pulse. She was still alive.

Alice had an ugly bruise over her left eye, and her right arm was twisted at an odd angle. Her lips were parched. Jamie pulled a bottle of water from her pack. She put one hand under Alice's neck, lifting the woman's head so she could drink.

Alice took a big gulp of water reflexively, and then her eyes fluttered open. "Jamie?" she whispered hoarsely.

"Don't try to talk." Jamie urged her. She offered Alice another swig. Slowly, Alice regained her faculties. Jamie took some crackers from her pack and offered them to her. She devoured the food and asked for more. Alice was dirty and exhausted, still wearing the jumpsuit Stub had torn on their wedding night. Jamie washed the cut over her eye and applied some ointment and an adhesive bandage. Alice cried out when Jamie positioned her broken arm against her chest. She tore strips of cloth and immobilized the limb.

An hour later, Alice looked much better. Jamie had helped her change into a clean jumpsuit and had propped her up against the rock wall. With her immediate needs satisfied, Jamie asked her what had happened.

"After you found me on the beach trail, I went to the Lander and took some food and a blanket. I wasn't going back to the settlement. Stub was waiting for me." She trembled. "I went into the jungle. I had to get away from him. I walked for several hours and came upon this mountain. I thought there might be a cave, somewhere to hide." She pointed to the upper ridge with her good hand. "I was up there when the storm hit."

"You were out in the open?" Jamie shivered at the thought. She remembered the destruction wrought by the strong winds.

"There was a cleft in the rock. I saw the storm moving in from the sea and knew it was going to be bad. I wedged myself behind a big stone and stayed there."

"That was over a month ago."

"A month? I knew it was a long time, but I lost track. I rationed my food, eating as little as I could. I collected rainwater to drink."

"We thought you were dead."

"I did, too. I ran out of food a few days ago. I thought about coming down off the mountain and going back to the settlement, but Stub would have hurt me again. I decided to die."

"When did you fall?"

"I can't say exactly. I came out of the cleft to pee, and a piece of rock must have been dislodged by the storm. I was in the wrong place at the wrong time. There I was, squatting on the ledge, and it hit me. The next thing I knew I was down here. My arm hurt like hell, and I couldn't move it."

The two women sat in silence for several minutes. Jamie looked at her friend's matted hair. She took a comb from her side pocket and began to tease out the kinks. "We lost fifteen people in the storm," she said.

"Rusty?"

"He's alive, but he's not the same. He took your loss pretty hard."

"I feel badly about that. I suppose Stub survived."

"He did, but Carter dissolved the pairings. Your marriage has been annulled."

"Honest?"

Jamie cupped her friend's head in her hand, combing her hair gently. "It's true. Carter said couples could stay together if they wanted to, but you're free, Alice."

"Did Rusty and Bliss stay together?"

"Bliss wanted to, but Rusty refused. He's still in love with you." Jamie decided not to tell her about his suicide attempt. "You and Rusty have a chance."

"I want to, but I can't face Stub." Alice looked like a scared rabbit.

Jamie gave her a reassuring smile. "Vickie took care of him. He tried to rape me, and she broke his wrist. She told him she'd cut his balls off if he ever mistreated another woman. She was ferocious. I don't think you have to worry about him anymore."

Alice tried to laugh at the thought of Vickie slicing off the man's testicles, but her injured arm moved, and she winced in pain. "I do want to see Rusty," she gasped. She paused, waiting for the throbbing in her arm to subside. "How did you find me?"

"It's complicated. I was expelled from the settlement." Jamie told her about her dreams and how she had been accused of appropriating other people's memories. Alice looked at her friend suspiciously. "Don't worry, I can't read your mind. I just remember things."

"That's pretty weird, Jamie."

"I know. It's discouraging, too. I thought the memories were mine. I was hoping they were clues to who I was."

The sun settled in the east, and the ridge where the two women sat glowed in the horizontal shafts of light. The air was cool. Jamie unrolled her blanket, and they huddled under it. She wrapped her arm around her friend and smiled to herself. They were like two girlfriends on a sleepover. The fact that they were nestled on a narrow ledge, a hair's breadth from a hundred-meter drop, was just a bonus.

Alice pulled the blanket under her chin. "So you were kicked out of the settlement. That still doesn't tell me how you found me."

Jamie hesitated. She knew how crazy this part of her story would sound. "I walked south along the beach and then turned inland at a large river. There are strange plants in the jungle," she started. "They are the source of the jungle lights."

"The ones shaped like baskets?"

"That's right. We called them mantles. They glow when twilight falls. And here's the weird part: there's an alien presence in them." Alice gave her an indiscernible look. Jamie pleaded with her friend. "I know it sounds like I'm losing my mind, but they spoke to me."

"And they told you where I was." It wasn't a question.

"They gave me a vision. I saw this rocky hill. I saw you lying on the ledge. It was like they opened a channel between us, and your mind became a homing beacon, guiding me right to you." Alice was still for a moment. Jamie took her hand. It felt cold. "Do you believe me?"

"Yeah," her friend replied. "I had a strange dream last night. I knew you were coming."

* * *

Both women slept soundly. They awoke in the shadow of the mountain, the sun rising in the west. The morning breeze rippled through the jungle below them, and they could hear the faint clicking of the leaves, a concerto for alien wind chimes. The mountain distorted the flow of air, and a cool and gentle wind swept over them, a rare and welcome refreshment.

Alice looked better than she had the day before. The color had returned to her face, and she was moving with more energy. Jamie made a simple breakfast from her food supply, and Alice ate enthusiastically, another sign of her returning health.

"Do you think you can walk?" Jamie was wondering how they would ever get back to the settlement.

"If you help me up on my feet, I can make it."

Jamie offered her a hand, steadying herself on the rocky ledge. Alice rolled over until she was kneeling and gripped her friend's fingers tightly. Jamie leaned back, and the injured woman rose to her feet, unsteady at first and then with renewed confidence. Jamie stooped down and grabbed her pack. "We have to figure out how to get off this mountain," she mused.

* * *

The two women got back to the settlement the next day in the early afternoon. The main gate was closed. They stood outside the fence and shouted into the compound. Ben Beck appeared from behind the clinic building and trotted toward them. When he saw Jamie, a scowl appeared on his face. "What are you doing here?" he demanded. Then his demeanor changed. "Is that Alice?"

Within moments, the remaining colonists gathered at the entrance of the compound. Someone called for Rusty, and he came running as fast as his feet would carry him. Jamie stood back as Alice reached through the rails of the gate. Rusty threw himself at her with a primal cry of joy, hugging her with all his might. Bliss stood at a distance, grateful for Alice's safe return, but resigned to the fact that Rusty would never love her.

"I thought you were dead!" Rusty's eyes were red from lack of sleep, his face flooded with tears.

"Jamie found me."

"Let her in!" Vickie commanded. Ben unlatched the gate, and Alice slid through the gap between the posts.

Alice fell into Rusty's arms, wincing as he squeezed her. He relaxed his grip, seeing the bandage on her arm. He almost dropped his hands, but she stopped him. "Don't let me go," she pleaded.

The gate was still open, and Jamie started to follow Alice, but Vickie put her hand up. She was wearing her military face. "Not you, Jamie. You're still not welcome here." Ben closed the gate and engaged the latch.

Carter emerged from the back of the crowd. He took one look at Jamie and stepped back. He looked like a primitive hunter facing a mountain lion with his bare hands. He wore a mask of crazed paranoia. He looked away from her, his eyes darting from person to person. "Get away from us! I'll order Vickie to kill you if you don't leave!" Vickie grimaced and then looked at Jamie. A crack formed in her stern military demeanor, and she silently pleaded with her to follow Carter's orders.

Jamie squared her shoulders, knowing she had nothing more to lose. "There's intelligent life here." Silence swept over the settlement. Carter's eyes narrowed. He glanced at her again, unable to hide a look of sheer panic. Even Rusty turned his attention away from Alice. Jamie pressed up against the rails and reached through the perimeter fence in a pleading gesture. "You've got to listen to me. An entity spoke to me in the jungle and told me where to find Alice."

"You're lying!" Olivia snarled.

"But I found her. She was on a mountain southwest of here. There's no way I could have known that."

"And why in God's name would aliens help us?" Olivia was scared.

"I don't know."

Vickie's eyes narrowed, her inner warrior returned. She gripped her sidearm, unconvinced. "What do they look like?"

"They are the mantle plants."

Carter had moved closer, unconsciously drawn by Jamie's news. He pushed against the gate. "Plants can't speak!"

Jamie agreed. "They didn't talk. They spoke with ideas that flowed into my mind."

"They've brainwashed her!" Olivia cried. She clutched Carter's elbow. "They might attack us, honey."

Vickie stepped toward the gate. She was all business. "Do you think they are hostile?"

Jamie shook her head emphatically. "They won't hurt us."

"And you believed them?" Stub growled.

"They're instruments of Satan!" Olivia snorted.

Carter ignored her. His eyes lit up. "They knew where Alice was?"

"They did."

Carter turned to Ben. "Let her in!"

Ben looked at Vickie. She nodded, confirming the order. He opened the gate, and Jamie entered the compound. Bliss and Thomas wasted no time welcoming her with smiles and hugs. Carter insisted that everyone gather at the fire circle. This time, Jamie was given a place to sit. Carter knelt down before Jamie, as if he was consulting an oracle. "Where was this mantle?"

Jamie was taken aback by the man's intense interest. His fear was gone, and he drew close to her with immense curiosity. She felt uncomfortable and cleared her throat nervously. "I went south on the beach until I reached a large river. I followed it inland and found the mantle in a clearing. It was huge, easily twice as high as the ones we saw on your expedition." Carter was taking in her every word. "I camped there for the night. When the lights appeared, I heard the entity in my mind."

Carter leapt to his feet and began to pace back and forth in the circle, rubbing his hands incessantly. "We're going to mount another expedition." His eyes blazed with a passion born of insanity. "We're all going to go." There was an erratic bounce in his step, reminiscent of his crazed dance in the jungle. "Jamie will speak to the aliens in the mantle. She'll force them to tell us where Hip and the others are."

"Hip is dead, Carter." Olivia said it softly.

"Silence!" Everyone flinched as Carter lunged at her. Olivia cowered in her seat. He glared at her while pointing his finger at Jamie."They showed her where to find Alice, didn't they? They'll lead us to Hip. I know it! We will leave tomorrow. There will be no discussion about it!"

* * *

Everyone gathered at the gate at first light. They filed through the entrance. Ben took up the rear and pulled the gate closed behind them. They stood on the beach trail, the trees arching over the path. Carter raised his walking stick like Moses parting the Red Sea. "Be prepared for anything," he said with a voice quivering with maniacal fervor. "We were lucky on the last journey. I'm certain there are many dangers out there." Vickie rolled her eyes.

They retraced Jamie's route along the seashore, hiking southward through the heat of the day. Bliss walked next to her. "Carter's gotten worse since you left," she said quietly.

"I noticed." Jamie replied. "Why have the rest of you put up with it?"

"He's in charge. We can't disobey him."

"He's crazy. You've got to disobey him."

"He'll get better." Bliss threw her head back, raising her chin confidently. "He took Hip's death really bad, you know? He's got to get it out of his system."

Jamie snorted. "By dragging all of us out here? By making his denial the sole focus of our dialogue with a new life form? He needs sedation."

Bliss gestured toward Olivia, who was trudging through

the sand next to Carter. "Olivia has been real close to him the last few days." Bliss nodded like she was trying to convince herself. "She's helped him."

"Olivia only helps Olivia, Bliss. She wants to be our queen. She'll do anything to prop up her own importance."

"I don't know, Jamie." Bliss wasn't used to being decisive.

"Olivia is no help to him at all. She's just reinforcing his delusions."

"Carter is a good man. He won't do any harm, Jamie. We all know what's going on. We can deal with it."

Jamie studied Bliss's face. She was looking down at the sand, following the tracks left by the person in front of her. Bliss couldn't see Carter's flaws. She had not seen his unfettered rage. She hadn't seen the way he had destroyed the mantle plant on the first expedition. Her friend wanted desperately for things to be better, for their world to be happy and bright. Jamie sighed. "I hope so, Bliss." She knew Carter was leading them toward disaster.

* * *

They made camp on the warm sands as the sun dipped low on the horizon. The sky resolved into deeper shades of violet, and Alathea's rings became more prominent, their golden bands shimmering through the planet's atmosphere. Rusty and Alice were inseparable. Rachel the medic had tended to Alice's broken arm, and it was cradled in a proper sling. Jamie had been concerned about her friend's injuries, but Alice's reunion with her lover had infused her with new energy, and she had kept up with the group.

The murmur of conversations as everyone settled in for the night reminded Jamie of their first evening on Alathea.

The chatter was charged with anxiety and expectancy. Jamie wondered what would happen the following night when they stood before the large mantle that had guided her to Alice. She knew the mantle would not lead them to Hip. He was dead, lying in a simple grave on the north end of the settlement compound. What would Carter do?

CHAPTER SEVENTEEN
Chaos

T he next day, they stood on the bank of the wide river, where it emptied into the alien sea. Its waters popped and gurgled over occasional rocks that protruded above the waterline, creating eddy currents across the turbulent surface. Bliss dipped her hand into the water. She withdrew it and flicked her fingers at Thomas. He ducked reflexively as the droplets cascaded over his face.

"Stop that!" He laughed, cupping one hand and scooping it down into the river. He scraped the surface and sent a showing spray in Bliss's direction. She dodged, but not fast enough, the water spattering her midriff.

Jamie smiled at their playfulness and turned back to the group. Rusty had Alice wrapped in his arms. He was looking directly at Jamie. His face became hard as their eyes met. He glanced down at Alice, then looked up again and gave Jamie a subtle nod. It was an olive branch. She turned away, still wounded by how he had ostracized her.

Carter's eyes never left the river, gauging the width and depth of the water. "How do we cross it?" he asked.

"We don't," Jamie replied. "This is where I went inland."

Carter nodded, directing them to follow the tributary into the jungle. The colonists formed a column, walking two abreast. Bliss made a point of walking next to Thomas, while Rusty and Alice followed behind them. Jamie took the lead as they pressed onward along the river's edge. The mouth of the river disappeared behind them, and soon they were threading their way along the narrow strip of land that separated the jungle and the river. At first, the bank was covered with the ubiquitous crimson sod, making it easy to walk. After a while, their path was pinched off by tall bulrushes, which clogged the space between the water and the trees.

"Look at the cat tails!" exclaimed Thomas. He reached for one of the tall plants that crowded the riverbank. "We used to make torches out of these when I was a kid!" Jamie saw a glimpse of the boy in the man. He plucked one of the stems and ran his finger across the thick, furry head, which resembled a hotdog. Bliss stepped to his side and reached across him to touch the plant. Her hand brushed his fingers.

"We'll have to move away from the riverbank," Jamie said flatly. "It's too hard to walk through the tall plants." She ducked between two trees, and the others followed her. They began to work their way through the jungle. At first, they meandered between the trees, tracing their way between the roots. Carter grew impatient with their slow progress, and they began to climb over the long wooden cylinders. The roots were larger in this part of the jungle. Jamie remembered listening to the rushing sound within them. Their size was probably due to the proximity of the river.

They came to the first mantle plant in the late morning. Surprisingly, Carter let them linger in the small clearing. Those who had never seen the odd plants stood with wonder laced with fear. They all realized this was the alien life form with extrasensory powers. Bliss walked right up to the mantle and marveled at its intricately woven bulb. "It's like a wicker

201

Easter egg sitting in a big bird's nest, you know?" she observed. "Where does the light come from?"

Thomas stepped quickly to her side. Their hips met. He described how the mantle ignited, first with a tiny spark and then a controlled eruption of plasma. Jamie couldn't help but notice how the two shared each other's personal space. They had become a couple, the holy man and the bimbo. Jamie chastised herself for characterizing her friend in such an unkindly manner, but the words had popped into her head, and they fit. She watched as the two orbited the mantle plant. Bliss would turn quickly to him, expressing her delight in some discovery. Thomas was attentive, authentically interested in her. There was a kindness between them, not a bad basis for a love affair and whatever lay beyond it.

Olivia jabbed at the mantle's lantern with a stern finger. "Don't!" shouted Jamie, but she was too late. Olivia's uncompromising finger punched a jagged hole into the bulb, sending shards of delicate fibers in all directions. "It's very fragile," Jamie told her.

"I can see that!" she snapped. "I would think aliens would be heartier."

Rusty sat on the far side of the mantle, his digital canvas in his lap. Alice was perched over his shoulder, watching him sketch. Jamie came around behind them, careful to remain out of Rusty's line of sight. She was curious, but still unsure of him. Alice smiled as she approached. Jamie leaned over her. Rusty was replicating the pattern in the mantle's woven basket in amazing detail.

"Are they all like this?" Rusty asked without taking his eyes off the plant. Jamie was startled. She hadn't expected him to speak to her.

"Each one is different," Alice responded. "They're like

snowflakes."

Jamie kicked herself. Rusty hadn't seen her at all. The question had been for Alice. She backed away quietly and almost bumped into Carter. She recoiled from him, stepping back as she regained her balance. Carter was incapable of apologizing, a single focus driving him. "Is this the one that spoke to you?"

"No. It's still a few hours away."

Carter shrugged impatiently. "These things all look alike to me. How will you recognize the right one?"

Jamie could tell that Carter had no interest in the mantles. He didn't notice their uniqueness and seemed indifferent to the wondrous fire that erupted inside their fragile body. He was a man possessed by a concern that dwarfed all others: the recovery of Hip. He saw the mantle as a means to an end, a way to find his dead friend. Jamie doubted resurrection was in the aliens' skill set.

"Well?" Carter glared at her impatiently. "How do you pick out the one that talks?"

Jamie snapped out of her muse. "The one that communicated with me was very large, twice the size of this one."

"Must be their leader," Carter murmured. "He should have the answers."

Jamie was astonished. She had seen nothing to suggest any sort of hierarchy among the mantles, and there was no clue to their gender. Carter was drawing conclusions from nonexistent facts.

"Break's over! Let's get moving, people!" Carter's voice was shrill. He made wild gestures with his walking stick, urging everyone to take up their packs and continue into the jungle. He swung his body drunkenly and overcorrected as he pivoted toward Jamie. "Okay, Miss Mind Reader, show us the way."

* * *

Jamie kept her thoughts to herself as the morning wore on. They were on a fool's errand. Everyone knew it, but no one dared question Carter. He had everyone under his thumb, pushing them forward by the sheer force of his crazed will. She could not discern the future, but she knew they were doomed if something wasn't done about Carter.

Midday came and went. Carter refused to stop for lunch, demanding that everyone eat as they walked. Even Olivia was losing her grip on the man. She demanded that they stop for a potty break, and he did so grudgingly. The stern woman was still zipping up her jumpsuit when Carter compelled them to move on. Finally, Jamie could see the clearing up ahead of them. The giant mantle squatted in the middle of the glade. A tangle of vine-like stems formed the familiar "bird's nest" under the massive basket, whose narrow end reached for the sky.

Everyone dropped their packs gratefully. Some collapsed to the ground, while others perched on the massive tree roots which radiated out from the mantle. They were all exhausted except Carter, who bounced around the clearing with enthusiasm.

Jamie was sitting near the plant's base, swigging water from her bottle, when Carter nudged her with his foot. "Talk to it," he commanded. "Make it tell us where Hip is."

"It communicates when it is glowing," she countered. "We can't do anything until then."

Carter looked up at the sky, twisting his fingers into a knot. "How long until twilight?"

Vickie checked her watch. She had adjusted it to coincide with Alathea's thirty-two hour rotational period. "About four hours, sir."

"Damn it!" Carter was itchy and breathless, unable to contain his unrealistic excitement. He was worse than a child on Christmas Eve.

* * *

The rest of the day wore on intolerably, at a snail's pace. Jamie sat by herself. She could tell there was a lingering anxiety among the others. They weren't near her by choice. It was Carter who had compelled everyone to come on this expedition. All things being equal, damn few of them would have been within a kilometer of her. Bliss and Thomas were the exceptions, but presently they were sitting on the other side of the clearing, preoccupied with each other. They were long past friendship. She envied them.

Thoughts of Hip sifted into Jamie's consciousness. She remembered caressing his leg in the clinic and her hopes for a deeper relationship with the man. The sum total of their fleeting romance was a single touch. Nevertheless, she yearned for him more deeply than Carter did. He had been a kind man, a generous spirit. He had put the welfare of others ahead of himself. She wondered if Hip could have opened his heart to her and embraced her as a mate. She would have been thrilled to have his hand in hers, have his life surround her. Jamie sighed. Hip was an intensely loyal man. His guilt over his wife's death had run deep and cold within him. As fond as he was of her, he would never have been able to let go of his sorrow. Hip would have remained faithful to his wife, no matter how long he might have lived.

Jamie glanced across the clearing at Carter. He sat sullenly by Olivia's side, fingering his walking stick and eyeing the mantle suspiciously. She marveled at the way Hip had been able to reason with the man. She remembered countless occasions when he would take Carter aside and speak to him in low tones, cajoling him into a good decision. She remembered how angry Hip had been when Carter planned the lottery. Hip had been the voice of reason. If Hip were still alive, Carter would be in his right mind. They would be back in the settlement, building a new society instead of traipsing around in the jungle on a wild goose chase.

"Jamie?" She sat up, her back as straight as a ramrod. The voice was coming from behind her. It was Rusty. She turned quickly, her eyes first settling on his shock of red hair, then on the bandages still covering his damaged wrists. She nodded to him, but every cell of her body was on high alert. "Do you mind?" He gestured to the space next to her. Jamie shrugged.

Rusty settled down on the sod beside her. He crossed his legs and let his arms fall into his lap. There was an awkward silence. Jamie waited, unwilling to speak to him. "Thanks for finding Alice," he began. Jamie didn't move. "I..." his voice trailed off as he searched for the right words. "I haven't been myself lately." He looked up at her, hoping for some sign that she was listening. Jamie was a human stone. "I'm sorry for how I reacted to you in the clinic."

Jamie wondered what she was supposed to say. She had been trying to comfort the man. The realization that her memories actually belonged to Rusty was as traumatic to her as it was to him. Nobody had looked at it from her point of view, except Thomas and Bliss.

"I wanted to die." Rusty continued. "I was mad at you for stopping me. Then you started talking about Camille..." He grew silent again, a sea of pain lapping on the shoreline of his heart. Jamie stole a quick peek. The man was shaking. Their eyes met for an instant. "I was wrong about you. I shouldn't have told Carter to throw you out of the community." Jamie felt a lump rising in her throat. She turned her head, her cold eyes measuring his sincerity. "I don't know if we can be friends again," he continued. "But I know I can't stand being your enemy."

Rusty dropped his chin and looked down at his wrist bandages. Jamie looked at them again. Suddenly, she realized he couldn't look her in the face. The man was ashamed. Something melted in her. She felt his pain as if it was her own. She reached over and touched his hand, the artist's hand, the slender fingers that put a stylus to canvas, translating reality into sublime beauty. She heard Rusty suck in a jagged breath. Slowly, he looked up, offering her a look of contrition. "I'm trying to understand, Rusty," she said softly. Jamie wanted her words to convey the truth she was feeling. "I need some time." She paused. "But I still want to be your friend."

Rusty's eyes glistened. He nodded slowly as Jamie withdrew her hand. She couldn't forgive him yet, but she knew that time would come.

* * *

When dinner was over, and daylight was finally yielding to the coming night, Carter compelled everyone to settle into a circle around the mantle plant. He insisted on everyone holding hands. Jamie refused. The whole thing was too bazaar, like some kind of séance. A silence descended over the group as twilight began to fall. Several members of the group were nervous, having never been in the jungle after dark. Bliss clung to Thomas, and Olivia struggled to maintain her bitchy attitude. Rusty sat quietly next to Alice, his hand on her knee.

The mantle ignited, and startled exclamations rippled through the group. Everyone was bathed in the intense green light. The massive plant was brighter by an order of magnitude than any other mantle they had seen. "Be quiet!" Carter demanded, cutting off everyone's sense of wonder. He turned to Jamie. "Speak to it!"

Jamie cleared her mind. She could sense the murmurings as they wandered gently into her consciousness. The idea returned to her. "We are glad you found your friend on the mountain," it said softly. "You have brought all of your companions with you. We are honored."

Jamie relaxed as the link between her mind and the mantle plant coalesced, forming a bridge of intellectual awareness. She reached out toward the pulsating light and spread her fingers, as if to embrace the photons as they burst from the fragile plant. "It's good to be with you," she whispered.

"Ask it where Hip is!" Carter interrupted.

Jamie was submerged in the idea's presence, unprovoked by the man's insistence. "Where is the one we call Hip?" she asked. A part of her wished the alien presence could reverse time and resurrect her friend.

"You already know the answer to that question. Hip died in the storm. His body was placed in the ground, according to your custom."

"I know," she said meekly. "Some of us believe he is still alive."

"His body is dead, but his memories live."

Jamie had no time to consider what the idea meant. Carter was hovering over her, his anger threatening. Somehow she had to mollify him. "How can I comfort those who do not believe this?"

"Delusion is Carter's opiate. He must accept his pain and guilt if he is to face reality. That is the only path that will lead him to sanity."

Carter grabbed Jamie's arm. She flinched as the outer world collided with her inner dialogue. "What did it say? Where is Hip?"

Jamie excused herself from the idea and turned to Carter. She braced herself for the rage that was imminent and spoke to him with a firm and steady voice. "Hip is dead. His body is where we buried it in the compound."

Blood coursed into Carter's face as his anger erupted. He was holding his walking stick in one hand. "No!" He raised the stick. "This alien is reading our minds! It's trying to seduce us with lies! We must stop it! Stop them all!" He swung the stick. Jamie ducked, the shaft whistling centimeters over her head and shattering the mantle's basket.

There were screams as the light was snuffed out, the brilliant plasma erupting from its disintegrated vessel and evaporating into the air above the clearing. Pieces of unraveled weave showered over everyone. Carter was beside himself, raging at the jungle, smashing every last vestige of the delicate plant. He stomped the broken pieces into the crimson grass. Jamie fell to the ground. It was like her breath was sucked out of her lungs, leaving her gasping for air. The idea collapsed in her consciousness and for a brief, horrifying moment, she could hear the mantle scream.

* * *

Everyone settled in for the night after Carter's outburst. No one dared to challenge the man. Jamie pulled the blanket around her shoulders, pleading for sleep to come and take her away from the sound she had heard in her mind. The scream that echoed within her was laced with astonishment and sadness. The idea's last expression was utter disbelief in Carter's inhumanity. Every mantle in the jungle had extinguished when Carter immolated the giant lantern, casting the clearing and perhaps the entire hemisphere into darkness.

Jamie was numb. She had been fully linked with the alien being. She had felt Carter's blow in her mind. A flash of pain had shot through her as the thought-bridge collapsed, leaving a horrific void. Then there was the painful and utter silence. Her mind shut down, unable to think and reason. It was as if a piece of her own living force had died with the plant.

* * *

Jamie stirred as the first fingers of morning light began to sift their way down to the jungle floor. Leaves were already beginning to fall from the nearby trees, transforming the red grass into a dull brown carpet of hard, fibrous triangles. Carter was straddling one of the thick roots like a warrior on his armored steed. His walking stick was propped next to him, and he was hard at work, whittling one just like it. Jamie looked down at the ground beneath his feet. A dozen more staffs were piled there. Carter was making weapons.

The other's stirred. One by one they rose from their blankets, wandering off into the wood to pee. Carter handed a walking stick to each of them as they returned to the clearing.

"What are you doing, Carter?" Jamie asked.

The man pulled himself up straight and ran his fingers through his tangled hair. He had a wild look in his eyes, and his temper was barely in check. "Today we are going to kill the aliens. We will comb the jungle and destroy every mantle we find."

"No!" Jamie shouted. "You can't do that."

"I can, and I will, Lizzie." His eyes blazed at her.

Something clicked in Jamie's head. "What did you call me?"

"Jamie."

"No you didn't. You called me Lizzie."

Carter shuddered. "Whatever."

Jamie remembered the dream where she was running in the forest. Her little sister was chasing her. She remembered calling to her and hiding behind a tree that stood on the rim of a deep canyon. The puzzle pieces began to snap together. She took a step toward him. "Your name isn't Carter, is it?"

"That's ridiculous!" shouted the man.

"Your name is Howard."

Carter froze. Jamie knew it was the truth. "How do you know that?" he gasped.

Jamie's voice softened. "It wasn't your fault."

"What are you talking about?"

"Lizzie. Your little sister."

Carter dropped his bundle of walking sticks. Jamie held fast, pressing her fear down, refusing to be overcome by it. "The day Lizzie died. She was chasing you in the forest. She fell over the cliff."

The blood drained from Carter's face. "You can't possibly know that!"

"I remember it like it was yesterday. You've been beating yourself up for years over that day. It was an accident. It wasn't your fault."

Carter spread his hands. He gave her an evil smile. "You don't know anything! You might remember what happened, but you don't know the whole story."

Jamie stepped even closer to him. "I know you enjoyed watching her fall." A look of fear crossed the man's face.

"You were young, Carter. You didn't realize how final death was. You were twisted by the guilt."

Carter reached for her, grabbing her shoulder with one hand and clamping the other over her mouth. "These aliens are attacking our minds. I can feel it!" He swung Jamie around so she was in front of him. He wrapped his arm across her chest, looking at the startled colonists. They were stunned. "Listen to her! She's already been possessed! We must defend ourselves!" He threw Jamie to the ground. "We'll sweep the jungle and kill them all!"

"You're crazy." Jamie scrambled to her feet. She turned to Vickie. "Can't you see it? He's lost his mind. Don't do this. These mantle plants are living beings. They mean us no harm!"

Carter stooped down and grabbed his staff. He raised it menacingly. "I'll kill you if you get in our way."

Rusty stepped in front of Jamie, facing Carter. "You aren't going to hurt her."

"Who's going to stop me, little artist man?" Carter swung his walking stick and struck Rusty on the side of the head. There was a resounding "Crack!" as he fell to the ground. Alice screamed and rushed to his side. Blood was flowing down his cheek.

"There's no place for you here." Carter tried to jab Jamie in the stomach, but she sidestepped his thrust and stepped back. He cursed at her and raised the staff like a club.

"Stop it!" Jamie shouted. "I'll go!"

Alice was helping Rusty to his feet. "We're going with her," she announced.

Carter curled his lip into a sneer. "That is fine by me!"

Thomas and Bliss stepped forward. "We're leaving, too."

212

Thomas said.

"Makes sense," said the madman. "First you abandon God, and now you abandon me!" The two couples joined Jamie at the edge of the clearing. Carter glared at the rest of the colonists. "Any other traitors?" No one moved. He swiveled toward Jamie and her friends. "Get out of here!"

They grabbed their packs and blankets and left the others in the clearing. Jamie wanted to turn back and stop Carter from his deadly campaign, but Thomas restrained her. "Vickie and Ben have real weapons, Jamie. You'll get yourself killed."

She felt a wave of despair wash over her. The aliens were about to experience the ugly side of humanity. They had no superior firepower, no lethal technology that threatened the human race. They were helpless in the face of Carter's brutality. Jamie bent over and threw up, the acidic bile burning her throat.

CHAPTER EIGHTEEN
Alexia

J amie and the others resolved to go back to the
settlement. She led her companions back to the
seashore, and they turned northward. No one spoke
during the long trek. Jamie let the others go on ahead of her
as they padded their way through the pale green sand. There
were five of them, leaving eleven others in Carter's group.

The rift among the colonists frightened her. Every person
was needed if they were going to survive. They had to heal
the rupture in the community. Jamie hoped Carter would
calm down after his rant in the jungle. She stopped short.
What was she thinking? Waiting for Carter to regain his sanity
was a fool's errand. How long could sane people put up with
a leader like Carter? History was rife with examples from
Berlin to Jonestown. People had a habit of looking the other
way, hoping for the best, adapting to the dysfunctional, and
deferring their own sense of right and wrong in order to avoid
confrontation.

Jamie thought of Carter's genocidal crusade. Her heart
ached. Contact with the alien had been like dipping her toe
into a deep pool of knowledge. There was so much more to
learn, a deeper friendship to fathom. Now, Carter was waging

a meaningless war, wiping out a humble race of mental giants. Her sense of loss was staggering.

Jamie remembered the first time she had seen a mantle plant. She remembered touching it, how easy it had been to crumble the lacing of its basket. The strange plant held such magnificent light in its fragile bag of sticks. The mantles were much like them. She and her companions were fragile creatures, skin and bone. Each of them held a burning ember, a value, a talent, a dream. How easily things were broken.

Suddenly, Jamie was startled by a mental flash. She could feel the mantles dying. She shivered at the thought of the carnage taking place in the jungle. Carter and the others were hacking the delicate plants into firewood. Distant whispers called out to her. She sensed pain and sorrow, but no anger. How could these living things face such aggression without enmity? She heard indistinct voices. Then she heard a single word. "Why?" the idea asked. "Why?" She had no answer.

* * *

Jamie and her four companions were back in the compound, sitting around the barren fire circle. "What are we going to do?" Thomas knit his fingers together tightly. Bliss clung to his arm, a serious expression etched on her face.

Alice rubbed a sore muscle in her left thigh. "I've been thinking about that." She gave her friends a hard look. "We've got to shake Carter out of his denial. As long as he believes Hip is alive, he's going to keep looking for him. His quest is more important than our survival."

"But how do we do that?" Bliss asked. "He's really set on it."

"I don't think it's possible," Jamie mused. "He's crazy. We have to stop him, remove him from power."

"There's a way, but none of you are going to like it." Alice's mouth was drawn into a thin line. Her eyes were hard, her expression chiseled.

"How?" Jamie was skeptical.

"We exhume Hip's body." Alice gestured toward the lone grave at the north end of the compound. "We show it to Carter. He'll have to accept it."

Jamie's heart skipped a beat as she thought of the man she had almost loved. Seeing Hip's corpse after being in the ground for weeks would be repulsive. He hadn't been embalmed. His body would be bloated. There would be an awful smell. She even wondered if he would be recognizable. She shuttered at the thought of seeing his body like that. Still, Alice's idea had merit.

"It might work." Thomas rubbed his hands together unconsciously.

Jamie nodded her head, a knot of anxiety choking her. "Let's do it."

* * *

They dug into the dense, fibrous sod and gently pulled Hip's body from its resting place. Jamie wept openly as they prepared their friend's remains for viewing. Their greatest fears were realized, his corpse bloated and discolored by death. Bliss brought a pail of water from the shore, and they carefully washed Hip's body, making it as presentable as they could. Alice found some fragrant spices in one of the supply sheds, and they applied them like salve to mask the odor of death and decay. Jamie found a fresh jumpsuit, and they slid it over his cold, lifeless flesh. Finally, Rusty and Thomas laid Hip on a blanket and propped his head up on a cushion. It was the best they could do.

* * *

The others returned as twilight was falling on the compound. Carter marched through the main gate with his head held high. He brandished his walking stick like a monarch's scepter. Olivia was by his side, basking in the artificial glow of her little man. They were exhausted warriors, having poured themselves out on the field of battle. They had vanquished their helpless foe, crushing the innocent and snuffing out the alien voices of wisdom and reason.

Carter drew to a stop when he saw Jamie and her companions sitting around the fire circle. He called Vickie to his side and muttered a few words to her under his breath. The security officer didn't look happy, but she followed his orders, ripping the Velcro closure open on her sidearm. Carter raised his staff. "Jamie, I want you to leave! You are no longer one of us."

Jamie got to her feet and walked purposefully toward them. She wanted to yell back at him, curse him for killing the mantles. However, she held her emotions close, remaining calm. "We have something to show you, Carter." She didn't dare call him Howard.

Carter met her gaze and drove his staff into the ground in front of him. "Get out! I want nothing to do with you!" he said firmly. Vickie drew her weapon unwillingly. She pointed it toward the ground.

"We found Hip," Jamie said softly.

"What?" It was clear that Carter had not expected this. He dropped his walking stick and took a step forward. "What did you say?"

Jamie spoke a little louder. "We found Hip."

Carter rushed toward her. The threatening look on his

face was replaced with boyish excitement. "Where is he?"

Jamie gestured toward the north end of the compound. "He's back there."

Carter pushed past her and ran toward the place where Hip's body lay. He fell to his knees and threw his arms around the corpse. "Hip! Where have you been?" His words morphed into deep guttural sobs. He cradled his friend's body, rocking it back and forth.

Jamie and the others circled around Hip's body. Vickie put her sidearm back in its holster. They stood solemnly, waiting for Carter to pour out all the grief that had been tormenting him. Finally, Carter pulled himself up and looked closely at Hip's swollen face. He wiped one of his tears from the dead man's cheek and straightened a crease in the blanket that was covering the body. He got to his feet slowly, shaking his head. Then he turned to Jamie. "Your trick almost worked," he said softly. "You had me going for a minute, but I'm too smart for you."

There was a collective gasp. Vickie's face had a grayish cast. Olivia was speechless. "What do you mean?" Jamie asked him.

"That isn't Hip!" he shouted. Everyone took a step back, rage returning to Carter's face. "I don't know who that is," he said flatly. "That man is dead. Hip is alive!"

Thomas rolled his eyes. Even Olivia seemed crestfallen by Carter's refusal to accept his friend's death. Carter grabbed Jamie by the shoulders. He shook her with blind fury. "Get out of my settlement. Go out there and die!" He pushed her out of the circle, toward the main gate.

"If she goes, we all go!" shouted Bliss. Thomas stepped to her side, his arms folded in defiance.

Carter wheeled around to face them. "Not this time. The rest of you are needed here. Vickie? Ben? Confine these two!" He gestured toward Bliss and Thomas. Then he whipped around to face Rusty and Alice. "You two go with them. Jamie is on her own. She's been the cause of all our trouble!" Vickie looked sick, but she did as she was told, hustling the two couples toward the shed where Jamie had taken refuge during the storm. Bliss gazed defiantly at Ben Beck as she passed him. The guard looked down at the ground, embarrassed.

Jamie turned away from them and walked dejectedly toward the gate. There was nothing else she could do. The second expedition had only been a temporary reprieve. Carter still feared her. Confronting him with his sister Lizzie's death had been a calculated risk, and it had backfired. She had burned the bridge between them. She knew her fate was sealed.

"Stop!" Carter's voice was shrill. Jamie paused, but didn't turn around. "Leave the jumpsuit," he commanded. Jamie turned around, a look of disbelief on her face. "We need it here," he said. Stub was grinning, his crooked teeth a ragged patch of white in the faltering light.

Jamie didn't utter a word. She turned around and unzipped the suit. She let it fall over her shoulders. She pushed the loose fabric away from her hips and let the jumpsuit fall to the ground. Jamie stepped out of the suit and kicked it aside. Then she stood motionless in front of them. She made no attempt to cover herself, but stood defiantly with her feet planted wide on the worn crimson grass. Olivia turned away in embarrassment. Jamie gave everyone a piercing glare, daring them to see every inch of her and what they had permitted Carter to do. Then, she turned and walked slowly out of the compound.

* * *

The evening breeze blew gently over Jamie's skin, but she did not feel it. She had no food, no clothing, no shelter. She might last a few days, but she would die naked and alone. She walked listlessly along the beach trail and paused as it opened out upon the seashore. The mirror moon and her opaque sister cast milky light on the sand, now a shade of gray in the twilight. Should she walk into the surf and swim as long as she could until she drowned? Jamie wasn't suicidal. It was a cruel joke. She had known other times like this, times when her despair had tempted her with taking her own life. It had scoffed at her, reminding her of how easy it would be. Even so, she could never act on such thoughts. It wasn't in her.

Jamie made her way to the mouth of the small river. Its contents cascaded over the waterfall, its sound a soothing lullaby. She found her flat rock near the river's edge. She had spent hours there, trying to remember who she was. She sat on it. The stone was still warm from the long afternoon sun and felt good on her skin. She leaned back on her palms, facing the sea. Her eyes were locked on the far horizon, the sounds of the surf washing over her. There was no hope, she reasoned. Whatever life she once lived on Earth was lost to her. Perhaps it didn't matter. For all intents and purposes, she had died in hibernation. For the first time, Jamie ceased worrying about who she was.

Jamie thought about the rest of the colonists, how they had stared at her as she surrendered her clothing and stood before them. Figuratively, they were all naked. Their days were numbered. Food supplies were running low. There were no crops in the garden to sustain them. Carter would preside over the slow and agonizing death of every man and woman. Alathea would hardly notice that they had ever been there. Her ocean would continue to lap against her shores. The mantles would multiply somehow and repopulate the jungle.

Storms would howl across her alien landscape and wipe away all evidence of their presence. She thought again of Rusty's story about keeping balance. What had he said? "This too shall pass." Homeostasis, nature's great balancer, would win in the end. Alathea would be the only survivor.

The evening breeze kicked up a mild chop, and the light from the moons and the golden rings sparkled on the ocean's surface like tiny diamonds. Jamie remembered seeing Rusty and Alice playing in the water. She was glad that she had joined them. Jamie lowered herself down upon the stone. Its warmth permeated her back, relaxing her muscles. She rocked her hips and pointed her toes. She took in the expanse of heaven, the stars peeking out from their places in the firmament. Then, having drunk in their beauty, she closed her eyes.

"We are here," said the idea. Jamie's eyes snapped open. She didn't expect the inner voice to speak. Her heart raced, and she felt a surge of euphoria as the idea returned to her mind. "We are here, young one." The idea was more distinct, now. The willowy boundary between them dissolved like a morning fog, and Jamie was surrounded by the alien presence.

Jamie was confused. She had seen Carter destroy the large mantle plant. The voices had been truncated by his brutal slashes. "We are not part of the mantle." The presence had read her thoughts. The idea's intimacy radiated warmth throughout her body like a long, slow coupling with a trusted lover.

Jamie closed her eyes again and imagined what she wanted to say. "You spoke to me when the mantles were glowing."

"That is true," replied the idea. "The mantles amplified our thoughts. They made it easier for you to hear us. You know our voices now. You can listen on your own."

221

Jamie thought again. "I heard the mantles dying."

"Your friend Carter and the others caused great damage, but they did not kill them."

A wave of relief coursed through her. "The mantles survived?"

"They are broken, but they are not dead. They will grow back, and their children will bear leaves again."

"The dead trees will live?"

The idea sighed, an immense mental breath. "They shed their leaves, much like the trees on your Earth once did. They look dead, but they are sleeping, waiting for life to flow once more."

Jamie sensed the incredible expanse of the alien's knowledge. She felt like an explorer, standing at the water's edge of an iceberg and sensing a fraction of what was hidden beneath the surface. "How do you know this?"

"We have spoken to the mantles. We have learned from their memories."

"How can plants remember?" Jamie wondered.

"It's not so strange, young one. The trees on your Earth remember the seasons. They record their memories in their rings."

Jamie struggled to shed her preconceived notions. She had assumed her dreams had revealed her missing memories, but they had not. She believed the mantle plants were the aliens, but she was mistaken. Now she realized how little she knew about the idea. Nothing was how it first appeared. "If you aren't the mantle plants, what are you?"

"Look up, child," whispered the idea.

Jamie opened her eyes. The stars now blazed in the

heavens. The mirrored moon and her sister hugged the far horizon. Alathea's golden rings shimmered in the darkened sky. "You are the rings?"

"We resemble planetary rings when we embrace a world."

Jamie wondered if she had fallen asleep. Perhaps she was dreaming. She pinched her forearm, and it stung. She was awake. Jamie looked up at the rings. She had become used to the golden light that caressed the landscape after sunset. She looked at the sea and the sand. Then her eyes drifted across the river and finally came to rest on her body. She imagined what she must look like from the aliens' point of view. She was a tiny sack of naked flesh on a warm stone. They couldn't be impressed. Talking to her was like carrying on a conversation with a hamburger in a skillet. "Why are you talking to me?"

"We are very old," said the idea. "We followed your spacecraft from Earth. We travel like the cosmic dust that flows through space on the solar winds. When we saw you settle into orbit around this planet, we coalesced into our present form. We are your students. We wish to learn from you."

Jamie laughed out loud. "What are you studying, frustration? I know a lot about that."

The idea laughed and then grew serious. "You have many memories."

"The only recollections I have belong to other people." Jamie couldn't hide her emptiness.

"There is much more to you than you know, young one." The idea whispered with a godlike voice." You have a depth beyond your imagining."

"Then tell me who I am and why I'm here!" Jamie was

desperate.

"You already know who you are," the idea replied.

"No I don't!" Jamie exclaimed. "I can't remember."

"Open your mind," urged the Rings.

Jamie reached back into her memories. She remembered Carter's two expeditions into the jungle. She remembered the violent storm. She remembered landing on Alathea. She felt a curtain begin to drop, separating her from her past. She thought of the days on the pod ship and pushed back to the moments after she woke up from hibernation. She strained to remember something before that, but she could not.

The alien presence stood with her like a sentinel in her mind. "Don't struggle, young one. Your past will come back to you." The Rings of Alathea soothed her.

"There's a wall," Jamie said softly. "It's been there ever since I woke on the pod ship. I can't get around it."

The idea whispered in her mind. "Describe the wall."

Jamie had been so focused on her missing memories; she had never considered the barrier that was keeping them from her. "It's like a curtain, made of a thick, gauzy material. It's black."

"What kind of black?" probed the idea.

"How should I know? It's dark."

"How dark?" asked the Rings.

Jamie was exasperated. "I said it's black." She scrunched her face as she concentrated on the barrier. "Wait. It's not black." She corrected herself. "It's grayish." The curtain shimmered as faint shadows began to move across its dark surface. It was like looking at a photographic negative. There were blurry images beyond the wall, indistinct suggestions of her former life.

The dark wall became as white as snow. Jamie squinted with her mind to see the image. Suddenly, the vision surrounded her, enveloping her in the scene. Beneath her, the flat stone was transformed into an operating table, and the surrounding landscape became a gleaming white room. Doctors were gathered around her.

"What are they doing to me?" she gasped.

"Don't you remember?" asked the Rings.

She did. "They put something into my head."

"You received a great gift."

"What was it?"

"Perhaps it would be easier if we showed you."

Jamie awoke in a dream. She was back on Earth, before the pod ship had launched. This time, the flat stone was a bed. A serious man with sad eyes stood next to her. He was holding her hand. The man was trembling. "You need to know something before you go," he was saying. "Your implant is different from the others. Each colonist was given an injection containing billions of artificial memory cells. Each was given a different piece of our collective knowledge. They have no idea what they are carrying. Together, you possess the chronicle of human history. You, my dear, are the nexus. You are the one who will bring everyone's knowledge together when you settle on your new world." Jamie shuttered at the memory, then she studied the man's face. He was her father.

Memories of Jamie's childhood flooded back to her. She remembered her parents, eating a meal at their beach house, the first young man to kiss her. She could see the faces of her girlhood friends, hear the echoes of her favorite music, taste the cake at her sixteenth birthday party. "Poppa!" She opened her eyes. The Rings of Alathea greeted her above the ocean's gentle waves. She was alone on the rock by the gurgling stream. She buried her face in her hands.

Nothing could have prepared her for what happened next. Jamie felt a great vault opening in her mind. She guessed that everything in the mental depository was part of the device the doctors had placed in her skull. Beyond the door was an avalanche of experience; billions of strangers' lives were unfolding before her. Jamie felt like she was drowning. She felt herself sinking into a sea of endless voices, each calling to her like a desperate carnival barker at a cerebral county fair. She gasped for breath, her survival instincts kicking in. "Make it stop!" she screamed.

The Rings spoke softly. "You must not look at everything at once. It will destroy you."

Jamie struggled to quiet her mind, but the immensity of the knowledge was stunning. The door of the vault closed, and she breathed easier.

"Concentrate on this memory," urged the idea.

Alathea's Rings directed Jamie to a place in the far recesses of her mind. She saw an ornate doorway with nine glass panels. A foyer lay beyond it. There was a hardwood floor and a mahogany desk. Jamie put her palm on the door, and it opened effortlessly. She stepped over the threshold and found herself in an enormous library. A room beyond the foyer held more books than she could count. They were ancient volumes made of paper and ink, the bindings embossed with gold and silver lettering.

A cheerful woman with an impish smile walked up to her. "Welcome!" she said. "Let me tell you about my library. I can tell you have never been here before." The woman said it kindly, without any hint of superiority. "For those unfamiliar with libraries, this place is overwhelming. All you see is a mass of books, all blurring together, offending the eye and confounding the mind. However, I am a librarian. I see every single volume. Each book has a title and an author. Each book has a story to tell. Each one has a point of view. Taken one at a time, these treasures will expand your universe."

Jamie emerged from the vision. The Rings were waiting for her. "You must discipline your mind to survive," the idea said. "Microscopic memory will allow you to focus on each memory in fine detail. Macroscopic memory will protect you from the minutia and allow you to see the broad scope of history. Both points of view are essential for wisdom, but you must learn the difference between them. That way, the memories will not overwhelm you."

Thus far, Jamie's dreams and memories had taken shape mysteriously, as if cued by some external force. Now, she guided her thoughts to Earth, summoning the memories to appear. Her mind's darkened screen flashed with new imagery. Jamie saw storm clouds churning over a city. It was a scene of pure chaos. She heard people screaming and weeping. Somewhere a congregation was singing a hymn. There were looters breaking the windows out of shops along a deserted street, strewn with garbage. Religious extremists were announcing the end of time. A mother cowered behind a dumpster, squeezing her children to her breast.

Jamie sucked in a breath. "It was horrible," she managed. "It was of the final week before the launch. Society had crumbled. We were afraid people would find us. We had to hide from them, or they would kill us." Jamie's eyes filled with tears. "It was either them or us. We had to choose." She put her hands to her face. She wanted to forget the terrible scenes that unfolded in her mind.

The Rings of Alathea wept. "A asteroid was on a collision course with Earth. You had to leave to survive. You weren't saving yourselves. You were preserving your species."

Jamie looked at the wall again. Now it was a dirty white. Pale, ghostlike images phased in and out on its surface. "I remember getting on the ship," she murmured.

"There were ten pod ships." The idea's voice was soft, almost reverent. "Four of them launched successfully. Your ship was the only one to survive."

Jamie remembered standing on the launch pad and looking up into the night sky. The crescent moon was dwarfed by the asteroid, which assaulted the landscape with a cold and foreboding light. She had paused briefly outside the hatch, taking in her last glimpse of Earth. "There was so much death," she whispered sadly. She felt a great weight of grief as she thought of the Earth, now shattered and lifeless. "Everything they experienced, all their knowledge and wisdom are gone." Her hands were shaking. "Could you have stopped it?"

There was a pause. The Rings of Alathea shimmered, as if they were taking a deep breath. The sadness that she had felt a moment before was replaced with despair. "We do not have such power," said the idea. "We live in the realm of ideas, not action." Another pause. "You may consider yourself insignificant and vulnerable, but you are wrong. Human beings can act in the material world. You can cause a change. We listen and we speak, but we have no way of manipulating the cosmos."

"You must have been able to do something!" Jamie's anger was kindled. The aliens had been there. They had watched the Earth die and didn't lift a proverbial finger.

The idea trembled in her mind. "We whispered to your

people, but they did not hear us."

"Maybe you should have spoken louder," Jamie snapped.

"There were no mantles on Earth. Humanity did not know what to listen for."

The wall in Jamie's mind grew dark again. The images faded from view, disconnecting her from the past. She shivered, the icy fingers of utter solitude gripping her. "So you are telling me that we are the only human beings left in the universe."

"We fear that is so, young one."

"There are only sixteen of us left."

"Yes," said the Rings.

"And my own people have left me to die." Jamie glared at the Rings.

"They are driven by their fear."

"So am I," Jamie declared. "I'm just like them."

"You are wrong. Their fear drives them away from the truth. You are willing to be afraid in order to discover the truth. We have much to learn from you." The idea paused as if conferring with some unknown associate. "You and your companions possess many stories."

Jamie thought of all the colonists who had died, first those who did not wake from hibernation, and then those who had perished in the storm. She thought of Hip. Her heart ached as a great sense of loss swept over her. "Many of us have died. We have lost most of the stories."

"That is not true, young one. Death doesn't destroy the artificial cells. You can still access their memories."

"But there are thirty-three dead bodies still on the pod

ship. It's in orbit. I can't reach them."

The Rings of Alathea pulsed their golden light across the sky. "You are wrong, young one. Their knowledge is not lost. You hold the key."

"Why are you so interested in us?" Jamie asked.

"We want to hear your stories," breathed the idea. "Every living thing has a story. We cherish them because they point us toward the truth."

Jamie thought of Stub. "We have some pretty messed-up stories."

"Even tragic tales reveal a truth."

A new question took shape in Jamie's mind. It was a question she had been asking for a long time. "Is my name Jameson Stryker?"

"No," said the Rings. "Jameson Stryker was a wealthy banker. He didn't know about the implants and bribed his way onto the pod ship. You were going to be left behind, but your father and mother stopped him from boarding, and they placed you in his hibernation pod."

Jamie felt like she was approaching a holy place, a mooring for her little boat in the midst of a shivering gale. She prayed she wasn't dreaming, caught in a heartless illusion. She needed this to be real. She was desperate. "Do you know my name?"

"We do." Jamie looked up at the Rings. They seemed to brighten. "Your name is Alexia. It means 'protector,'" whispered the idea. "You are the protector of stories."

She repeated it softly to herself. The name was like music. It rang true in her memory, like a cherished song from her youth. "Alexia," she repeated it again, a smile forming on her lips.

Suddenly, there was a distant scream. The sound cut the night, fracturing her conversation with the Rings. It was a woman's voice, coming from the compound. She looked in the direction of the sound. There was another cry. It was Bliss. "You must go back to the settlement," urged the idea. It was a mental imperative commanding her full attention. The Rings told her what she already knew. "Your friend is in danger." Alexia did not want to leave, but she leapt from the rock and ran like a gazelle across the darkened beach.

CHAPTER NINETEEN
Death Sentence

Alexia ran the full length of the beach trail. The main gate was open, and she rushed into the compound. The glow of several lanterns illuminated the front of the storage shed where she and Bliss had ridden out the storm. Most of the colonists were gathered there. Alexia crept forward, keeping in the shadows. No one noticed her. Their attention was drawn to Carter, who was brandishing his walking stick like a sword. Bliss was on the ground in front of him, several red welts on her bare back.

"You have been disobedient before," Carter observed, taking in the old scars that traced jagged lines across her spine. He planted a foot in the small of her back and pushed her down to the ground. She cried out in pain. "You should have learned your lesson." Bliss shielded her breasts with her arms, a look of terror on her face. She pulled herself back up on her knees, crouching in anticipation of the next blow.

"Stay down!" Carter struck her again with the staff. Bliss collapsed but struggled to get up again. "You will not disobey me!" Carter hit her harder this time, and she went down a third time. Vickie took a step toward him. "Stay back!" the man thundered. "I'm in command here, and I'm not finished

232

with this bitch!" There was a murderous expression on his face. He raised his walking stick over his head. Bliss tried to pull herself into a ball, but her injuries wouldn't permit it. She cried out like a wounded animal.

Alexia watched helplessly. She wracked her brain, trying to think of a way to stop Carter. She had nothing: no weapon, no clothes, no plan. Her friends were imprisoned in the shed. If she uttered a word, the colonists would descend upon her, and she'd be of no use to anyone.

Carter towered over Bliss. The young woman lay motionless at his feet, blood trickling from the wounds on her back. Either she had stopped defying him, or she was unconscious. Bliss's face was turned away from Alexia, and she could not tell. Carter's rage had turned into a detached malevolence. He was a stone-cold killer. His eyes were dead, witnessing to his total disregard for human life. She had seen that look before.

A memory snapped into place. Alexia remembered Carter floating among the hibernation chambers on the pod ship. His eyes had the same look, his face chiseled with determination. In her original dream, she had been the one who turned off Captain Chamberlain's life support system. Now the vision was different. Alexia remembered what the Rings had told her. She was seeing Carter's memory, and he was the killer.

Alexia was shaken out of her muse by a gasp from the crowd. Carter had raised his walking stick over his head. Bliss was awake, now cringing below him and covering her head with bruised arms. Carter was caught in the lantern light, his shadow larger than life on the storage shed, a monster poised to strike.

"Stop!" Alexia yelled. Everyone turned toward the sound. The lantern lights swung in her direction, plucking her out of the darkness with their intense beams. Alexia froze. She felt their eyes on her. She was like a deer caught in headlights.

Stub was standing nearby. He grinned lustfully. "This show's gettin' better and better."

Carter's staff had come to a standstill in mid-swing. He turned, hefting the stick in his hand. His eyes narrowed when he saw Alexia. Forgetting Bliss, he walked slowly toward her. The crowd parted as he approached. Alexia held her ground. If she had been wearing any clothes and had a weapon, she might have felt like David facing Goliath. Carter stopped less than a meter from her, slapping the walking stick into the open palm of his hand. The wood resonated a meaty, thumping sound.

"You're going to be sorry you came back, Jamie." Death was in his voice.

A shiver went up Alexia's spine. Every fiber of her being was telling her to run. "My name isn't Jamie," she said, her voice cracking.

"Oh! Say it isn't so!" Carter glanced at those surrounding them, urging everyone to see the absurdity of her response. He turned back to her. Death wore a smile. "We've been calling you Jamie for a long time now. You've been answering to it."

"Jameson Stryker was a wealthy man who tried to buy his way onto our ship. He almost succeeded, but he failed. My parents put me in his hibernation chamber."

Carter laughed. "So who are you?" The light from one of the lanterns caught Alexia in the eyes, making it impossible for her to see Carter's face. His body obscured most of the light, and once again he was a menacing silhouette, resembling the shadow beast with the raised club. He slammed his walking stick into the ground at her feet. "I said who are you!" he shouted.

"My name is Alexia."

Carter raised his walking stick and lowered it slowly toward Alexia's bare shoulder. She tried unsuccessfully to knock it away, to shield herself from a blow that never came. "I dub thee," Carter taunted her with a faux English accent, "Alexia the naked!" There was a round of laughter as he pulled the staff back.

Alexia held her ground. She raised her voice above the catcalls. "I know why I got amnesia," she began. "We are all carrying artificial memory cells that were put into our bodies before launch. Those who sent us out here put something in my head to coordinate all the information we carry."

"Look at her!" Carter laughed. "She's lost her mind!"

Alexia pointed up to the rings arching overhead. "The Rings are a life form. They have followed us from Earth. They told me about what was done to us."

Carter's voice took on a mocking tone. "Sweet Jesus, girl. First you tell us the mantle plants are aliens. Now you say it's those damned rings! There's something wrong with you. Don't expect me, or any of us, to believe one word you're saying."

The voice of the Rings whispered in Alexia's mind. She felt a breath of tranquility sweep over her. She squared her shoulders and dropped her hands to her sides. She smiled serenely at Carter. The light from one of the lamps spilled onto his face. The man's grin had faltered. "I know about you, Carter," she said slowly. "Why don't you tell everyone how you killed Captain Chamberlain while the rest of us were in hibernation?"

The color drained from Carter's face. "You're crazy," he

said, but his voice had lost its power.

Alexia's eyes grew wide as the complete recollection appeared in her mind. Carter misinterpreted her facial expression and grinned again, believing he had discredited her. She took a step toward him. "You killed all of them!" she said. His grin vanished like a mirage over cooling quicksand. She drew even closer. "You turned off the life support systems on all those helpless people. You're a damn murderer."

Carter was turning red. Alexia couldn't tell if it was anger or shame, probably the former. "When will you stop making up stories about us?" He waved his stick menacingly. He looked at the others who stood spellbound by Alexia's accusation. "You were all asleep. Why didn't I kill you too?" Alexia could hear a hint of anxiety in his voice as he turned back to her. "Why didn't I kill you?" She could feel his hot saliva on her breasts as he spit the words at her. "You couldn't know what happened up there on the pod ship."

"It's the truth, isn't it?" she asked.

"I'll determine what's true, Jamie."

"My name is Alexia."

"You're crazy." Carter repeated the accusation like a broken record. He paused as words failed him. Alexia could see the veins in his neck expand as his blood pressure skyrocketed. Then his eyes became glassy. "Those aliens have invaded your mind," he shouted. "You are a danger to us!" He turned to Vickie. "Tie her to the wall over there!" He gestured toward the fence that skirted the southern end of the compound.

Vickie scowled, a look of disapproval on her face. Then she acquiesced and nodded to Ben Beck. He and another security guard grabbed Alexia by the arms. She resisted, but the men overpowered her. They dragged her to a fencepost and tied her arms behind her back. The wood scraped her skin from her shoulder blades to her buttocks, and she grimaced. Ben Beck leaned close to her. She braced herself for a sexual assault. It never came. "I'm sorry things turned out this way," he whispered. He stooped down in front of her and tied her feet, then gave her a sympathetic glance before stepping away.

Carter strode purposefully across the compound and stopped in front of Alexia. The colonists flanked him, their lantern lights directed toward her. Alexia's back was pressed against the post, her arms pulled tightly behind her. Her legs straddled the base of the column. She was totally exposed. Carter studied Alexia's body for a moment, as if she was a bug tacked to a piece of cardboard. She met his gaze with all the courage she could muster. "We are in a very precarious situation here," he began with restored confidence. "We can't have you around here anymore, but you keep showing up. I send you away, and like a bad penny, you come back." He poked her in the breast. Alexia could smell his breath. "Your actions have threatened the survival of our settlement. I hereby declare you an enemy of this colony and sentence you to death."

There was a collective gasp. Alexia's knees buckled. She slumped against the post. Her eyes lost their fire. She was defeated.

"You can't do that!" It was Vickie. Her hands were balled into fists as she stepped toward Carter. "She deserves a fair trial."

"Says who?" he replied.

"Says human decency, Carter!"

"I am the captain. I am the one in command." He was

full of irrational bluster as insanity rose up in him again. He stepped next to Alexia, intentionally brushing her breast with his elbow as he turned to face the colonists. "This woman will be put to death at first light."

"I won't follow that order!" Vickie thundered.

Carter smiled. "I didn't expect you would. You are relieved of command." He looked into the crowd. "Stub? You're the new security chief. You will execute this woman at dawn."

Alexia watched in horror as Stub Andrews sauntered to the front of the crowd. Stub was an engineer, not a trained soldier. He was a cruel and violent man, a womanizer. How could Carter choose him? Then Alexia remembered how Carter had defended Stub when Alice was beaten. Carter had been sympathetic to him all along.

Stub grinned at Alexia, his face resembling that of a rutting bull. "Can I sleep with her, sir?" She closed her eyes.

"No. She is to remain where she is." Alexia opened her eyes. Stub was disappointed. He looked like he needed a cold shower. Carter was studying her intently, and then he pivoted toward his new security chief. "Tell me, Stub. Can you carry out my order? Will you put her to death in the morning?"

"Yes, sir. I'll do it, sir!"

Carter nodded with satisfaction, then addressed the crowd. "We will gather here in the morning to witness the execution. There'll be no more dissent in this community! This is what happens to those who challenge me!"

Vickie's face became as hardened steel, her inner warrior rising up. She lunged at Carter, knocking the walking stick from his hand and wrapping her powerful fingers around his throat. He was caught off-guard and fell to the ground. Vickie rode him to the turf like a jockey on a fallen horse. He tried to strike back, but he was no match for her. She was a fighter, trained to perfection and driven by honor.

Alexia watched Carter's face turn red and then blue as Vickie choked him. She had no doubt that the woman was going to kill him. Suddenly, something flashed through the lantern light. Stub had retrieved Carter's walking stick and brought it down hard on Vickie's head. There was a resounding crack as wood met bone. Vickie released her grip on Carter's neck and crumpled to the ground next to him.

"That's for breakin' my wrist, bitch!" Stub hissed triumphantly. He raised the staff and struck her head again. There was a sickening crunch. Vickie didn't move.

Carter was gasping for air. Everyone stood around him in stunned silence. The settlement, once believed to be a haven of safety, was now the realm of a madman and a thug. Alexia could see the fear in their eyes. No one would question Carter again.

The crowd thinned as the colonists escaped to their quarters. Olivia and Stub helped Carter get to his feet. Rachel Bennett and Ben Beck rushed to Vickie's side. They knelt beside her, the medic assessing the extent of her injuries. "I think her skull is cracked," Rachel reported.

"I don't care if she's dead!" Carter's voice was raspy. "You and Ben lock her in the shed with the other prisoners. She'll be executed with our little mind reader in the morning."

* * *

There were no lights over the jungle that night. The mirrored moon and her sister set early, leaving the Rings alone in the sky with the stars. Alexia's shoulders ached. The rough surface of the fencepost dug into her back. She pulled at her restraints until her hands were numb. She refused to

239

accept her fate. She was Alexia, the guardian of humanity's stories. Somehow, she had to survive.

Alexia's soul blazed in fierce defiance. She tipped her chin up. The Rings of Alathea hung silently over her. There were no mutterings, no disembodied voice whispering in her mind. She listened to her heartbeat. It was pounding in her chest. She willed herself to relax. She tried to clear a space in her mind, a space devoid of her present peril. She needed a safe harbor, a place to think.

Something moved in the shadows. Alexia's eyes snapped wide open. Was it her imagination? No. There it was again. A shape. It was a person. Her heart rate jumped, the pounding exploding in her head like a bass drum. She unconsciously pulled her arms, willing them to break free from their bindings, but they remained wrapped around the fencepost behind her.

My God, Alexia thought. It's Stub coming back. She dry-heaved, a dribble of sputum cascading down her chin. He would rape her, perhaps cut her. She screamed silently into the night, not wanting to draw any further attention to herself. The shadow moved closer. It was headed directly for her. Panic distorted her mind.

Alexia felt herself drowning in a sea of fear. She imagined herself pumping her arms to push herself up above the surface of the danger engulfing her, but she could not. She held her breath, trying to keep the terror from entering her body and her mind, but at last she had to draw in a great lungful of air, and the horror swept over her and into her like an avalanche of frozen snow. Alexia stifled another scream and convulsed in her restraints. Her bladder let go and hot urine coursed down her legs. She whimpered and then surrendered. She was just a piece of meat tied to a stick.

The shadow moved closer. Alexia closed her eyes,

pleading to the Rings and the idea that had told her who she was. She would detach her mind from her body. She would will herself into a coma and sleep through whatever Stub would do to her. She would retreat into the castle's keep of her psyche and protect her inner sanity from the outer chaos that was sure to come.

"Jamie?" It was a woman's voice, muffled by the protective layers Alexia had wrapped around her mind. She opened her eyes and peeked through her lashes. Rachel Bennett was standing in front of her, a concerned look written on her face. The woman's lips moved, but her words were out of synch. "I'm sorry I frightened you." The medic's voice was clearer now. Alexia flinched involuntarily as she relaxed her guard. Rachel's lips moved again. "I need your help."

Alexia smiled weakly. She took a breath; the pungent odor of urine hung over her, and she laughed. "That's really funny," she managed.

"I'm serious." Concern covered Rachel's face. "We've got a couple of really sick people. They're going to die if we don't do something."

Alexia's eyes narrowed. "Vickie?"

"She's got a fractured skull. I don't have the training or the equipment to care for her." Alexia slumped against her restraints. Rachel put a hand on her shoulder. "The other one is Bliss," she said. "Carter hit her really hard, and she's got internal injuries. I think there's some bleeding in her gut. She needs serious medical attention." The woman bit her lip. "I wish Hip were here."

Alexia felt helpless. Vickie had saved her from Stub. She was lying near death in the shed because she had stood up for her again. Bliss was her best friend. The voluptuous woman

241

had no guile. She was guilty of innocence, but nothing else. Both needed her, and she was powerless. "What could I possibly do?" Alexia whispered.

Rachel was worn and exhausted. "Vickie's a goner. Without the medical equipment on the Lander, I can't do anything except pump her full of drugs and keep her comfortable. Bliss is another story. If I knew what to do, I might be able to repair the damage."

"I'm not a doctor," Alexia breathed.

"You said they put artificial memory cells in us. If that's true, then we have the knowledge to save Bliss." Rachel was desperate, a physician fighting for her patient. "Can you really coordinate all that information? Are you the librarian? Do you know where to find the medical procedures?"

"I don't know." Alexia felt empty. "I really don't know."

"You can remember things that happened to us." Rachel was not going to give up.

"Those memories just came to me. I have no control over them. I have no idea how to access the knowledge."

A sound drifted across the compound. It came from the shed where Alexia's friends were being held. It was Thomas. "Rachel!" he hissed in a loud whisper. "Get back here! Bliss needs you!"

Rachel looked back at the shed. "I've got to go." She turned again to Alexia and sighed. "It was worth a try." The medic pivoted on her heel and disappeared into the darkness.

Alexia cursed herself. Life was swirling around her like a cyclone, and she was a bystander, unable to change the events sweeping past. Deep within her, something surrendered. She felt a wave of cold resignation pour over her. Carter was in total control of the settlement and had sealed her fate.

Nothing would stop the inexorable chain of events that would unfold in the morning. Everyone would gather around her naked body and gawk at her for one last time. Carter would make a speech, reminding everyone of their duty to be loyal to his command. Stub would make an obscene comment, and then he would put a bullet in her head. There might be a prick of pain as she lost consciousness. Finally, she would confront the grand mystery of death, and everything would come to an end.

* * *

Alexia must have been sleeping when the alien presence returned. "There is a way, young one," it whispered. "You can still save your friends."

"Stop tormenting me!" Alexia shouted. She was sure that she had gone mad, the victim of some schizophrenic spell.

"You already know how to do it," the Rings replied, either ignoring or unaware of her protestations. "You must remember. Your implant is the key."

"I don't know what you're talking about."

"Remember," said the idea.

All at once, Alexia remembered her mother. She was beautiful. She had long blond hair that lay on her shoulders like silk. Her smile was like the sun, full of warmth and light. She touched Alexia's hand, her skin soft and gentle. "Your implant will connect with the ship's intellect," she was saying. "It will permit you to access all the information we have placed in you, as well as everyone else." Alexia looked into her mother's face. She had never felt such love before. "I love you, Alexia." She felt her mother's kiss on her forehead, and then the memory drifted away into the shadows of her mind.

A glimmer of hope cut through the dark night of Alexia's

243

soul. "I can communicate with the pod ship's intellect?"

"You must reach out with your thoughts," said the Rings.

Alexia quieted her mind and saw the dark wall that had separated her from her memories. It shimmered with diffuse images, and then a series of doors appeared. In an instant, the image surrounded her, and she was standing in a large room, the doors spread out in front of her. Each held its own secret. Alexia felt the cold fingers of fear. Perhaps one would reveal a horror beyond her imagining. She shut the thought from her mind and pushed fear out of the way. She heard the echo of her mother's voice in the cathedral of her soul. Alexia had to remain focused on what she had told her.

Each door sent a different set of sensations through her mind. There was the vault door she had entered when she was by the river. She shuttered as she remembered the avalanche of memories that threatened to bury her. She stood before it, examining the huge hinges and the great wheel that disengaged the lock. She could hear whispers emerging from it, and she quickly moved on. She saw a smaller door with a shiny surface, like Alathea's mirrored moon. Instinctively, she knew this door would reveal her memories. She wanted to linger there and open it, but her mother's voice called like a siren, beckoning her onward. Alexia passed several more portals and then stopped in front of a small metal door. She knew her destiny lay beyond it.

Alexia opened the door. There was no light, only a narrow corridor disappearing into the darkness. She felt, rather than saw it. She crossed the threshold and found herself floating, then moving through the passageway at ever-increasing speed. Nameless things flashed by her at a dizzying pace. A light appeared, in the distance. It filtered down the narrow channel, glinting off protuberances in the walls, defining to her rapid movement. Then, as if she was pressed into the palm of a giant hand, she came to a standstill.

Another door stood before her. She touched it, and the portal swung toward her. Light spilled out of the opening, dancing and flickering. She floated through it and heard chirping voices, muttering back and forth to each other. They spoke so rapidly; she could not make out what they were saying. Then she heard her mother's voice again.

"Welcome, Alexia."

"Mom?"

"Your mother created me. I am the pod ship's intellect."

Alexia smiled in her mind. It was like touching a piece of her mother's jewelry or smelling her scent on a pillow. Engaging with something her mother made was like touching her hand. It was a happy reminder of a long-forgotten joy.

"Do you need me for something, Alexia?"

The intellect's question was like a key turning in the cylinder of a lock. All at once, Alexia knew why she was there and what needed to be done. "Yes, we have to transfer the ship's log over to Lander B."

"Done," the intellect replied.

"Does the log include the status postings of the hibernation pods?"

"It does," came the answer.

"Good." Alexia held her breath. "How good of a pilot are you?"

CHAPTER TWENTY
Redemption

I n the morning, Alexia watched all the colonists gather around her in the south end of the compound. The prisoners had been released from the shed to witness the execution. Rusty and Alice stood off to one side with Thomas next to them. Alice had been crying. Ben Beck was standing watch behind the trio, his face flush with shame. Thomas kept looking back at the prison shed. Bliss was lying there, and his heart was torn.

Carter stood next to Alexia, like the host of a morbid game show. "I understand Vickie is unable to appear before us," he intoned.

Rachel Bennett stood straight as a ramrod, her hands clutched behind her back. "She's still unconscious, sir," she reported. "I don't expect her to live."

Carter turned toward Alexia. "That leaves us with Jamie."

"My name is Alexia."

He ignored her. "I have warned you about your memories. It's obvious to me and everyone else that you are being controlled by a hostile presence."

"You are the one who's hostile," said Alexia. "You beat Bliss. She's almost dead. You destroyed the mantle plants. They did nothing to you."

"So you don't deny being under their influence?" Carter was intent on discrediting her.

"I do deny it. The mantles helped me hear the aliens in the Rings."

"And the so-called aliens planted lies in your mind, untruths that you have been spewing for days, accusing us of things we never did."

"They aren't lies, and I can prove it. The ship's log will show that you woke up before the rest of us. You killed Captain Chamberlain and then disabled the life support systems on half of the hibernation pods."

Carter began to chuckle. "You'll say anything to save your life, won't you? That log was lost when the Lander was swept out to sea. The only other copy is in orbit. What are you going to do, flap your arms and return to the pod ship?"

"I don't need to." Alexia was calm. She looked directly into Carter's eyes. He flinched, but she was the only one who saw it.

Carter turned away from her and looked at the colonists. "I have determined that this woman is a danger to all of us. Stub? Are you ready to carry out the sentence?"

The new security chief stepped forward. He had Vickie's sidearm strapped around his waist. The belt was tight, making him look like an hourglass. He fumbled with the Velcro strap holding the weapon in place. "Yes, sir!" he said enthusiastically. "I'll be happy..."

Alexia cut off Stub's response with a strong and steady voice. "What about my defense?"

"You have no defense." Carter snapped.

"Says you." Alexia offered him a confident smile.

"Quiet!" Carter thundered. "The prisoner will not speak, unless spoken to."

She was getting under his skin. "I can prove that you killed Captain Chamberlain and half of the colonists. You are the one on trial here."

"I said shut up!" he screamed. Alexia could see the blood vessels bulging in Carter's neck. She met his murderous glare with a steady gaze.

Stub finally got Vickie's weapon free from its holster and leveled it at Alexia. She could see his hand shaking. The man was full of bluster, but he'd never killed before. One of Stub's memories flowed easily into her mind.

"Your mother should never have abused you, Stub." The words struck him like a lightning bolt. He lowered the gun, crestfallen. "She was sick and twisted. It wasn't your fault."

"Shoot her, Stub!" Carter knew he was losing control.

"Let her speak, Carter." Olivia had been standing quietly in the crowd. Now she stepped toward Stub. He was raising his weapon again, but she put her hand on his arm. "No, Stub. It's only fair. I think we all want to know what Jamie has to say."

Carter tried to shut the woman down. "That won't be necessary, Olivia. There is no evidence to back her claim. It's her word against mine, and we all know how unreliable her memory has been." Stub pushed Olivia's arm away and took aim again.

A sudden breeze whipped the branches of the trees at the jungle's edge. The leaves clattered loudly. Then there was a rumble overhead. Everyone jumped, thinking that another storm was going to strike. They looked up, but there wasn't a cloud in the sky.

"Don't be afraid," Alexia announced coolly.

"What are you doing?" Carter was frightened.

"I couldn't go up to the pod ship and collect my evidence," she said. "So I instructed the ship's intellect to bring it to me."

Lander B appeared over the tree tops, her thrusters thundering in the tropical air. She pirouetted like a ballet dancer and then rapidly approached the settlement. The leaves on the trees slapped together more loudly as the great ship distorted the air, her engine nacelles pivoting to slow her horizontal motion. Her fuselage blotted out the sun, casting a shadow over the compound.

The ship came to a stop, hovering thirty meters over Alexia's head. "Don't move," she cautioned. The ship is going to land right behind you." She looked up at the Lander and nodded her head. Everyone froze as the Lander responded to Alexia's command. The ship's landing gear extended, and it settled down like a feather in the middle of the compound, the hull and wings towering over the sheds and perimeter fence.

"Kill her, Stub!" Carter shouted.

Stub had turned away from Alexia to watch the ship land. Now he turned back to her, raising his weapon a third time. "You don't want to do this, Stub," Alexia said calmly. The man hesitated. Suddenly, Rusty and Alice lunged toward him. Ben made no attempt to stop them. Rusty tackled the ugly little man, and Alice pulled the gun from his hand. Stub's eyes grew wide as he saw the hatred in Alice's face. She raised the gun up like a hammer and bludgeoned him in the head repeatedly.

Carter was beside himself. He rushed at Alexia, ready to kill her with his bare hands. Ben rushed toward them, his sidearm drawn. He reached Carter as the man locked his hands around her neck. Ben jammed the cold steel of the weapon into his face. "Let her go." Carter dropped his hands. "This has gone too far." The security guard hit Carter in the head with the butt of his weapon. The man crumpled to the ground, unconscious. "Stay there!" he said. Ben turned back toward the crowd. "Thomas! Get over here and free Jamie, or Alexia, or whatever her name is!" Then he turned his attention to Stub. Rusty and Alice stepped back as he approached, unsure of what the man would do. "You did what I should have done a long time ago," he muttered. Then Ben knelt down and zipped a set of restraints on Stub's wrists.

Thomas reached behind Alexia and released her hands. A moment later, she was free. Her arms and legs burned like fire, but there was no time to delay. She hobbled toward Rachel Bennett. "We have to get to the Lander's intellect," she said. Rachel helped her walk unsteadily toward the belly of the Lander. Alexia envisioned the hatch in her mind, and it opened.

"How did you do that?" Rachel was amazed.

"My implant allows me to communicate with the intellect. That's why the ship's here."

They climbed the ramp into the Lander and then inched their way forward through the cramped passageways toward the flight deck. "What are we going to do?" Rachel asked.

"It's what you are going to do." Alexia smiled. "You're going to save Vickie and Bliss." Alexia led her to the intellect's control surface. "Sit down," she said gently. The display came alive and thousands of medical images and texts began to flash across the screen.

"What's that?" Rachel asked.

"It's coming from Hip's artificial memory cells. Before we left Earth, you were all injected with them. Hip was given all the medical wisdom that humanity has amassed over the centuries. His body is dead, but we can still access the knowledge." Alexia placed her hands on the woman's temples and pressed gently. She closed her eyes, retreating into the inner recesses of her mind. She found Rachel's door and opened it. "Relax. I am not able to control you. All I can do is open the neural pathways that will expand your memory. In a moment, you will become aware of the knowledge Hip carried."

Rachel's expression changed. She sucked in a breath. Then her eyes flashed open, as if she had just seen something of indescribable beauty. "My God!" she gasped. "I see it!"

Alexia removed her hands from her head. "Now Doctor Bennett, go save your patients." Rachel rose from her seat and headed back toward the hold for additional medical supplies. Alexia paused, her thoughts lingering in the afterglow of Hip's knowledge. She missed her friend. Even though he was dead, the kind physician was still saving lives.

* * *

There was a new atmosphere of hope in the settlement. Lander B had brought additional supplies, which gave them a second chance for survival. Tents had already been removed from her hold and were pitched in the compound. Ben Beck pressed Carter and Stub into service, compelling them to dig graves for the thirty-three dead colonists on the Lander. Their bodies would be interred next to Hip in the morning.

As twilight fell, the mantles' lights lit the jungle once more. Alexia invited everyone to go to the beach, where they made a fire on the sand. She sat by the water, listening to the waves caress the shore. Carter stared at the fire, a sullen expression on his face. Rusty and Alice sat side by side, their arms wrapped around each other's waist.

Everyone looked up as Thomas and Rachel emerged from the beach trail. They were speaking quietly to each other as they approached the fire. Thomas circled the group and sank down on the sand next to Alexia. Rachel opened her palms toward the flames, warming her hands. There was an expectant hush as everyone waited for her to speak. Finally, she looked up and smiled broadly. "Vickie and Bliss are resting comfortably," she began. "Their prognosis is excellent." Everyone cheered except Carter and Stub.

Alexia watched quietly, drinking in the presence of her companions. Even now, as they sat like ancient ones around this simple fire, she could sense their memories, their knowledge. The glow of the fire grew brighter as the breeze blew in from the alien sea. The flickering light danced on their faces. She could tell their fear was receding into a sense of awe. They had glimpsed the immense gift they carried. Alexia vowed silently to treat them and their memories with respect and compassion. The Rings whispered in her mind. "Now you understand, Alexia. When you listen to the story of another without expectation or manipulation, you learn to cherish them." She smiled and looked up. The rays from Alathea's setting sun were still glistening on the golden Rings.

EPILOGUE

Alexia didn't know if she was breaking through a chrysalis or sensing her final glimpse of light through a shroud of death. The light was diffuse, milky white. She could hear moaning. Distant guttural murmuring emanated from the edges of her consciousness. The last wisps of a half-forgotten dream slipped away through overwhelming physical sensations. She felt her chest heaving, her hands groping, her head tilting back, her toes fisting as she squeezed her buttocks and tensed her leg muscles. Every joint ached. The sounds were closer now. They were synchronized with her rising shoulders. She could feel something between her lips. Dry lips. Parched throat. Leathery tongue slapping against hard plastic. She was making the sounds.

"Wake up, sleepy head."

Alexia's eyes opened. She saw the curved lid of her hibernation pod in the dim light of the pod chamber. Hip was grinning at her. She could feel the echoes of her dream dying away. "You're alive," she murmured. Her eyes filled with tears, and her heart sang with joy as she gripped her husband's hand. "You're still alive."

"I hope so." Hip laughed. "I've been waiting fifty years to

give you a kiss." He bent over the pod and kissed his wife.

Alexia reached up and cupped her hand around his neck. His kiss tasted good. "In my dream, you died during a storm." Hip frowned. "You had been married before and lost your wife."

"Not in this lifetime, beautiful." He gave her a radiant smile. "I'm alive, and I'm all yours." He kissed her again.

"Have we arrived?" she asked.

"We're in orbit. All safe and sound." Hip squeezed her hand. "I ran a diagnostic as you were waking up. You're in perfect health."

* * *

Alexia floated through the crew cabin on her way to the flight deck. She saw two of her companions holding hands by the large view port. Their destination hung below them, an alien planet chosen for its Earth-like characteristics. In a few weeks, they would be establishing a new colony there. Something about it reminded Alexia of her dream. She gazed at the planet, its golden rings shimmering in the sun. She shook off the feeling of déjà vu and took in the breathtaking panorama. She couldn't find the words to express how she felt. Alexia glanced at Rusty and Alice. It was good to have an artist and a poet with them. Science alone could never describe the wonders they would behold.

Alexia entered the flight deck and nodded toward the captain. Vickie smiled in return. "Good to see you. Did you sleep well?"

"I had a weird dream." Alexia took her seat behind Vickie. She cleared her mind and felt the ship's intellect flow into her consciousness. She immersed herself in the familiar cascade of information. She was the crew's cybrarian, charged with fielding the immense knowledge of the ship's intellect.

A chime sounded, and Hip's face appeared on the intercom screen. "Vickie? We've got a problem back here."

Vickie swiveled in her seat and gave Alexia a concerned look. Then she acknowledged Hip. "What is it?"

"We have a mystery guest on board." Alexia closed the mental link with the intellect and gazed at her husband's image. He was scratching his head. "We're supposed to have a Jameson Stryker with us, but he's not here. There's a woman in his hibernation pod."

About the Author

Dan Moore lives with his wife Diana near Syracuse, New York. He is a freelance video producer and the proud father of two sons, two daughters-in-law and three grandsons. Dan caught the Science Fiction bug by reading Robert Heinlein's "Spaceman Jones" when he was in high school.

Contact Dan:

Dan@meridiansshadow.com

www.danmoore.com

www.meridiansshadow.com